# COMMENTS BY THREE AVID READERS:

"I got it (reading) done way earlier than I thought .... that is a good thing!  I didn't want to put it down.  . . . The beginning and ending (especially ending) was my favorite."

—J.J. Dahl, Esq. – Board Certified Marital and Family Law Attorney

"In my humble opinion, this story is heads above the other of yours that I have read.  The writing seems to have matured (I mean this only in the best of ways) and is far more interesting to read.  . . . BEST YET. You even got better as you wrote this story. Very good ending. "

—N. Ray, Senior Editor, New Business America

"In Shelby's Way...Maybe, our heroine descends from being the highly desirable wife of a breathtakingly handsome Hollywood stuntman to the bereft abandoned wife and mother of a sweet little eight year old girl.  Can Shelby survive in a place that values money, power and sex above all else?  Can Shelby make a new life for her beloved daughter and overcome her own deeply felt insecurities? Will she succumb to life's temptations or will she rise above . . . ?  . . . . . . . . . .Maybe?"

'I highly recommend Shelby's Way...Maybe for book clubs.  The difficulties facing single mothers and women who have been abandoned or widowed often time live in the shadows.'  Powerful discussion subject.

—Carol Diesl, BS in Ed., MS in ED.,  AAS in Nursing, RN;
and former Book Club president for six years

PRIOR WORKS:

YOURS FOREVER . . . MAYBE
    Publisher:     LANE UNLIMITED
                ISBN      978-0-692-74806-0
    Published:    12-13-2011
WASTED . . . MAYBE
    Publisher:     LANE UNLIMITED
                ISBN      978-0-578-47553-0
    Published:    03-14-2013

# Shelby's Way…Maybe

## Listen to Your Heart and Find Your Way

Katherine [MK] Mitchell

ISBN: 978-0-578-47554-7

This book is printed on acid-free paper.

This book is a work of fiction. Places, events, and situations in this book are purely fictional and any resemblance to actual persons, living or dead, is coincidental.

Printed in the United States of America

*I dedicate this novel
to my husband and my loving daughter*

# ACKNOWLEDGMENTS

I thank the late Charles Y. Nakamura, Emeritus Professor UCLA Department of Psychology, for steadfastly standing by and encouraging me through many years until his passing; N. Ray, Senior Editor, New Business America, for appreciating my talent and investing precious time in my support; J.J. Dahl, Esq., Board Certified Marital and Family Law Attorney, for going from employer to the most accessible, supportive friend one can ever have; Carol Diesl, Book Club President, for being a most enthusiastic champion of my work; and Karen A. Clark, my mentor and angel who watches over me.   I am enriched by each of them and grateful.

I praise my husband for bearing with me throughout the years.  His life would be easier if I could live without writing.

# CHAPTER 1

"Oh, to be rich!" she whispered with a wicked sparkle in her eyes.

"We're getting there, babe," he said.

"By *there*, you mean like this?" Shelby gestured to the extravagant party, the luxurious home. "I could learn to live with it."

"You might have to."

"Oh, why the hell not, Boyd? Let's go all the way to the stars." Her eyes were gleaming with childlike anticipation as she leaned close to his ear. "And the people? Can we have all the beautiful people, too?" Her chuckle punctuated the sweet imagery.

"And what would you do with all the beautiful people?" he asked.

Shelby smiled a mysterious smile, and made an exaggerated motion with her arms. "I would put them on our bookshelves. Every time I wanted to have a good talk—while you were working, of course—I would take one off the shelf and ask questions and find out things."

"I always like your fantasy world," he said. Her big eyes and perfect skin were accentuated by the shortest blonde tresses. Pretending to rearrange some wispy longish strands of hair, he playfully caressed her neck.

The striking couple, Shelby and Boyd, did not go unnoticed. While her eyes were drinking in the minute details of the stunning hillside home and the glamorous crowd, several of the guests had them under scrutiny. The red mini dress lightly draped around her toned body, the espadrille high heel wedge beach sandals elongating her already long legs. She was the envy of the less well-shaped women. But their jealousy went beyond Shelby's looks. They coveted her eye-catching husband, Boyd, a man simply beyond handsome, beautifully built and sexy to one and all, women and men. He was accustomed to being watched.

Someone filled up Shelby's champagne glass. She nodded her thanks, pre-occupied with the amazing views of the Pacific Ocean on one side and the sprawling Los Angeles cityscape toward the other.

A super-thin woman in a designer beach gown floated over to them. *Was it a slinky evening gown or a designer beach dress?* In her mind Shelby determined it had to have been the latter, since the woman was wearing it to a pool party. Shelby noticed earlier that a few guests, as well as the hostess, were displaying wide black armbands.

"Boyd, how are you?"

"Great, Elisabeth." They kissed on the cheek. "This is my wife, Shelby. She loves your house."

"So do we. Later on I'll give you a tour," she said to Shelby.

"And the armband? What gives?" asked Boyd.

"Oh, don't you know? We're still mourning the loss of the Colonies," Elisabeth said with a wide grin.

"Clever touch," said Boyd.

"Let me introduce you around. Anyone you don't know?"

"I worked for some of these people." Just as he spoke, a handsome, wiry man, George Eckert, stopped by. The aura of success made him appear taller than he was.

"Elisabeth, your husband is a genius with what he did to this place." George was eager to share his excitement. "I remember seeing it before your restoration. It was done by Buff & Hensman, wasn't it? I know their work. They must have had a field day doing so many glass walls and creating the indoor-outdoor flow."

Elisabeth was glowing with pride at his praise.

"Oh, dear. You must tell Malcolm. He'll be ever so proud to hear this from you."

George turned to Boyd. "Boyd, good to see you."

"It's been a while," said Boyd. "This is my wife, Shelby." Then he turned to Shelby. "Meet George Eckert."

George shook her hand. "This is the most I've ever heard Boyd talk."

"I know. He's too smart to talk. I'm not that smart," she said with a shy smirk.

Before George could answer, a striking woman, a true showstopper in her forties, waltzed into the little group wearing a body-hugging Rudi. The Rudi

Gernreich originals for Harmon Knits were still coming out and making a splash, even though the notorious American designer pursued other endeavors. *A Rudi* was a definite status symbol, and the man with the colorful personality was considered a national treasure by many.

"This is Nancy, my ex-wife and current friend," said George.

"First rule of divorce: never forget who butters your bread," said Nancy. "I'm more than a current friend. I'm his best friend." She kissed him on the cheek, but her eyes were measuring up each detail of Boyd's body.

"And you are?" she asked.

"Boyd Carpenter, Nancy. One of the finest stuntmen in Hollywood," said George, "and his wife, Shelby."

"Well then, it makes sense that I would recognize the body but not the face, hm?" said Nancy. Flirtatiously closing in on Boyd, she gave Shelby a dismissive glance.

"Nancy's not good at looking into people's eyes, but she's harmless," George added and Elisabeth laughed out loud.

"Don't insult me, dear," said Nancy. "Being harmless is not exactly endearing."

But George was already past that thought because Sidney Marshall joined the group. He turned to Boyd.

"Boyd, let me introduce you to Sidney Marshall, the world-renowned author, in case you didn't know," he said, not expecting the physical guy to be much of a reader.

Shelby's face lit up. "Oh, Mr. Marshall! Oh—" she said, but no other words escaped her. His face opened into a wide, ear-to-ear smile. She felt electricity burst through her body under his glance. She was glad to hear George continue with the conversation and to know that she did not have to participate.

"Boyd, I want you to know that I'll be doing Sidney's next novel. You'll definitely work on it."

"That can wait, George," said Nancy. "Work can wait. This is a party."

Shelby watched the curious group interact. She was familiar with the books of Sidney Marshall, the author famous for sexy action-packed romantic stories. Blue sweater or blue shirt, his pictures were all over the covers of his books, and he was all over the talk shows. Sidney had a distinctive voice: rich, smooth, and soft, memorable for his uniquely precise enunciation. Familiar for what appeared to be a perpetual twinkle in his eyes, the witty man in his middle years exuded casual elegance.

He reached to shake hands all around.

"It does match your eyes," said Shelby. At everyone's questioning look, she explained: "Someone asked him on Johnny Carson why he wore blue so much. That's all."

"Very observant of detail," Sidney said. His appreciative look was nothing new to Shelby. Men saw something in her that she didn't see.

Sidney glanced toward George. "You make me proud. One after the other, you turn all my novels into nothing less than blockbusters. Good man."

"First comes the written word, Sidney. Don't forget that. I just put them on film."

"While you boys are talking business, I'll take this young man to the terrace and show him the sights," said Nancy. Turning to Boyd, she continued, "You can't have an opinion, dear. You're an actor, right? In George's world decisions are made about you, not by you." She did not wait for approval.

"Right," said Boyd. "So show me the sights. I'll be right back, Shel."

"I wouldn't be too sure. I have a lot to show you," said Nancy brazenly, taking him by the hand and dragging him to the railing. The minimalist home with its clean lines and open flow was out of the ordinary in every sense. It was cool and sleek, yet surprisingly inviting.

Shelby could hear only part of their conversation as they moved slowly away from the group.

"There's an upstairs also, Boyd, yes?" She gave him a sly look while repeating his name. "That'll leave you speechless."

Shelby was powerless as she watched them disappear from sight.

"Well, young lady. You're stuck with us," said Sidney.

"I like brainy people," she said, grabbing a hors d'oeuvre off a tray passing by. "Boyd is more the mingling type."

"Nancy came with us, George," said Sidney somewhat apologetically. "It was decided by my wife."

He looked at Shelby. "What an interesting name you have. Shelby," he said then turned to George.

"A car?"

"A Ford," said George. "A Mustang."

"Could be Cobra," said Sidney.

"Or GT. But I'm sure she has heard that before from less brainy people."

"Not that one, the GT. That took real brains." She got a kick out of the slight bantering. "But don't call me GT, OK?"

Amidst the chuckles, George looked toward the partying crowd milling all around.

"Sidney, GT, look at my date," said George pointing to a young beauty sitting on the edge of the pool, dangling her feet in the water while tolerating the attentions of a talkative man.

"GT?" mumbled Shelby with a disapproving grimace. *No, thanks,* she thought, but let it go.

"There she is." George pointed toward the girl. "Marci."

"Pretty," said Shelby, as if she were one of the guys.

"Very. And young," said Sidney. "Have I seen her in anything?"

"No," said George. "You'll be surprised to hear that she is not an actress, nor a model. She is not looking for a part in our movie."

"Why would anybody who wants nothing date you?" Sidney joked.

"I wonder about that. Actually, she did ask me to read something she wrote."

"A writer?" said Sidney.

"Poetry, I think. No competition for you."

"Watch out, my friend; writers don't go away. Not ever. Writers stick like crazy glue," he said in his grand manner. "They endear themselves until you have no choice but to give," he emphasized with a mysterious smile.

Shelby lost interest. This was not exactly the brainy talk she expected. "It was good to meet you," she said and turned away from them, curiously checking out the crowd, trying to see where Boyd might be.

"We're probably boring you," said Sidney. "We always get caught up in our work. You see, George here has just finished producing the movie of my last novel and . . ."

"We usually talk about the next one," said George.

"I'm still writing it."

"Then we have nothing," said George.

"Oh, don't change your ways on account of me," she said.

"I've been wondering about those black armbands," said George.

"Funny," said Shelby. "Loss of the Colonies," she chuckled.

"Witty. The English have a wonderful off-the-wall kind of wit," said Sidney. "How do you know Elisabeth?" he asked George.

"Mel, her husband and our host, is on the board of our production company. You've seen him at meetings."

"He must not have impressed me. But now I'll remember him."

"I thought you knew Mel," said George.

"I don't know anyone here. I think my agent puts my name on every invitation list because he doesn't think I'll go, but it makes him look good." Sidney liked to hear himself talk. Turning to Shelby he continued, "You know, writers write. I come out after each book is finished, smell the flowers, and then back to the dungeons I go."

"But you said you're writing now," said Shelby. "Yet you're out and about."

"My wife wanted to come."

"Luckily, your wife is very likeable and a great mixer."

"I almost forgot something, Shelby, while talking about the life of a writer. There is another mandatory outing. They need me at book signings. They'll have me doing one at Brentano's next Wednesday. Come if you can," he said. "Around one o'clock."

"I've never been to one. Maybe I'll stop in."

"I'll have a book for you."

The food trays were circulating. "I've had too much champagne. I think I need some ice water," said Shelby. "Excuse me."

She walked away from the men and saw Boyd and Nancy cozying on the dance floor. She took a deep breath and turned her attention to the bar. Glass of ice water in hand, she started for the staircase. *Why not?* she thought. *Curiosity is a good thing*. She knew that the house was not all that big. Standing at the top of the stairs, she absorbed the overall impression. *How sweet*. The master bedroom suite dominated the entire second floor, continuing into a bathroom that took Shelby's breath away. She had never seen a bidet before and was compelled to turn it on.

"Oops," she was surprised by the sudden oncoming force of the water spraying toward her face. "Aha, so that's how it works."

Just for the fun of it, she used the toilet. *That's where rich people pee*, she thought. There were no doors, only cleverly angled walls separating each area, and the suite ended in the rooftop lounge deck with a fireplace and an open loft office overlooking what seemed like the whole world. "Ah," was all she could say. "Ah."

She looked down to the party around the pool. Boyd was not in sight. She went downstairs, then made her way through the people, the conversation groups, the cozy nooks and crannies of the main level. No Boyd.

As the party thinned out, she kept checking her watch. She saw Sidney and George saying goodbye to each other. Then they spotted her.

"If I were you, I'd go home," said Sidney.

"Do you have the car?" said George.

"I have the keys." said Shelby.

George's date came over and smiled. "I'm ready."

"Don't worry, I'm sure someone will give him a ride," said Sidney. "See you all." He walked away.

Shelby just stood there, motionless. She walked around once more. The maids were picking up the spoils of the party. People were leaving, hugging and saying their goodbyes.

She walked out of the house. Leaning against the moss green 1973 Mach 1, Boyd's beloved Mustang, she waited. The sun was setting. Elisabeth came outside.

"Hello, dear," she said. "There's no one else inside. Can you drive home?"

Shelby looked at her. Nodded. "Yes, thank you. Nice party."

She got into the car and drove away.

The night would not end. Darkness all around, Shelby sat on the patio bench, staring into the black backyard. She had no tears. She was in deep shock, numb as if anesthetized.

The rising sun forced her into good parent mode. She was grateful to be able to hide behind the busy façade of motherhood. The needs of the dependent child had to come first, compressing all her other emotions and storing them somewhere in the back of her someplace, her backburner. Wherever.

Days came and went. Hard, dark, mean days. She survived the wrenching feelings of disbelief, the incomprehensible puzzlement, the inherent denial, but not the anger. Some instinct in her brain yelled *Enough!* The sound got louder and louder: *Enough, ENOUGH!*

Three days had passed.

Shelby handed the keys to the valet at the Beverly Wilshire Hotel. She marched through the lobby, through the automatic door directly into Brentano's book store. There was a line for Sidney's autographs. He was charming in his element. Shelby walked right up to the table, stood in front of him with hands on hips, challenging.

"Boyd, my husband if you recall, hasn't been home in days. Since Sunday. Any ideas? The last thing I heard him say was 'I'll be right back, Shel,' then off he went with your friend."

The nearby people listened eagerly, anticipating being first-hand witnesses to some Hollywood scandal.

Sidney smiled, excused himself from the fans, and guided her to a private corner.

"Didn't you see him with Nancy? They were pretty obvious. Such naiveté. I thought you'd know," he said.

"You brought her."

"She's a friend of my wife's."

"She didn't have a car."

"Nancy dials the telephone and hires a car whenever she desires. She came with us but didn't go home with us."

"My husband didn't go home with me. He vanished from the party." Shelby looked at him, and if eyes could kill, he would be a dead man.

"Nancy's rather impossible to resist."

"That's my husband she took. Doesn't that mean anything to her?"

"She has a way about her. Let it run its course," he said, matter-of-factly. "Would you like a book?"

"Is that your sense of humor?"

"It's a gift."

"You're joking, I hope," she said, turning sharply.

"Shelby," he called to her. "I have lunch at the Ocean Avenue Seafood in Santa Monica every third Thursday. Come by. We can talk."

"That'll be the day."

"Writers are good listeners. They know about people," he said.

"Forget it, Mr. Marshall."

"Sidney to my friends," he said, but she was gone before he finished his sentence. Sidney returned to his adoring public.

# CHAPTER 2

$S$ helby seemed to be on autopilot. Her car made all the correct turns through Beverly Hills to Sunset Boulevard. She was blind to the restaurants and shops lining the boulevard as she traveled the famous section nicknamed Sunset Strip. The traffic light at the Laurel Canyon Boulevard intersection was longer than the others and her impatience brought her back to reality.

The winding canyon road climbed higher and higher. At Lookout Mountain Avenue Shelby turned onto the narrow Horseshoe Canyon Road and kept going through some dirt road, until she reached a wider, paved Tianna Road.

Shelby arrived home. The house was a Scandinavian design chalet that was built as a guest house some years earlier on the lot of an architect. He designed it and in lieu of guests, he decided to lease it out. Boyd and Shelby were thrilled with the good rental deal on the unique building and loved being surrounded by the lush trees and foliage of the Hollywood Hills.

Greeted by the familiar picture of her daughter and the babysitter was calming to Shelby. Pamela, a beautiful, self-confident eight-year-old, and Thelma, a family friend who was helping out, were finishing Pamela's homework. Thelma was an attractive, sturdy woman in her late fifties, dressed in bright color-coordinated pants and top. Her hair and nails were done. She had the look of a woman who had never left the popular psychedelic free love decade of her youth, the 1960s. She was a student of color psychology guide books and a believer in all their rules.

Pamela, clearly raised with a lot of love, was as alarmed as Thelma when they saw Shelby's tear-filled eyes and runny makeup. Pamela rushed to embrace her mother. Thelma's arms completed the group hug.

Shelby kicked her shoes off in the foyer and collapsed on the living room couch. She sat there, staring, looking from Pamela to Thelma.

"I don't know what to do. Your father apparently went away somewhere with some lady who he likes better than us."

She pulled Pamela next to her and put an arm around her. "I would like to explain this to you, honey, but I can't. I don't understand it myself. I know a mother should know things, but I don't know what's happening." She took a tissue out of her purse and blew her nose. "Sit down, Thelma. Please."

"I feel like *small me*. Invisible."

"I remember when your mother told me how you used to say that you felt like a *small me*. You would cringe down and stay that way for a while. Then, as if some magical truth took control of your mind, you would walk around, stretch your neck toward the sky and take a deep breath. Your nostrils widening, you would grit your teeth and say 'giraffe!' Giraffe! And you made yourself appear a strong *large me*," said Thelma. Her neck was stretched up high as she relayed the story.

"Well, not today," said Shelby. "There's no giraffe in sight."

Thelma sat down next to Shelby and took her hand in hers.

"You'll have to find out what happened. Do you know anyone who knows the woman?"

"Come to think of it, I just told the man off. "

"What do you mean?" asked Thelma.

"I was rude and mean to him. Sidney Marshall."

"The author?" Shelby nodded. "I love his books," said Thelma.

"I used to," said Shelby. "But now I hate everything about him. To have friends who steal people's husbands."

Thelma was preparing to leave. "I can't stay for dinner with you. Arnie is home early tonight and he said we should go to the movies."

Shelby nodded and wouldn't stop, as if her head was attached to some yoyo.

"You have to call him—Sidney Marshall—and ask him what he knows or what he can find out."

"You're right."

"Give him a call. He's a writer. A good writer," said Thelma, getting her purse.

"Yeah, yeah, and writers are good listeners and writers know people, yeah, yeah. I don't have his number." Shelby helplessly paced around the living room. I don't even know the names of the people, the house and the address where the party was. I don't know anything," she started to cry again. "It's always Boyd who knows everything."

"I can't leave you in this state."

"I'll take care of Mommy," said Pamela.

Shelby smiled at her daughter. They were the spitting image of each other. Pamela was the *mini mom*. She had the long legs, big sparkling eyes, pixie nose, and long neck of her mother.

"That's right, we can do this together," said Shelby. "How sweet."

"Oh, Thelma, the brain just kicked in. I know where Sidney Marshall is having lunch next Thursday. If Boyd isn't home by then, I'll go see him."

"He'll be home by then. I bet you," said Thelma. "You OK?"

"Yes, thank you. We'll be just fine. Pamela and I. You have a nice evening with your husband."

Shelby walked her to the door and said goodbye.

Pamela watched her mother and waited. Shelby sat down again and looked lost.

"Thelma and I made some stew," said the little girl, trying to please. "You know, she did it, mostly."

"How sweet," Shelby said. "It smells good."

"Would you like some wine?" asked Pamela.

"You bet I would," said Shelby. "But I'd better pour it myself."

Shelby and Pamela went to the bright, small kitchen. Pamela set the breakfast nook table. She took care of details, folding the napkins just so. "See, Mommy, I make it very pretty. The way you like it."

This brought on another flood of tears. "Are you going to cry before we eat?" said Pamela.

"Nah. I think I'm done."

The Ocean Avenue Seafood restaurant was a popular eatery in Santa Monica for some years but Shelby had never been there. She found it easily. She drove by a few times, too nervous to go in. She pulled into a parking spot to watch the front entrance. A metallic blue Bentley Mulsanne stopped in front of the valet and Sidney Marshall got out of it. Shelby's fist tightened as she watched the man disappear inside. She sat there for several minutes then drove into a public parking lot and walked back to the restaurant.

She looked around hesitantly inside the busy upscale eatery. There was no hostess at the front desk. She waited, trying to appear nonchalant. Out of nowhere the Maître D' appeared.

"Welcome, Miss. How can I help you?"

Shelby was tentative but since she could not see into the dining room, she had to answer. "I'm looking for someone," she said softly.

"Are you expected?"

"Oh no. Not me. I mean," she took a deep breath. "I'm here to see Mr. Marshall."

There, she said it and the world did not end. She looked into the man's eyes and her demeanor took on strength. "Please tell him Shelby Carpenter would like to see him for a minute." She kept her eyes on him and the man did as he was told.

Sidney rose out of the center of his semicircular booth as he saw her approaching. A waiter was placing a glass of wine in front of him. When the waiter saw the new arrival, he immediately hurried off only to return with a plush chair positioning it directly opposite Sidney.

"Hello, Shelby," Sidney said.

"Hello."

"I'm glad you came. Can you stay?"

"I'll be quick."

"Please sit down. Will you join me?"

Shelby started to lower herself into the booth, keeping her eyes on the man. He gestured that she should take the chair.

"It's the *eye-to-eye theory*. Very important. I have to see the eyes otherwise I don't like to converse." He stopped for a beat as if waiting for Shelby's comment. There was none. "Would you like some wine?"

"Who drinks in the daytime anymore?"

"Those who can. Or the privileged few," he said.

"Conceited, aren't we?" she snapped while making a childish grimace.

"Yeah. Sometimes," he said, taking it in stride and signaled the waiter, pointing at his glass of wine.

"Are you still angry with me?" he asked.

"I embarrassed you."

"I'm too big to be embarrassed." This made her laugh out loud.

"Yes, it is conceit," she said.

"Feisty. I knew you would be," he said. "Now, do you have time for a chat?"

The wine arrived. "Notice I didn't order a whole bottle. One glass is good for the digestion." He lifted his glass and when she didn't lift hers, he took a sip. "Would you like to order?"

"No. Nah, I don't think so," she was back in her *small me* mode. She followed instructions, did as she was told, took the menu from Sidney. *Why am I so polite?* she wondered to herself.

"Share a bite with me?" he said.

"Well, I didn't mean to disturb you."

"Too late for that," he said.

"Are you flirting with me?"

"I have a God-given flirtatious nature, but you can take it or leave it."

"Well, I don't want you to eat alone. I have God-given good manners." Shelby proceeded to check the menu. In the meantime, Sidney pointed to the platter of bite-size seafood.

"I'm famished," he said. "What's mine is yours, please help yourself."

"I'll have what you have," she said and stared at the glass of wine. She felt her *small me* coming on again and tensed up. She knew she had to put an end to that.

"You seem so calm." She looked into his eyes and imagined Boyd sitting across from her. That always made her comfortable.

"My characters are crazy. That's a trick of the trade," he smiled and studied her. "All my anxieties play through my characters."

The waiter placed artfully arranged fish tacos on the table for starters. Following that he served her a sample of the pan roasted sea scallops. Her face lit up when it hit her palate.

"Whoa," she gushed.

"Well, Mr. Marshall—"

"Sidney, remember? We're sharing a meal, breaking bread," he said. "Let's see some respect," he joked.

"Well, Sidney, here it goes." She raised her glass to his and took a big gulp of the wine.

"Love this wine. I'm glad drinking at lunch is not *passé.*"

"I'm glad you came," he said.

"It's not a social visit," she said a little too quickly. She noticed the smile in his eyes. She spared a small smile admitting *that was dumb.*

"That was dumb. Of course it's social. But before I put both feet in my mouth—"

Sidney interrupted her. "Boyd went to Kenya with Nancy," he said and stuffed a huge oyster in his mouth. He watched her. Completely taken aback by the news, she reached for the wine as if it could save her.

"Kenya? Africa?"

He didn't say anything. He waited until she digested the news.

"I don't suppose he'll be back for dinner. I was to going cook his favorite."

She got up, took her purse. Sidney rose out of his seat politely and looked after her marching to the exit. He stood still. Two minutes later Shelby returned.

"I was rude. I shouldn't let you eat alone." she said.

"By all means."

"I'm really not a drama queen, Sidney. I just don't have any idea what to do." she said, lowering herself back in her seat.

Looking at his attentive eyes and finding listening ears, Shelby's mouth started to run, pouring out her heart to him. She could not stop herself.

"I thought my whole life was set up, going forward, perfect with Boyd's rising success, you know, the Hollywood scene, and now *small me* showed up. *Small me* hasn't been around for years and years. Since I met Boyd."

Sidney watched her eating, listened until there was a break so that he could speak. "*Small me*? Who's *small me*?"

Shelby's smile lit up the room. "Used to be me," she said. Sidney found out that Shelby was an introverted nerdy girl until graduating from college where she became Ms. Popularity after performing Salomé's Veil Dance in a school production. The dance ended in her near nude body on the floor in front of the ruling monarch.

"I was a regular Rita Hayworth in Salomé."

"And there was no more *small you*?"

"Rarely."

She couldn't stop talking as if a floodgate broke open.

"No one ever listened when I talked," she said.

"Where did Boyd come in the picture?"

"They were shooting a movie on our street and Boyd saw me come home. He invited himself inside and you know how no one can resist him. He swept me off my feet. My mother, too. My dad not so much until he asked him for my hand. Formally. Dad liked that respectful stuff."

Sidney listened to her closely, watched her every move, smiled at some of her expressions, watched the way she leaned into the conversation, displaying body language that underscored her words. His courteous nodding seemed to prod her on.

"Boyd likes that I don't know anything about anything. That I'm not smart. That I don't speak up. That he is the boss," she chuckled. "I do what I'm told. He is very much like my dad. Speak when spoken to kind of a man. 'You're beautiful,' he'd say. 'Like children, you should be seen not heard.'"

Sidney stopped chewing, stopped swallowing, but could not stop staring at her.

"What?" he said with disbelief.

"He likes smart people; he just doesn't want me to be smart."

"It's mind-boggling. So old-fashioned. I'm surprised people still think like that. This is the 1980s. When will they get with it?"

"Well, people do," she said, sounding somewhat wise. "There are all kinds of people, all different people. That's how he wants Pamela to be raised. He doesn't want any more children so he wouldn't deform my body," she said all in one breath.

"You seem to be too bright not to have a voice, Shelby."

Sidney was fascinated by Shelby. "Boyd is always in charge. Everything is done right. I make everything pretty. That's my job: pretty. Now I have to figure out how to do things without him."

"He'll be back, I'm sure," he said.

"Not in my bed, Sidney. No siree." Her body stiffened. She took on a defiant stance; she locked eyes with him and held it until she was ready for the next bite of fish from her plate.

# CHAPTER 3

Shelby knew deep in her heart that she could never trust Boyd again. She contained her anger and did not discuss her problem with anyone since she ran off her mouth to Sidney. During the day when Pamela was in school, Shelby gathered all his clothes, shoes, and belongings. She put most of them in large plastic trash bags and called the nearest charity to come pick them up. She separated his casual clothes from the famous labels that he wore so well and delivered those to the best designer consignment shop on Fairfax Avenue. Among the labels were Bottega Veneta leather, Armani, and Versace, but true to being the quintessential Californian, Boyd favored Zachary Prell, Travis Mathew, and other contemporaries. No matter what he wore, Boyd looked great. She loved him so much. What's going to happen to me now? Life looked bleak. Protecting Pamela became her escape and heartfelt mission.

Shelby flashed on scenes from the movies where the wronged woman, in a dramatic manner, would throw the man's things out the window and all the neighbors would know what had happened. At this point in time, she didn't see the humor. Sadness would linger around her without the smallest sign of it fading away. The Laurel Canyon lifestyle catered to privacy. The residents kept to themselves. Neighbors didn't know what was going on in her life and that was her choice.

Hanging on the doorframe between the master bedroom and bath spa like mistletoe was a sparkling sterling silver medallion about two inches in diameter. Shelby took it off the door, held it in her hand.

*"I'll love you as long as I'll live; I'll live as long as I love you — B."*

She looked at it. Read it out loud. Threw it in one of the large trash bags and watched it be swallowed up by the assortment. She walked away to continue gathering the giveaways. As she lined up the bags on the front porch the bell rang. The sign on the side of the pick-up truck said "St. Vincent de Paul Charitable Organization." She pointed to the bags and the driver loaded them on the open truck. He was preparing a receipt for her. She came running.

"Please, wait a minute," she yelled. She ran quickly to the bags. She reached into one of them that seemed to be all the way in the back. Miraculously, her hand found the medallion. She took it out.

"Thank you," she said to the man. "Thank you." She went inside.

After all this, she ran some errands before arriving at the main gate of Pinecrest, the private school on Sherman Way where Pamela was a student. The children waiting for their rides were under the supervision of a full-sized young woman. A tunic top featuring the Pinecrest emblem covered her ample body, revealing only jean pants and nondescript tennis shoes. Pamela seemed to be saying her best goodbye to the staffer. "Kiss-kiss-hug-hug, see you tomorrow," said the little girl, waving as she got into Shelby's car.

They headed north on Ventura Freeway to Malibu Canyon.

"Mommy, are we going to the beach? We don't have our bathing suits," said Pamela observing the road her mother was traveling.

"I thought we should have a nice dinner in a special place."

"I like nice dinners." Pamela reflected Shelby to a T.

"Me, too," said Shelby and negotiated the curvy Malibu Canyon down to Pacific Coast Highway and right to the Beau Rivage Restaurant. Other early diners had started coming into the prestigious romantic favorite. Shelby and Pamela waited at the front desk. The old world European setting featured a fireplace, ocean view tables, and a friendly outdoor patio dining area.

"Maybe we'll stay around long enough to see the sunset," said Shelby. "It's very romantic."

"Mommy, it's only me."

Shelby smiled. "Could I ever forget that? You're the most important person in my life." Shelby gave Pamela's shoulder a little squeeze. Pamela grinned. She got a kick out of her mother making strange comments like this.

"Boyd Carpenter," Shelby announced to the hostess.

"Will you wait for Mr. Carpenter or would you like to be seated?" she asked.

"We would like to be seated. He may be late. He's in Kenya."

"How interesting. He's on the set," said the hostess, as if she was in the know. Carrying three menus she seated them at a primary table in view of the fireplace.

"Is this the table you reserved?"

"Yes, this is Boyd's favorite table," Shelby replied.

The waitress immediately appeared with finger food sized vegetables in a citrus cream to prepare their palate for the oncoming orgy of tastes and textures. European specialties were also explained to Pamela and they both listened intently before making their choices. Shelby waited for the glass of their rich, dark house Malbec and Pamela had a virgin cocktail. They touched glasses, sipped on their drinks, and enjoyed the majestic surroundings.

"Is daddy in the real Kenya or on a set, Mommy?"

"Someone told me he is in the real Kenya in Africa. In some famous club with famous people."

Pamela absorbed the information and seemed to have no problem accepting it. Their appetizers came. They turned their attention to the food, ooh-ing and ah-ing as they tasted the distinctive dishes.

"Did you want to go with him?" she asked her mother.

"I would have gone with him anywhere. But no, this time he went with other people. He didn't say a word to me." Shelby took a deep breath. "Just went. Left. How do you feel about that?" said Shelby.

"When is he coming back?"

"I don't think he will be living with us when he comes back."

The silence indicated that Pamela was thinking. "I don't like it."

"I don't like it either," said Shelby. "But he wants to be with somebody else, not me." She swallowed a tear. "He has made his decision and went away with her. There is nothing I can do, Pamela."

They were quiet during most of the main course. Pamela didn't look at her mother. "Does he want to divorce us?" she asked.

"Not you, honey. He loves you more than anyone. He'd never leave you."

"Where will I live?"

"You'll live with me, honey. I have decided to give up the house in the Canyon and move into grandma and grandpa's house in Encino."

"But it's for sale!" said Pamela.

"It was but I spoke to the realtor who handled it. I told her what had happened and she took it off the market."

Shelby seemed to be talking to herself more than to anyone else. Pamela's thoughts were centering on her own needs.

"Mommy, I think I will miss grandma and grandpa living in their house but not with them."

"Honey, I miss my parents too. But maybe living in their house will make us remember them better. All the things we did with them while they were alive, all the good times we had with them."

"And the monkey bar they put in for me. And Mommy, how they kept talking about a little brother for me?" Pamela's excitement grew as she envisioned her future.

"Not likely, Pamela," said Shelby. The tears welling in her eyes were unnoticed by the child.

"You know, with him gone, I'll get a job. Some things will change but everything will be OK."

"Do I have to change schools?"

"No."

"Will I take the school bus?"

"We shall see. You shouldn't worry. It'll be fun living in grandma and grandpa's house." Shelby looked away to holdback her tears.

"But what about Thelma? She's not going away, is she?"

"No, honey. Thelma will stay around. You know, Thelma is very much like your grandmother was. They were best friends since their high school days."

"High school?" said Pamela.

Shelby caught her humor. "Yes, they had high schools way back then," she said. "Smart aleck."

The waitress came to take dessert orders.

"I'd like an Irish Coffee," Shelby said.

"Anything else?"

"How about an apple strudel or a peach tart for my daughter?"

"Peach tart, Mommy, please, thank you." After the waitress walked away, Pamela said, "I like this place a lot."

"It was your father's and my favorite restaurant. Many memories come to mind."

When they finished, the hostess stopped by to pick up the untouched third menu.

"Looks like your husband did not make it after all," she said.

"No. He didn't. He's in Kenya."

Shelby took Pamela by the hand. Pamela looked to the hostess and said, "That's in Africa."

The hostess nodded in agreement but wasn't sure just what exactly was going on.

Carrying their shoes in one hand and holding each other with the other, Shelby and Pamela headed out to the sand.

"Whoa!" shrieked Pamela with delight. "The sand tickles me," she squealed. She dipped her toes into the ocean and her laughter filled Shelby's heart.

Shelby was lingering in bed, staring at the ceiling. She remembered her parents' old fashioned decoration, old light fixtures, good dark wood furniture and of course, the knick-knacks. Those were gone. She moved the furniture she and Boyd had bought into the Encino house from Laurel Canyon. She stopped liking them after all that had happened and planned on having an auction house sell them as soon as they could be replaced. She wanted new furniture suitable for their new lives. This was something else for the back-burner. She was down and for the first time in her life she knew what feeling lonely meant.

Day after day, Shelby's only joy was Pamela. Was she a precocious child or just bright and alert? Shelby delighted in the way she didn't have to do baby talk and could communicate with Pamela on an intelligent level. Whatever she did not understand, she would ask. They talked about everything that was on their minds. Mostly on Pamela's. She seemed to have accepted the fact that her father would not live with them when he returned but she could spend a lot of time with him no matter where he lived. At first she suggested to her mother that she forgive him since, in her estimation, coming back would mean that he liked her again. Pamela escalated her methods even pleading with Shelby to take him back. But Shelby stood her ground. It was weeks later that Pamela gave up and finally allowed Shelby to do whatever she needed for herself, even though Shelby had no idea what those needs were. What *herself* really was? She never had to define her identity before. Didn't know how.

"Thirty years old," she said to herself, "and no one ever asked me if I know who I am. I couldn't have answered. I still can't." Although she halted the ongoing dialogue in her head, she knew she would have to resolve this question soon.

In the meantime, first things first. A job.

Shelby was hoping to find a job located conveniently to Encino making it an easier drive for her. She called on every newspaper ad for a job in the West-wood or Santa Monica areas, just off or near the San Diego Freeway. Her second interview was in a Beverly Hills investment firm. Unsuccessful. She never even got a passing grade from the office manager, a tall, skinny spinster. It was too far for Shelby to drive anyway which in her mind justified that failure.

She was pretty anxious about her interview at the June Scott real estate office in Beverly Hills. She thought she did well but they told her they would let her know. By then she knew that meant a polite *No*.

Learning little-by-little she still did not want to think about running out of money and getting to the point when a time crunch would drive her job search.

It was a beautiful sunny day. Leaving the Beverly Hills interview as she turned on Wilshire Boulevard from Rodeo Drive Shelby noticed a sign in the window of Brentano's book store. "Meet The Author - Book signing Today — 1:00 p.m." Her heart seemed to skip a beat with the memory of Sidney and her subsequent confrontation with him. Moving with the traffic she caught a quick glimpse of the photo of a young woman, apparently the featured author that day. She was relieved. Somewhere deep in the back of her mind she expected Sidney's face in the window display. Even without his picture, his magnetic aura tugged at her. She continued driving west on Wilshire Boulevard and before she knew it she was in Santa Monica, parking in the public lot, walking into the Ocean Avenue Seafood restaurant.

The same Maître D' greeted her inside as when she entered for the first time. His face lit up.

"Hello again, Miss. Is Mr. Marshall expecting you?"

"I don't think so. This is a surprise. Please ask him if he would see Shelby?"

She was also surprised on learning that Sidney was there. *Guess this is the third Thursday of the month.*

After a brief moment the Maître D' returned. "Please, follow me." She did all the way to Sidney's table.

Sidney had the biggest smile on his face. He welcomed her with open arms. She never felt more appreciated than at that moment. Shelby had a chance to pour out her heart. Sidney had a chance to bring her up to date on his professional progress. Together and separately, they had elevated each other's day, perhaps life.

They made no plans. She didn't know she had an open invitation. But Shelby saw him again on the spur of a moment and it was always as if he were waiting for her. He seemed to want to know the most miniscule details of her life. He wanted to understand why someone as gorgeous was not showing off her beauty by modeling? Why she would accept being secondary to her husband? Sidney's curiosity spurred her on.

Suddenly she said "I almost forgot, Thelma is not picking up Pamela today. I gotta run."

"Thelma?"

"My babysitter. My friend. Bye." Shelby hurried out of the restaurant.

# CHAPTER 4

*T*hings were not going so well for Thelma. Arnie, her husband, a tall, slim man of 70, was preparing a light dinner and setting the salad on the table in the breakfast nook. Thelma came in from the garage with grocery bags and started to put the purchases away. She looked at the ready table.

"Nice job, Arnie, but it doesn't look like you washed this Romaine."

"It was washed three times, just read the packaging," he said.

"I don't trust the packaging. I like to wash my own lettuce."

"Then go, wash it," said Arnie. He dumped the salad into the colander and walked out of the kitchen.

The sliding glass doors opened from the kitchen leading to the U-shaped courtyard. An attractive roll-out canopy provided added shade and reached over the swim spa in the center. The screen covering the entire courtyard ended at the high wall in the back that completed the *outdoor* section of the property. A life-like mural depicting a Continental sidewalk café brought a smile to anyone's face on entering. Thelma and Arnie had created a secluded private world of their own. The courtyard opened on one side to a separate one-bedroom and bath wing that was independent of the rest of the home. On the other side of the U-shape the main house bent around from kitchen to a large great room, a study and the master bedroom. A favorite relaxation spot was the extended patio that, like a bird cage, sat on the golf course. Thelma loved their house. Arnie was also proud of it. It was comfortable; it was home in every way.

"Now why would you do that, Arnie?" she called after him. "What's wrong with you?"

"Nothing's wrong with me," he said, raising his voice as he returned. "I want to help and it's not good enough for you."

Thelma looked vulnerable. "I like it when you help but after all these years together you should know my habits. I know yours. I pay attention," she said. "And you know that I can't stand it when you raise your voice. Yelling is not going to make you right."

"I'm not going to be pussy-whipped."

"Doing things around the house my way is not going to emasculate you. It'll just mean that we are growing together."

Thelma stepped closer to Arnie. "This must be what happens when people marry late in life. Agree?"

Just as she said that the telephone on the wall rang. Thelma picked it up. "Hello," she said. "Hi, sweetie. Yes, I can be there. Bye."

"Was that Shelby?"

"Yes."

"Don't you think you're spending too much time with her?"

"I have to help Shelby. She's like my own daughter. Her mother was my best friend and I am not going to let her down when she needs me."

"You have your own daughter."

"She doesn't need me," said Thelma.

Time out. She headed for the bedroom. She took her bathing suit off the hook on the back of the bathroom door. Undressing, she looked at her nakedness in the full-length mirror. She saw the skin that was once tight and smooth now wrinkled around the neck and loose around her waist. What happened? What else will happen? She did not understand the deterioration of the body while her brain remained sharp as ever.

She poured her loose skin into the skirted swimsuit and went through the bedroom, slid the full size glass door open, stepped outside, and entered the swim spa. Eyes closed, she tried to calm herself.

Arnie came out of the kitchen, sat down on the chase lounge and watched her. He always enjoyed the way she moved and appreciated how she took care of herself. Neither spoke. She swam against the current, resting her eyes on the colorful life-like wall mural depicting a happy place.

"I don't like to fight, Thelma. I really don't. I like it here, living with you."

She didn't answer. Maybe she didn't really hear him.

"I love you," he said.

"I would not marry you now, the way you are now. The way you have changed. You used to love everything about me and now, you're just not the same person I married." Thelma did not look at him. He was silent for a few minutes.

"Thelma," he said. "I'm going inside, finish the salad and set the table, OK?"

"OK. I'll just go another ten minutes. Thank you, Arnie."

"Let's never fight again, Thelma. I don't like it."

"I don't either. Why can't you just agree? Say 'Yes, dear,'" she said.

"Then I'll be a . . . pussy."

"No, dear. You'll be an agreeable, sweet husband."

# CHAPTER 5

"You are young and fresh. That suits me," he said to Shelby. "Younger than springtime," he winked. "I don't like old people around me."

"You mean your contemporaries?"

"They know what I know," Sidney replied.

She stopped eating and waited for more insight from Sidney. None came. He slurped the British Columbian oysters from the iced shellfish platter in front of him with great appreciation. Followed by shrimp and black mussels he leaned back, graciously allowing time for conversation.

"Help yourself, Shelby. Just dig in any time," he said.

"Funny that you want younger people, who know nothing." She saw humor in that. He didn't. She put a couple of the appetizers on her plate. She smacked her lips; she approved of the delicate tastes.

"Not funny. Far from it. It's important. Younger people know young things. I don't want to read in the newspaper about what's going on, what everyone is doing. I don't want to watch the news to find out what's a trend. I want to create the trend. I want to *be* the trend! What if I want to make it a verb: *trending?* That would be a cute word," he said in an aside. "I want to live it and do it and trend it and make it my own." As usual, Sidney was satisfied with himself.

"I doubt that'll ever be a word. Cute or not. *Trending,*" said Shelby.

"I wonder. I like words. I like inventing words. For instance, look at something like *bum.* It's a *bummer. Bumming.* What do you think? Cute?"

"It'll never happen."

He looked into her eyes and raised one eyebrow suggestively, Rudolph Valentino style. "Here's another: *style, styling.* What do you think?"

"It's probably true. Writers often create words."

"Or styles," said Sidney. "Create styles, coin words."

"That's sage," said Shelby.

"I agree. And modest."

"So?" Shelby grinned.

"So? Do you know what's fascinating about you? You are young, but smart and getting smarter."

"I'm not that smart."

"You just can't see how smart you are. I am able to see it more and more," he said.

"How sweet."

"You bet it's sweet."

"Could your smarts be rubbing off?" she said.

He chuckled. "Maybe. Or maybe yours are coming out. You realize that we can talk about many things, but you're also a woman with womanly ways."

"That doesn't sound like good English. Is it? Womanly ways?"

"Yes, that's correct," he said. "Trust me."

"Maybe it just sounds old."

"There you go. That's what I mean. I learn youth from you."

"We're both learning," she said. "I have a question."

"Go ahead."

"Being in a public place with you makes me wonder: what do people think of us?"

"Shelby, my dear, when you see a married man in some dark, out-of-the-way restaurant where no one would recognize him, he is hiding something. If you see him in a well-known place with a woman, everyone assumes that he is having a business lunch. So people think nothing of us."

Shelby laughed. "I learn the old stuff from you, don't I? Good thing I'm not your lover. I'd feel guilty." She sipped on the glass of white in front of her, then reached for a notepad in her hobo bag. "If I take this out it will look like I'm taking notes and doing something business-like."

"We don't have to go that far," he said, also laughing.

A handsome man wearing the latest Italian Canali jacket over well fitting jeans and an open collar shirt came to their table.

"Sidney, my friend, you make these Thursdays special," he said.

"Jeffrey, how are you? You remember Shelby Carpenter?"

Jeffrey leaned down to shake Shelby's hand. "Jeffrey King, Shelby. You met him a few weeks ago when you were here before," Sidney said.

"Yes, of course I remember. You're the owner. This is a wonderful place."

"We try. I'm on my way to the kitchen. If you haven't ordered yet I'll have my man prepare an inimitable dish for you," said Jeffrey. "Not even on the menu yet," he said reaching out to shake with Sidney. "You'll like it. I'll have them split it in two."

Amid smiles, Jeffrey King took his leave and headed to the open kitchen in the back of the dining room.

"Good man," Sidney said.

"Good food," Shelby said.

"We don't want to disappoint your palate."

"You never do, Sidney." She was pensive. "I like the way you take charge. I don't like to think for myself."

"Don't go backwards, sweetheart. You have to think for yourself. I like it when you do."

Shelby listened. "Thank you. I needed that."

"When we finish, I want you to follow me to my place. I want to show you something."

"Your etchings?"

"That one is too old, even for me," he said with a twinkle in his eyes.

Shelby studied the older man across the table from her. He was tall even when sitting down. His posture, the angle at which he held his head, the gaze of his eyes that swept the restaurant, and his elegant *California casual* wardrobe, all spoke of absolute self-confidence. He owned the world. Shelby was impressed with every-thing about him from the moment she met him at the July Fourth party. It was heralded as a pool party, a casual gathering, but casual for the show business crowd is not the same as it is for ordinary people. Showbiz casual is still designer casual.

The Maître D' came by. "Excuse me, Mr. Marshall. There is an Alexandra Novak here to see you."

Sidney nodded. "Thank you. We're expecting her," he said.

Alexandra was at least forty with stunning red hair and a great deal of arti-ficial enhancements that contrasted with Shelby's natural young appearance. The women looked at each other and nodded. Sidney rose to introduce them but kept it brief.

"Alexandra, this is Shelby. Shelby, this is Alexandra." Then he turned to Alexandra, "Please sit down." She did not sit. She handed him a large manila case tied with a ribbon.

"Here it is, Sidney. The others are on your desk," she said with a deep smoker's voice. "Anything else?"

"No. I'll see you at the meeting tomorrow." Sidney was formal.

"Right. Nice to meet you," she said to Shelby and headed toward the exit. Shelby looked after her. *I bet there's a dumb blonde under all that red hair,* Shelby thought. *I should know, 'cause I am one. Look at her sway that butt in rhythm in those high heels. She knows she is being watched.* Shelby stopped her catty mind play and turned her attention back to lunch.

"Now we are officially confirmed as business acquaintances as far as anyone watching is concerned. But I assure you, no one cares at a restaurant like this. People are hep."

"Hip," she corrected him.

"Hip, you're right. I enjoy seeing you," he said.

"I like it, too."

"But as a man—"

"A married man, don't forget," she interrupted.

"I never forget that, Shelby, honey. I take pleasure in my marriage. It's a good thing."

Shelby was relieved. "Then we're good?"

"Very good. We're very good," he said. "Ready to go now?"

She followed the Bentley as Sidney drove the short distance to a condominium complex on Ocean Front Walk.

Sidney waited for her to park the *Mach 1* in the visitor spot.

"Nice car. It should be a *Shelby GT*," he said.

"Nice car," she said pointing at his Bentley. "And it matches your eyes."

"You don't forget a thing, do you?"

Sidney carried the large Manila envelope as they walked to the elevator that took them to the top floor. Although there was no one around still Sidney seemed quick about unlocking the door and gesturing her inside.

"Welcome to my *pied-a-terre*," he said with a certain amount of pride, arms wide open to welcome and embrace her. Shelby glanced around the well-appointed lavishly decorated spacious one-bedroom condominium. Everything he needed when he was away from home. Mirrored walls and huge windows added a special sparkle to the sunny living room. Shelby walked around noticing details that caught her attention. The alcove wall was a full length window and from his desk Sidney could see the ocean in its ever-changing yet never changing beauty. He placed the envelope on the coffee table and walked her to the terrace. The view to the Pacific was soothing. The couple of glasses of wine Shelby had at lunch made her dreamy. He put his arm around her. She let him. The sense of safety felt heavenly. Not since Boyd did she experience the protective energy of a man's arms. She closed her eyes. Sidney kissed her lips. She lingered then pulled back much slower than she thought.

"No, Sidney. Please, no," she whispered. "That's not who we are."

"We could be."

"No. Not really."

Sidney moved away from her. "Well, Shelby, my dear. I have waited for you for a long time. I can wait some more."

He stepped inside, got the chilled *Calloway Fumé Blanc* from the refrigerator and the frosted glasses from the freezer. He uncorked the bottle, poured and rejoined her on the terrace.

"I keep remembering when we met. The first time I saw you," he said. "And the party, the English woman, the wife of the chief of George's production company?"

"Yes, Elisabeth," she said.

"And the black armbands. That was priceless. Lots of fun."

"That was funny except that's where Boyd was swooped up by the rich divorcée. The vulture and the prey. Not so funny. 'I'll be right back, Shel' was the last thing he said to me."

"The irony is that none of us was supposed to be there. Nancy is friends with my wife and she drove to the party with us. George, her ex-husband, who produced the movies of a couple of my novels, only came to show off his date."

"Whatever," she said. "Boyd didn't like parties. Rarely went."

"Kismet. You and I were destined to meet."

Thinking about how Boyd left her immediately after meeting the woman changed Shelby's mood considerably. She went inside. Sidney followed. "Here we are appreciating each other, filling a void."

"What void?"

"Maybe void is the wrong word. Maybe what we are appreciating, or what I am appreciating, is the potential of new excitement, new feelings in my life. A writer has to experience life in order to write well about it. So it's not a void but it's actually an opening."

"Maybe not for both of us," she said.

"It could be." He raised his glass. "To many more perfect times." He waited a beat then added "together." Shelby's mind was on the wonderful lightness of the dry wine as they touched glasses.

One thought lead to another. She did not understand whether or not she should take the road her imprudent feelings wandered. Part of her wanted to get away from the man but not all of her. The lonely woman within wanted to stay. Shelby was confused.

"Let me see if I can cheer you up," he said.

Sidney opened up the Manila envelope on the table, undid the decorative ribbon bearing his initials that tied the bulky pages together. Shelby watched him wondering what he was doing. He got a pen and wrote on the front page of the contents of the envelope then retied the ribbon and ceremoniously handed her the thick document.

"This is the new novel I've just finished and which is about to come out in print," he spoke with tenderness as if he were handing over a newborn baby. Shelby trembled with excitement.

"Your manuscript? I can't believe it," she whispered. "Your autographed manuscript!" She read the autograph once and then read it out loud. "For Shelby who's not afraid to dream __ Love, Sidney Marshall."

She didn't look at the date but she knew she would remember it forever. With mischief in her eyes she gave him a quick kiss on the lips. "Thank you, Sidney. I will cherish this, always."

Only minutes earlier Shelby had spotted several Manila envelopes like hers. She looked at him without saying anything. He saw her look but said nothing. Another sip of wine later she walked past him and sat down on the couch. He slid close to her. He kissed her and she found his lips irresistible. He tasted good, he smelled good, his touch was caring and he exuded a *going home kind of warmth*. She stopped thinking and let herself go with the moment. He responded to the change in her attitude with hopes rising. But it ended as suddenly as it started. It ended abruptly when she reminded herself of where she was and with whom. She pulled out of his embrace.

"You know, I admire your amazing writing, your unique lifestyle and I am blown away by the autographed manuscript. I don't care how many copies exist. I'm just honored to be your friend." She placed the manuscript back in the envelope and into her spacious hobo sack.

"It's a very limited edition," he said pointing to the pile on the desk. "Only ten. They're numbered."

"How sweet," she said gently caressing the book. "I'll probably have a leather cover made for it."

"I'd like to pay for that. Just let me know how much." He then took his wallet and pulled out several bills. "Better yet, why don't you take this now?"

Shelby laughed out loud. "Don't ruin the moment, Sidney. I don't care why your publicist came to the restaurant to deliver my copy when you had all these here. Oops, the brain just kicked in," she said with her laughter turning to a smile. "She brought them up here, didn't she? She has a key."

"As I said nothing to hide." He grinned mysteriously. "She works with me. She is running my publicity campaign. Besides, I couldn't be sure you would come up here, could I."

"Right."

"I'm a good salesman," he concluded.

"I'm a pushover."

"Whichever or both. You are here and now. That's what matters."

"She is beautiful," said Shelby.

"Yes. That helps things. Don't you think? Smart and beautiful, that's how I like my women. But you sound jealous. I like that even more," he stretched out in the cushy lounge chair. "I'll wait. You'll come to me."

"Yeah, yeah," she laughed. "You'll make me an offer I can't refuse."

"Sounds like a plan," he laughed with her. "I was also thinking that with all that's going on about my new book, we should devise some kind of a code system. We could leave messages but no one else would know what they meant"

"Almost romantic."

"Clever, don't you think?" he said.

"Who needs it?"

"One never knows."

"Your wife probably doesn't care."

"She does," he said immediately.

Shelby realized by his tone that he and his wife were getting along just fine and there was no need for her to get brazen or smart-alecky.

"Hate to be a party pooper but I have to get going. Time to pick up Pamela and then get ready for my sixth job interview. But who's counting?" She took a deep breath, her mind weary. "It's a job in itself to get an interview then when they don't like me, I go crazy. Then it takes me days to put the pieces back together."

"Can I help?"

"How?" she asked.

"Well, what skills do you have?"

"Good wife. Does that count?" He didn't answer.

Shelby got her bag and bent down to give him another kiss. "Thank you, really. Very, very much," she said.

He walked her to her car. Neither of them was chatty.

"You know, Shelby, you wouldn't have to work at all. If you'd let me take care of you and Pamela. Think about it." He said that with the confidence of experience.

"Is that any way to raise a child," she said.

"It's not such a big deal."

"I don't have to think about it. And I appreciate it but as you know by now, that's not who I am. I may be a flake but I am a good mother."

She got into her car and waved to him as he closed the car door for her.

Shelby had always loved the beauty of Sunset Boulevard winding its way from Santa Monica to the San Diego Freeway and she took that route every chance she had. She was deep in thought as she drove to the San Fernando Valley. Her reflections always lead back to Boyd.

Madly in love with her husband every day throughout the years, Shelby could not get used to the idea that Boyd would be able to leave her. But he did. He went off with Nancy, George's ex. As a stuntman and stand-in for stars, Boyd was popular in the Hollywood industry and his professionalism was widely recognized. His working in the films George produced had no connection with Nancy. Shelby's mind *dazed out. Boyd will still work for George. Nancy will still be rich and friendly with George. The only person whose life was irreparably damaged was Shelby.* "The ignorant innocent idiot," she said out loud.

The divorce was uncontested by Shelby. She could not imagine how she could live with him after all this even if he did come back. She was still reeling with the pain for which her threshold was miniscule. *A weak woman,* she thought of herself. Principled, she did not believe in alimony of any kind as long as she felt she was capable of earning her own living. She didn't know that she was not capable of managing her money, learning to budget and stay afloat. As it worked out, her principles and her pride got her child support, period. Any job would have been OK and that's exactly what she looked for. A job. She was not sorry only disillusioned and weary.

Shelby pulled into the parents' pick-up lane in front of the main building of the sprawling private school. There were only a few kids still waiting for their ride. The full-sized young woman was there as before, supervising the students. Watching Pamela's body language Shelby perceived that Pamela was fond of the young woman so Shelby also smiled at her.

"See you tomorrow! Kiss-kiss-hug-hug," said Pamela and jumped into Shelby's car.

"Nice to see that you like your teacher so much," said Shelby.

"She's not a teacher. She is the lunch lady. She's so nice. She makes the sandwiches the way we want them; we just have to tell her in the morning. Then she puts our names on it and it's so fun!" Pamela was overflowing with enthusiasm.

Shelby drove into the side garage of the house on Bergamo Road. Ranch style, it wrapped around a flower garden in the back and overlooked one of the canyons beyond which one could see Ventura Boulevard below. A nice size yard featured several rose bushes as a natural fence. Off to one side a well maintained *monkey bar* indicated that this was a child-friendly home. A tool shed in a corner of the back yard was empty and step-by-step Pamela was making it into her playhouse.

Pamela jumped out of the car and ran to get the mail from the curbside mail box before going inside.

"We will have a serious talk tonight, Pamela," Shelby said as they went inside and put down their things.

"OK, Mom. I will put on my serious hat," said Pamela and checked to see whether she got a smile out of her mother. No, not tonight.

"It's a nice evening. We can have dinner outside," said Shelby, anticipating and getting Pamela's enthusiastic approval. Pamela rushed to throw her books in her room, washed her hands and started setting the table on the patio deck. The rose bushes were full of buds and sweet smell of flowers filled the air. A screened-in extended lanai seemed to be reaching out into the garden as if embracing all living things.

Shelby, at nearly thirty, looked so young it was hard to imagine she was a parent. Pamela poured herself a tall glass of tomato juice over ice and for her mother she brought a glass of red wine. They settled down. The pulled pork that cooked all day in the crock pot tasted wonderful. The sun was setting. It was a perfect night in every way but one. No Boyd.

"I only have to memorize a poem for homework. Can you believe it?" said Pamela.

"How come that's all?"

"Because, our homeroom teacher is getting married and she forgets what she's supposed to do." Pamela giggled.

"It'll catch up with you, honey," said Shelby.

She sipped on the wine and then turned serious.

"Pamela, honey, this will be new. All new to me and to you. This full-time job means I'll have to arrange for you to be dropped off after school. You may be alone sometimes until I get home."

"That'll be fun, Mom."

"You can't bring your friends home."

"Can I have Lorraine drop me off?"

"Who's Lorraine?" Shelby said.

"You saw her at school, Mom."

"Oh, the big girl supervising? The lunch lady?"

"She's not big. Bigger than you, but everyone is bigger than you, Mommy."

"I'm crazy about you, kid. Remind me to hug you when we get up from the table."

"You hug me all the time," said Pamela.

"You know how it goes: ten hugs a day keeps the doctor away."

"That's apples, Mom. One apple a day."

"That's too cutesy even for me. Go, study the poem and then I want to hear it."

# CHAPTER 6

Shelby clumsily climbed out of bed as the six o'clock news crept into her dreams. Oh, hell. It's morning already. She tightened the little string belt around her slinky nightgown, and without her eyes fully open, headed for the backyard. She practically attacked the kid's gym set, doing chin-ups and body swings. In just a few moments her eyes were as wide awake as her body. She was ready to soak up the freshness of the morning and enjoy the silence, interrupted only by the playful chirping of birds. She cut some roses and checked on the other bushes that were starting to bud. She appreciated that her parents planned out the rose garden carefully; each month one bush produced flowers while another was getting ready with new buds. She turned on the sprinklers and went back into the house to continue exercising. Her mind was already focused on taking Pamela to school and driving to the next job interview.

Everything around her was a reminder of how beautifully simple her life had been. How easy it was when she knew that her father made all the decisions, and then Boyd took over. She kept running into the dead-end question: "Now what?"

Inner peace eluding her, she grew increasingly tense. Thoughts of her recent past raced around in her mind. She didn't think she did anything wrong to bring on these horrible events but she was never sure. She had no one to talk to. No one. The neighbor woman down the street, Dana's obese mother, Hazel, was sweet and plain. Dana, an occasional playmate of Pamela, was a bit older than Pamela yet not even close to Pamela's sharpness and worldliness. Shelby couldn't stop smiling at the mere thought of little Pamela going on nine, becoming a responsible grownup before her time.

The divorce papers were delivered by messenger one day a few weeks after Boyd ran off with Nancy on the African adventure. In the papers Boyd offered one year of alimony giving her a chance to train for some work. He was also fair in refunding Shelby the penalty she had to pay on breaking their rental agreement on the Laurel Canyon house. The settlement documents took Pamela's needs into account. All Boyd wanted were his clothes. She signed the documents and added a note stating that his clothes were donated to charity. She put the papers into the postage prepaid overnight envelope and took it to the post office. She was done. She was running on empty.

The reality of rough times ahead created a dense fog in her brain. Her *small me* had to crawl out of the daze and somehow find the light. All along she knew she would not allow anything to interfere with Pamela's world, her self-image and security. Shelby knew she would have to climb out of this hole step by step but first had to figure out what the steps were. The matter of money was never her area of responsibility but now she would have to find the balance. The income and expense. How to be frugal and give up dinners at the Beau Rivage. How to keep her fears camouflaged by her fashionable outside, impressive figure, warm smile and whatever else people perceived her to be. That was it. The perception. Once she accepted that by living up to people's expectations she had the perfect façade behind which her private world could remain private. *Let them eat cake* she thought to herself and a cocky grin appeared on her face. That's what Boyd used to say indicating that he didn't care about anyone's opinion.

The appointment was in an office located in an area in which she absolutely did not want to work. *Why was she even going? Why? Because things were getting tight,* she thought. Driving, parking, taking the elevator, getting closer and closer to her destination she grew increasingly unhappy. A law firm in one of those sterile suites in the twin towers on Wilshire Boulevard, full of attorneys and insurance men. Full of suits and ties and vests. Yes, the more important the man was, the better his vest. The concept was funny when she read about them in stories or satirical articles but not so when it appeared to become her reality.

Her initial interview was strange. She didn't know what to expect in the first place and what she got was the unexpected. *I am applying for an office job but clearly, typing is not my strong suit,* Shelby thought to herself as she sat across from the man pre-screening her. *Should she tell him that up front, or when?* She remained quiet.

Richie, a short, good looking Latino man, the attorney's assistant, attempted to prepare her for the interview.

"Now, listen," he said. "The last receptionist we hired left in a month. She found a better-paying job. But Mr. Ross will like the fact that you have a kid. It makes you more responsible."

"Thank you for your help, Richie. I really appreciate it," said Shelby. "What else should I know?"

"He'll ask you what you're good at," he said.

"Not typing," she said.

"With the computers it isn't that obvious. Do you want to do a typing test?"

"If I have to."

"Yes. Mr. Ross likes tests. Do you want to do it on a typewriter or the computer?" He got up walked her to the reception area where there was an old electric typewriter and a not too new *magnetic card* word processor. He looked at her and gestured to sit.

"The mag card word processor is more efficient because it saves the text on the cards. It's less work to make changes," he said.

Shelby immediately sat down at the older Selectric typewriter where she sensed possible familiarity and stared at the keys laughing back at her. Richie shrugged his shoulder and reached for a timer. It was an ordinary kitchen timer. Shelby was bewildered when she saw him push the dial to the first notch marking one minute. She held back the smart aleck comment on the tip of her tongue.

"Start." he said.

Shelby started typing from the text on a stand by the side of the typewriter. The bell rang. Richie took the sheet out of the machine and started to count the words one-by-one.

"Forty-two," he said.

Shelby reached for her purse and got up. "Well, you can't win 'em all."

"Oh, wait," he said. "Try again. Maybe you just needed to warm up," he encouraged them. Once again, he set the timer on the one-minute notch and said "Start."

Shelby typed the same sentence, and this time went farther before the bell rang. Richie took it out of the typewriter and proceeded to count one word at a time.

"It's better. Forty-nine," he said.

"Not exactly sixty to eighty."

Richie seemed desperate.

"We can't give up. We have to make this work."

"How 'bout hiring the next applicant?" she suggested.

"There isn't one. Tell me, what are you good at?"

"I'm good at thinking," said Shelby. "Very good."

"What does that mean?"

"I can think well, very well for other people. Not so much for myself but very well for others. I can explain to them what to do and how to do. I can think for other people," she said with extra emphasis.

"He's not going to understand that."

"Attorneys are smart. He'll understand."

"Listen, I don't like interviewing. He doesn't like interviewing. He just needs a body at the front window."

"So much for the personal touch," she said.

"Just tell him what he wants to hear. That's what I do." Richie looked bored by the whole thing.

"Well, what?"

"Tell him you can file, you're good with clients, you're friendly on the phone, and you get everything done, even though you're a little rusty on the typewriter. That's what he'll like a lot." Richie seemed to have run out of ideas.

"OK. I will."

Then the attorney's door opened. The chubby, graying man stood waiting for Shelby to enter. With fingers crossed behind her back, she walked in.

The rest was history. She could not understand why she got hired, but she did. This was the job she didn't really want but had to take.

She was practically dancing down the long corridor to the elevator. In the lobby she went to the phone banks to call the school and ask them to let Pamela out earlier. In the car she sang all the way to Pamela's school.

Pamela was excited to be picked up early.

"I have a job, Pamela! Imagine, your mother a breadwinner," she said. "We have to celebrate. Let's get our gear."

"Beach?" said Pamela.

"This may be a little moment but it counts. There's nothing wrong with loving the little moments."

"I like to celebrate," Pamela said.

They changed into their beach clothes and headed north to beautifully rugged Malibu Canyon Road. The drive across the mountain was overpowering and Pamela learned to appreciate it through her mother's eyes. She noticed changes in some rock formations and in the vegetation growth, and their conversation underscored the child's awareness of the world around her. Once they parked at the Surfrider Beach they took the narrowing passage with flat rocks in the water leading through to the community named the Colony. Rolling their chase-lounge-cum-carry-all, they arrived at their destination. The area where they settled was not too close to any of the homes and enough distance away from the tourist spots. The shores of Malibu remained open to the public even though the expensive homes of the Colony were inside the gated community of the rich and famous. Pamela called the area her private island. Together Shelby and Pamela appeared as two young girls, one merely taller.

Pamela dug her favorite toy, a yo-yo, out of the beach bag and walking at the edge of the ocean she was masterfully manipulating it.

"Look, Mommy!" she yelled to Shelby, who applauded her artistry. Shelby opened a book, but instead of reading she preferred to watch her child. Enthralled by the ocean, Shelby was captivated and peaceful. A middle-aged woman walked toward them briskly, chasing a Bichon Frise and calling after her.

"Sophie, come!" She said it several times, but Sophie was heading for Pamela. The strong little animal took Pamela by surprise. Losing her footing, she fell back into the water. The little dog started to lick her face, making Pamela giggle and shriek. The lady caught up with them, put the leash on her dog and sat down in the sand next to Pamela.

"I'm Moira," she said.

"I'm Pamela. I'm going on nine. I love your dog."

"Yes, and it looks like she loves you, too. She's normally not good with strangers," said Moira.

"Do you live here?" asked Pamela.

"Yes, just a few houses over. Not actually live here. It's our weekend place."

"We only have one place," said Pamela.

"One place is enough," said Moira.

"I like our house. It used to belong to grandma and grandpa and then they died so Mommy was going to sell it. Then Daddy moved out of the house where we lived and Mommy and I," she pointed toward Shelby, "we moved into grandma and grandpa's house." She continued playing non-stop with the yo-yo as she spoke.

"One house is enough. I don't know what we would have done with two houses," Pamela added.

"Sometimes I don't know either. When my husband and I travel we have to lock up both of them."

"That's a big job, I bet," said Pamela.

"We have people to help but it is a big job, you're right."

"We sometime have neighbors help us too."

"That's nice," said Moira. She got up and this time her dog stood by her side as a well-trained animal would.

"She is a good dog," said Pamela.

"Yes, sometime when she comes out to the beach she goes crazy with the freedom. Just like people, you know the sun and the sea."

"I do that, too," said Pamela. She was laughing hard. "I go crazy when Mommy brings me out here to the sun and the sea." Pamela started to jump up and down and Sophie was jumping with her. When Pamela fell down in the sand, Sophie fell down next to her. Moira had the biggest smile on her face, clearly enjoying the child and her dog playing together. Shelby walked over.

"Looks like you're having fun without me," Shelby said. Pamela shrieked.

"Lots of fun, Mommy. Look at this great doggie. Sophie. Her name is Sophie." Pamela stood up and as she stood still, Sophie sat next her. "Oh, that's Moira," said Pamela. "She lives here," then she thought about it, "some of the time."

Shelby and Moira shook hands. "Good to meet you, Moira," said Shelby.

"I love the laughter of a child," said Moira. "Your sweet Pamela is one happy person," she added. Moira's large hazel eyes seemed to cloud up as she said that. She had the most exquisite snow white hair framing her face in a bob cut. A bright scarf flowed around her long neck, hiding possible wrinkles, and loosely hanging gauzy beach clothes kept the curves of her body a secret. No doubt she was a great beauty in her day, still carrying an aura of understated dignity.

Pamela stood next to her mother and Sophie quickly positioned herself next to Pamela.

"Looks like Sophie and Pamela have adopted each other. That's unusual. She doesn't mix well," said Moira. Her warm smile put everyone at ease.

"Yes, they are liking each other," said Shelby.

"Well, we'd better go our merry way and get ready for dinner. My husband should be here shortly."

"It was great to meet you and have a nice evening," said Shelby.

"I have an idea," said Moira. "We are closing up the house for a couple of months and will have a going away party next Sunday. Why don't you and your little girl come? There will be some other kids."

"Oh, I don't think that's necessary. Thank you, though," said Shelby.

"Mommy, please? Pretty, pretty please, please," whined Pamela.

"Well, two more people won't make any difference. Just think about it. I'll leave your name on the gate," she said. Then laughed, "You don't have to walk from the beach. Just drive right in."

"Where is your house?" asked Shelby.

"Oh, yes. I almost forgot. It's the fifth house on the left as you drive from the south gate," said Moira. "I hope to see you on Sunday." She turned around and Sophie followed her back to the house.

# CHAPTER 7

Unbeknownst to Shelby, on the other side of town a new force was innocently evolving and taking the form of a man. He was looking at himself in the mirror, checking that everything was exactly right this bright sunny morning. The sun shone through the dressing room reflecting in the gloss of the spacious bathroom. He double-checked his longish, well-styled hair and put on his jacket. He was the picture of the complete, impeccably dressed executive. The vested designer suit fit him perfectly. His warm pale blue eyes took a last look at his sleeping wife and then he swiftly turned, headed to the study to get his briefcase. All was accomplished.

Holding the briefcase, his near six-foot frame gained some height and strength. By the time he sat in the brand new Mercedes 450 SLC, he was The Attorney. One hundred percent lawyer. Counselor Jeremy Kiery. The man.

Driving through fashionable Brentwood, he was oblivious to the natural beauty of the early spring mornings in Los Angeles. The counselor was reflecting. He was almost into a little nostalgia trip, but "No," he checked himself. This was no time for softness; it was time to concentrate and run through the case in his mind once more.

Yes, he was already completely preoccupied with the upcoming court trial. No one could tell him that he was not in unquestionable control of himself, his thoughts, his emotions. Thirty or not, he was big time. No matter what anyone may say, his parents' money alone was not enough to get him here. He needed the constantly nagging mother, the militaristic father and their totally opposing styles of raising him, to chase him out of the house. He had to be an honor student, he had to be the youngest man ever to enter Harvard Law School, and he had to succeed fast to be sure that he could live on his own. He also had to marry fast in order to be able to concentrate on his career and not spend too much time on ladies.

Indeed, finally, at the ripe age of thirty, he was a success; partner in the illustrious law firm of Marx, Kiery, and Corvin. Good practice, too busy to hassle at home, and stuck with only monthly visits to his parents. Not too bad.

Oh, yes, the trial.

Shelby quickly adjusted to the routines of the small law office. The group of reasonably congenial people consisted of a law clerk and two paralegals who seemed to be more typists than researchers. There was Richie, the Man Friday who did everything for Mr. Ross and they hired her as a receptionist at the front window to direct traffic. It wasn't too hard to digest. Shelby knew she was retraining for a new life and did not mind too much being on the low rung of a new ladder.

She enjoyed wearing her fine clothing of another time to work. It made her different from most of the women and it also kept her focused. Dressing noticeably well was a prerequisite of being married to a rising Hollywood talent. Maintaining the image, her wardrobe kept improving. She liked it. Then he became a recognized name inside the industry and both of their clothes climbed into a higher category. Apparently people in the entertainment business were label conscious. Shelby did not know that Boyd was ripe for infidelity or whether or not he had cheated on her before. Nancy's timing was right on. She easily swooped him up, out of Shelby's life. How she could do that Shelby would never know. But that was then and this is now. As long as she didn't give up, she could make her own life comfortable in time.

It was five o'clock in the evening; she would get ready to go home at five thirty. She headed toward the ladies room through the boring, lifeless hallways of the boring, lifeless office building. As she turned the corner, she practically bumped into an extremely handsome young man and his friend. They were dressed straight out of a fashion magazine and one of them had the most gorgeous light blue bedroom eyes she had ever looked into. Lo and behold, Blue Eyes, looking at her, exclaimed, "I'm in love!"

She knew the statement was directed at her, though he spoke to his colleague. She smiled and said "How sweet."

She walked away without missing a beat, but Blue Eyes followed her. "What did you say?"

"I said, how sweet." She unlocked the ladies room door and entered. There was a satisfied smile on her face. Little strokes like this always helped. She knew she was attractive, but she was so lost she could not seriously think about a new man.

Several minutes later, her make-up and hair freshened, she exited the ladies room, and found Blue Eyes waiting.

"Why did you say you *how sweet*?"

"Just talking."

"No, it was more than just talking," he said.

"Because it's wonderful to be in love. It's even more wonderful that you're so free you can say how you feel when you see something pretty enough to move you. Goodnight." She was walking back to her office with him alongside. Before she opened the door she turned to him, "I think you're pretty, too." *Where did that come from?* She had no idea.

She disappeared behind the door and Jeremy was dumbfounded for a moment. What happened? He certainly had seen his share of attractive girls and women but this one had something special. There was kind of a bright light exuding from this woman practically piercing right through him. He felt warm and thrilled and could not describe his sudden overall vibrancy.

Upon returning, Shelby found a substantial pile of loose documents sitting in the middle of her desk. She could have screamed. The handwritten instructions said that she was to organize them in the binders according to the Tables of Contents so that Mr. Ross would have it ready for court in the morning.

"Oh my God," she said. She looked around. The office was emptying out. She was on her own. *That's what it is,* she thought to herself. *Working for a living means you have to swallow a lot of shit. Now it's my turn.* She called the school but no one could stay past six o'clock to wait for her. They suggested that one of their staffers could take Pamela home. Naturally, they would add the small charge to her account. Shelby agreed and worked as fast as she could. However, it was her innate need to make things pretty and because of her father's strict training of her, they had to be accurate. Check and double-check.

Finally, she was finished and could go home. On arrival, she had barley opened the garage door to the house when Pamela rushed to greet her.

"Mommy, this is Lorraine!" she was unstoppable. "Lorraine lives close and they let her bring me home. Isn't it great? We're friends." Pamela pointed to the oversized young woman standing behind her. She took Shelby by the hand and pulled her next to Lorraine waiting enthusiastically for them to be best friends.

"Thank you, Lorraine, for bringing her home." She searched in her purse for some cash.

"Please take this," said Shelby as she handed her a ten-dollar bill.

"No, thank you, Ma'am. Not necessary." Lorraine headed toward the front door. "But if this happens often you'll have to arrange for it and the school will charge you." There was a biting edge to her voice yet looking at Pamela's happy face Shelby figured that this young woman had to be nice. Kids and animals spot and intuitively react to bad people.

"It was an emergency. I didn't know it would come up," she said to Lorraine almost apologetically but Lorraine was already opening the door and done with her. She was gone.

# CHAPTER 8

"**H**ello, I'm home!" Lorraine hollered through the one-story home as she came in from the garage. There was no answer. She went into the spotless kitchen. She thought she heard the TV in the great room but that was often left on even when no one was paying attention. Unaware of anyone watching her, Lorraine took some fruit and crackers on a plate and started out through the glass sliding door.

"More food? You need more food?" the voice said.

"Get off my case, Arnie. My weight is none of your business," she said without looking at the man.

"I want the best for you," he said, coming into the kitchen and blocking her way to the sliding glass door.

"I don't even want to think about what you want," she said.

"All men are not sex fiends."

"You didn't know me when I was slim and pretty."

Arnie was at a loss. "I'm not a bad person," was all he could come up with.

"I don't care. You married my mother. That doesn't make you my father." Holding her tray of snacks, she walked by him. He didn't move.

"I mean well, Lorraine," he said in a quiet voice.

She ignored him and continued on her way through the courtyard, disappearing into her private domain and locking the door behind her. The guest wing or mother-in-law apartment of this house had a nice size bedroom, large walk-in closet and a full bath with a door that opened to the courtyard and another to the bedroom. The apartment's sliding doors also led to the courtyard so she could sit outdoors at one of the garden tables any time or take a dip in the swim spa. She loved her mother's house. She loved what her mother had done to it by converting the courtyard into a French café. Lorraine never used the lanai that was on the golf course side of the house just off the great room. Her world was pretty much the apartment and the courtyard since she moved in. She didn't like Arnie because the first time they met he made a snide sex-related remark. Although she wasn't sure whether or not it was directed at her, she didn't like it. She was upset over the thought that was behind it. She was upset by the fact that Arnie would say it in front of her. She never mentioned it to Thelma because she knew that her mother was afraid of being alone in her olden days.

Lorraine always planned on leaving and moving out on her own but so far her job at the school did not pay enough. Her plans to go to chef school were pending not only on costs but also on acceptance. She reluctantly moved in with Thelma after spending years away from her while living under the roof of her father and his various sleep-in women until he married one. His new young wife didn't want Lorraine in the house. She made that loud and clear repeatedly. As a result, Lorraine stayed out night after night, mixed with an unsavory crowd, testing the authorities and being one step away from legal troubles. She felt stuck. She felt that this was her life. Remembering how as a teenager she and her father conspired against her mother and practically forced her to let Lorraine move out and live with him. Lorraine anticipated that her life would be unsupervised and nothing but fun. It turned out differently. She was incapable of living without guidance and she inconvenienced her father by getting into trouble with the law. By the time she realized that she was better off in her mother's home, she was scared to admit it. But Thelma needed no explanations. She was a mother.

Lorraine began to understand what living in limbo meant. Only her dreams and the children around her in school kept her going.

She kicked off her shoes, washed her hands, switched on the stereo, changed into a sweat suit and curled up on her bed. She thought she saw Arnie settle at a table in front of her room with a newspaper but she knew he wouldn't stay long. He would want to watch some sport on TV. A well-used volume of *Joy of Cooking* waited for her. The book was full of markers and highlighted paragraphs. She started making more notes, she was checking on articles in a *Better Homes and Gardens* magazine. Leaning on the backboard of the bed her eyes came to rest on the shelving of the rattan corner unit in her room. Her work corner contained the working pieces of mirrors, tiny halogen mini bi-pin lights, colorful insets, small switches and other materials of a dream project. A smile filled her face as slowly but surely, she nodded off.

Lorraine didn't hear Thelma get home. Thelma was in a good mood.

"I love it when I can help out at the day care center. Those little tykes are great."

"You work too much," said Arnie. "You don't have to, so why do you?"

Thelma sat down at the kitchen table, watching Arnie heat up some interesting leftovers from a restaurant.

"We could spend more time together."

"Oh Arnie, you don't mean that. You like your sports and your action movies with blood and gore and your buddies. I like young children because they listen and do as they're told."

"Not like Lorraine?"

"What do you want with her? She's a grown woman."

"She's fat."

"When she decides to lose weight, she will."

"I hate fat." He said, raising his voice.

"Don't raise your voice. She'll hear us."

"Why do I have to watch myself in my own home?"

"Because she is my daughter and I love her, Arnie. That's why. I'm hoping that one day she'll love herself."

Thelma headed for the bedroom. Moments later, Arnie followed and found her crying on the bed.

"I don't want you to cry. I want us to be happy."

"We used to be happy," she said. "What happened?"

Arnie didn't have an answer. He walked out. Thelma called after him. "You have too much time on your hands. You're so smart with your business, you should put more time into it. Working part-time is not enough."

"It's enough, honey. I need a hug," he said. "Maybe we don't have enough of this. This hugging stuff," he said and squeezed Thelma around her waist, holding her tight until she gave in and kissed him.

"Little Jacuzzi before dinner?" he asked.

She smiled. "Well, maybe."

"I'll join you."

"No skinny dipping," she said and went to get her bathing suit.

As soon as Lorraine heard the loud conversation, she tensed. She couldn't handle it and left the house without saying a word. Neither Thelma nor Arnie heard her leave. She drove around having no destination in mind. Inadvertently, she found herself on Bergamo Road, in front of Shelby's house. She parked. It was not late. She didn't know exactly what she was doing there. She went to the front door. Hesitated. *Should I ring the bell? What would I say?* She peeked into the den through a narrow gap on the side window. Lorraine could see Shelby practicing on a Selectric typewriter. Lorraine stood there, watching for a few minutes, then walked back to her Pinto. Slowly driving down the hill, she pulled up in the parking lot of the La Reina on Ventura Boulevard. One of her favorite places, this theater was an old fashioned single-screen movie house. One just knew it had been there forever and had a rich atmosphere unlike the commercial multi-screens that had come into being lately. It didn't matter what was playing. Movies were the inevitable escape. She went inside.

# CHAPTER 9

$\mathcal{P}$amela's growing excitement amused Shelby on the drive to Moira's party and the child's enthusiasm bubbled over. She announced their names at the gate house to the Malibu Colony. Shelby realized she didn't know Moira's last name but those guards knew their stuff, they knew who was having a party on which day, so he figured out quickly where Shelby and Pamela were going.

"Look for the valet on the left, Miss," he said and placed a pass on the windshield.

Driving through the fashionable main thoroughfare of the Colony was a new experience. Shelby didn't realize how big and wide Moira's house was on the land side because on the beach side only the decking and the pool were prominent.

They got out of the car. Pamela was carrying a gift tied with multicolored ribbons. The door was opened for them by the houseman. Pamela immediately spotted Moira. She let go of Shelby's hand and ran toward the hostess.

"Moira," said Pamela. "We're here!" She reached to hug the woman and handed her the gift. Sophie materialized on hearing Pamela's voice and she and Pamela were jumping high together to the delight of the onlookers. Then Pamela watched Moira opening her gift.

"Looks like a treasure chest," she explained. Pamela looked around to see whether her mother was watching all of this. Shelby was standing nearby, happy to see Moira's display of delight. Inside the box was a chewy toy. "I bet that's for Sophie," said Moira.

"Yes. Look, this really is a *travel time mirror box* for travel. You know, you'll be traveling. Each mirror lights up when you touch it, see? Like this. You can always see when you put on your lipstick and eyelashes."

Moira hugged Pamela again. "This is wonderful. I love it."

"My friend Lorraine made it."

"It's really wonderful, Pamela. Thank you."

Sophie had been eying the little toy in Moira's hand ever since she heard her name. Moira tossed it toward her but she jumped too high and missed it. Moira handed the toy to Pamela who tossed it up in the air and the little dog caught it.

"See," said Pamela. "I tossed it higher and she had more time to catch it."

"I'm impressed. Why don't you go outside and meet the other children? There's food and drink just help yourself," said Moira.

Pamela and Sophie chased each other to the deck through the high-ceilinged, wide open great room of the beach house. The large area had a Mediterranean flavor. Sprinkled around true to the American touch were personal nick-knacks in the various conversational areas. Showcasing a classic South of France look the home featured salmon-tiled floors and exposed beam ceilings. The open layout of the kitchen was inviting to the guests who milled around, helping themselves to snacks while enjoying the company of one another. Large, ceiling to floor sliding glass doors to the terrace were wide open welcoming the gentle breeze from the ocean. Reflecting the taste of the owners, the outside play area also had a serene corner for rest and relaxation, a wet bar that was manned by an attractive bartender, patio table and chairs for meals *al fresco*, besides the narrow lap pool on the side that seemed to be stretching the entire length of the house.

Shelby's eyes were drinking in the understated sophistication. She had always loved and valued beautiful places and things, but without Boyd, she did not see any way of achieving great wealth. *Just be happy with what you have, the peace and comforts,* she said to herself. *It's one of those count your own blessings moment not the blessings of other person's* she thought. That settled her down. *How sweet.*

The small jovial crowd mingled with great ease. Neighbors were walking in from the beach side and the general merriment was unaffected, effortless.

"Let's get you a drink," said Moira guiding her to the outside bar. Sidney had already noticed Shelby and was at the ready next to the bartender.

Moira smiled. "My husband, Sidney," she said. "Sidney, this is Shelby Carpenter. I met her and her darling daughter, Pamela just a few days ago. They are my new friends."

"We've met before. Our paths have crossed." Shelby and Moira looked at him. *I wonder how he'll handle this,* Shelby thought.

"Since I don't get out very much, I remember the July Fourth party this past summer." Sidney looked to Shelby, who was nodding "Yes." He continued to his wife, "Elisabeth and Malcolm's place on top of Beverly Grove Drive, the house that you liked so much." He turned to Shelby. "We talked a while. I remember you had a unique name."

"Where was I?" asked Moira. "My job is to be the buffer and I try not to miss any groupies." She laughed a hearty laugh and was joined by Shelby and Sidney.

"You were nearby. This is Boyd Carpenter's wife," Sidney said.

Moira's face tightened. Shelby wondered to herself, "*How much did Moira and her friend Nancy talk about Boyd?*

"There were too many people there to remember. Don't even think about it. Forget it, OK?" said Shelby.

"You're as smart as you are beautiful," said Moira, then turned her attention to a tall, extremely handsome man in his thirties joining the group. He was being nudged by an attractive young woman.

"Hey, Mike," said Sidney.

"How are you?" said Moira.

"This is my wife, Mindy," said Mike. "She wanted to be introduced. She's an actress."

"Oh yes, yes. I remember seeing you in a TV movie, *Never is Now*, I think that was the title," said Moira.

"Yes, Mike's friend directed it," said Mindy.

"I've been lucky with Mike's friends." She was talking fast to make sure she was holding the attention of the listeners. She was afraid that if she stopped talking everyone would leave her alone. "When he met me he said I was perfect for the part." She looked around at the faces but no one spoke. "The director," she added.

"I hope you liked it. Everybody said that was good footage of me," Mindy continued and turned to Moira. "Did your husband see it? Oh, there you are," she said to Sidney. "You are the writer, right?" Sidney and Moira have seen and heard this many times before.

"Yes I am. I am the writer," said Sidney with a hint of facetiousness in his tone recognized only by those who knew him better. Shelby noticed boredom on Moira's face.

"I don't watch much television, sorry to say."

"I could send you the footage."

He heard his name being called from the terrace. "Excuse me. I'm being paged. But I'll look at your film when we're casting." Sidney headed outside and disappeared on his way toward the beach.

"Yes, Mindy. Don't worry. I'm sure he's happy to meet you, since he and Mike are such friends," said Moira, always watching Sidney's back. But not even Moira could stop Mindy from following Sidney outside.

"I'd better check on the kids," said Shelby.

Walking to the railing of the deck, she noticed that Mindy had already taken off her cover-up and walked around the pool strutting her stuff. She had a nice body but nothing extraordinary. *She's no showstopper*, thought Shelby to herself. *Stop being so catty. Why do you care?* She could not stop herself. To her relief, as she reached the edge of the open ended terrace, she saw Sidney and some of the other adults playing Frisbee with the children. Pamela was having a ball. Mindy walked down the steps and tried to run, catch and throw the Frisbee. Her movements were very graceful, but not her throws.

"Her aim needs improvement," said Mike. Shelby hadn't noticed when he came up next to her.

"Not if it doesn't help her career." She suddenly put her hand on her lips. "Oh my God, I'm so sorry. I am out of line."

"Shelby, right? This is public knowledge. Her career is very important to her," said Mike.

"It's just that sometimes I think that I am talking to myself, and then . . . There you are. Anyway, you're right. My ex-husband is a hockey aficionado and a huge fan of yours. He reads everything and we watched that *60 Minutes* segment with you and your wife," she said and pointed toward her on the sand. "Mindy."

"Yes, I know she's my wife," said Mike with a shadow of a smile at Shelby's embarrassed grimace. "And it's been written everywhere. No one sees her soft side. I'm the only person who understands her ambition."

"I'm sure she is kinder than she seems, but on *60 Minutes* where she was showing off her house and her Jacuzzi and her furniture and her chandelier and all that was hers—it seemed like you didn't exist. Boyd was really annoyed with her. That's my husband. Well, ex."

"Boyd?"

"Carpenter. He's a stuntman and a double. I doubt that you'd know him, but he's a big fan. I'm a big hockey fan, too."

"Call me next time we play in L.A. and I'll leave you some tickets," said Mike. "I'll give the box office your name. What is it?"

"Shelby. Shelby Carpenter."

"Yeah, great car."

"I've heard that once or twice before," she said, laughing. Sidney was showering off his feet and heading up the stairs with Mindy close behind.

"I'd better give Sidney his space," said Mike and went to stop Mindy from attaching herself to Sidney.

Sidney got another drink and had the bartender make a fresh one for Shelby. She took it and sat down, keeping an eye on the children. Pamela ran up to her carrying a Wonder Woman shaped piñata.

"Look, Mommy. I won! I won!"

"You might as well share it with the other kids, honey. We don't want all that sweet stuff in our house. I might eat it."

"And toys? You know the ones inside?"

"No toys either."

"If Moira is still down there, ask her to hang it for you guys so you can all go at it and break it," said Sidney.

Pamela ran back to the beach and they heard her calling out to Moira down by the water.

"Moira is special. She stood by me all this time, through thick and thin."

"Sounds like the way a marriage should be."

"Strange seeing you here," said Sidney.

"Ditto."

"We have nothing to hide," he said.

"Do you want to tell her?"

"No," came his quick answer.

"Then we do have something to hide."

"I need the feelings. You give me feelings."

"But Moira is so dear."

"Yes, that she is."

Shelby felt guilty. Shelby thought about how she did know Sidney, and they did have a relationship of sorts, but where was the guilt? Was it only because it was not out in the open? But it was, in a way. This dilemma didn't exist before today.

Moira came up from the beach. She took a drink from the bartender and joined Sidney and Shelby.

"Do you want to see Mindy's footage?"

"I let George and the casting director do that," said Sidney and went to greet another arriving guest.

"These actresses don't know that I handle a great deal of the casting for Sidney's movies. So, they play up to him. I look out for the actresses getting the small parts. They are the ones working on the producer and director and sometimes the writer. They are really more dangerous. Do they want the man or the part? They don't have to be better actors than most, they don't have to noticed for their work, they just have to be on the set with access to the man."

"I didn't think of that," said Shelby.

"The usual method of these girls is to get the married man away from his family and get pregnant. Baby on the way they get married and their financial future is secured no matter what happens to their marriage or career. No one is safe."

"Interesting thinking," said Shelby. *She doesn't know I am the one she should be watching out for,* she thought to herself. She couldn't take any more of this.

"Moira, we have to get going. Tomorrow is a school day. Thank you for having us and you have a great time in Europe."

Moira rose. "Let me tell Sidney you're leaving."

Shelby called down to Pamela who came reluctantly. "Do we have to go?"

"Please, honey, no scenes. Say goodbye to the kids and to Moira and let's go."

Sidney and Moira looked after them for a minute and then returned to their party.

# CHAPTER 10

*I*t was almost five-thirty. Shelby covered her typewriter. As she looked up to close her receptionist's window for the night, there was Jeremy Kiery in his full glory. Looking gorgeous, conquering, and irresistible with his boyish dimples.

"Ready?"

She was puzzled, thinking that maybe she forgot something. Did they have a date? But at the same time she instinctively, as if pulled into a magnetic field, picked up her purse and was, in fact, ready to follow him anywhere.

Even though he knew the answer, he asked, "A drink?"

"Let me tell my babysitter." She had no idea why she would go against all her rules. She had no idea why she found herself walking by his side and sitting very close to him in the intimate little lounge doing business on the ground level of one of the respectable office buildings. But she did and her heart was laughing with joy. She recognized the rare delights of experiencing being alive and responding without rationalizing.

They didn't need a drink to know that they were once and for all drawn to each other. The prelude was a mere formality. The heat, the irrepressible heat of Jeremy was too real. Playing with fire was a first for Shelby. It was wonderfully exciting.

"The best thing that could happen would be that we go to bed, find we are horrible together and never again give it a second thought." She came to the point and laughed.

"My dear, you're full of shit," he said, all-knowing.

"Baloney is the word to use with strangers."

"That's right. With strangers."

Each time she looked in his eyes she experienced the uncontrollable resurgence of stirring sensations. It had been far too long since she last felt this kind of erotic exhilaration. The sexual tension was thick enough to be cut with a knife. She was scared, but also curious and truly powerless in face of the overwhelming physical temptation.

"I have another theory." She attempted to make the wrong right once again. "I positively have no time for an affair, you know. I'm holding down a job; I can hardly keep up with raising a child and managing a household. Dating is the least important thing in my life."

"I want to get to know you. I need to get to know you." Jeremy was not kidding. He was warm, sensuous, and sincere.

"Married men are out." Shelby's voice was firm, her eyes looking straight at him, but her hands were trembling in his.

He walked her to her car. They kissed. The touch of their lips generated sparks that could start an inferno. This was the kind of sexuality she had only read about. Shelby knew she could not refuse him in the future. She was angry with herself for understanding herself. She wanted this man, and soon.

That night when Jeremy arrived home, he stayed in his car in the garage for several minutes before going inside. He took his wife by the hand, walked her into his study, sat her down, and with some difficulty said, "We have to sort out our lives, Karen. We have to start right now."

Karen, merely a lollypop short of being Lolita, looked at him bewildered. Jeremy used to be crazy about her child-like qualities. He would go home any time and find his cute toy waiting. He did just that. Went home any time. He had never taken her seriously, not since his college days when her agreeable ways were exactly what he needed. But she never changed, never grew. Now, when she gave him her sweeter-than-honey smile, she noticed a new intensity in his face.

"What do we have to do, Jer?"

"We have to take a look at ourselves and see who we are, what we want out of life, and how we go about it."

"I'm your wife. I want nothing out of life but you. You'll have to tell me how to go about it. I thought I was doing OK."

Her voice was as soothing as her smile. She was calm, not confused. Jeremy left the room.

Shelby arrived home and saw Lorraine's Pinto in the driveway. She hurried inside.

"Thank you so much, Lorraine," she said as she hugged Pamela. "I don't know how to thank you. I wanted to get you a gift but I don't know anything about you." Shelby smiled her friendliest smile but Lorraine remained sour.

"Don't worry about it, OK? I like your kid," she said. "Besides, Pamela seems to enjoy it when you work late." Turning to Pamela she cracked a smile. "See you tomorrow, kid. We'll test your recipe."

Lorraine left. Shelby started for the kitchen. Luckily, the slow cooker was ready with the Chicken Cacciatore. All they had to do was add the rice. Pamela volunteered.

"Is Lorraine always such a sourpuss?"

"She smiles when I'm around."

"What recipe was she talking about?"

"Well, Mommy. Lorraine wants to become a sandwich designer. You know, like a job. So we made up a crazy recipe and she said she will try it tomorrow at school. The kids like her sandwich surprises. I do too. But she's not going to tell anyone that I am working with her."

Shelby started to set the table. "Well, honey, I'm glad she likes you. She doesn't have to like me. It would be nice, though."

They had a quiet dinner.

"Mommy, you're not eating. Are you OK?"

Shelby didn't hear Pamela. Her mind was far away from Encino and her child. She was recalling the delicious taste of Jeremy's lips on hers and the shiver that traveled down her spine whenever she looked into his eyes.

"Everything is fine," she said suddenly.

"You're acting weird."

"Just have things on my mind, honey."

"Mother stuff?"

"Yes. Mother stuff."

That evening they read two chapters before Pamela fell asleep. Shelby tried but could not concentrate on the bookkeeping, her expense budget, or anything. She just stretched out on the couch and let herself get carried away about Jeremy, recalling those sweet sensations over and over again. *Life is OK after all.*

# CHAPTER 11

Shelby was doing a sloppy job of driving; the tears flooding her face obstructed her vision. She clutched a crumpled sheet of paper to the steering wheel. When she arrived at the attractive condominium complex on Ocean Front Walk, she parked in the underground garage and hurriedly rang the doorbell to Sidney's *pied-a-terre*. The home away from the mansion he called home in Holmby Hills, California. The apartment he called his office, his work space, and presumably, the site of forbidden trysts.

Sidney's face was grim when he opened the door. His mind was in a different world, in the world of his characters. His shirt unbuttoned to the waist, sleeves rolled to the elbows, his hair mussed and reading glasses on top of his head, he was in a state of disorder, the kind she had not seen before. Clearly he had been interrupted by the unexpected visitor. But seeing Shelby brought on a wide smile.

"I don't like surprises, but you're the kind I welcome," he said. Noticing her tear-filled eyes and runny make-up, he reached out to put his arms around her. Shelby did not really hear him as she held up the crumbled sheet of paper for him to see.

"Boyd is dead," she said trembling. "Look, the woman swooped him out of my life, dazzled him with her money and worldliness. Then took him on safari." Shelby was breathing heavily. "He died. Had an accident and died."

She gulped down the glass of water Sidney handed her.

"I can't believe it."

"I don't know what to say," he said. "I'm sorry."

Shelby sat down on the couch. He continued, "You told me you didn't love him anymore."

"You never stop loving your first love. Never. You even say that in the novels you have written that *first love is forever*."

"That's fiction, really. Life is different."

He picked up a tissue and moved close to wipe her tears. She let him touch her. Studied his face, inhaled his aroma.

"Even when you're working, you smell good," she said.

He kissed her. She stayed in his arms. Needy, she held on to him.

"I feel small," she said. "I feel I'm stuck," she added and welcomed his warm, exciting lips on hers. "I want to be loved, please, Sidney."

She looked to him with hope. "You don't have to mean it," she said.

"I mean it," he said and guided her to the bedroom. The sunshine brightened the large room. He gently laid her down, took off her shoes, pulled off the shoulder of the loose fitting sweater dress and looked admiringly at her perfect young body.

"I mean it," he said again, bringing moisture to her eyes.

"I know, Sidney. I mean it, too."

His love making was gentle, caring and reassuring. Exactly what she desired. She was not looking for fancy acrobatics and proof of eternal manhood. No bells and whistles. She was lost and needed the feeling of safety. Sidney was her safety and her feelings for him were confusing. Her feelings for herself were equally confusing. *Am I a loose woman making love with another woman's husband? But I don't want him for keeps. I am just borrowing him.* She buried her face in his chest following the *great crescendo* and listened to his breathing as it returned to normal. Sidney did not have to be great in bed. His aura alone was half his sex-appeal.

She got out of bed. He watched her lithe nudeness as she picked up her clothes.

"Thank you, Sidney. Thank you for giving me your life juices."

"That's a new one. I like it a lot. May I borrow it in my next book?"

"Oh, why not. Take my whole life story. It's yours."

Suddenly her thoughts took her in another direction. "Sidney, I don't want to have feelings for you."

"I understand." He sat up in bed, partially covered by the sheets. "This was friendly fucking," he said. "The kind of stuff friends do to help each other out."

She broke out laughing hard and loud. Sidney joined in.

"You ARE the writer. You can say anything and have an excuse," she said, still laughing. She did not see his face, his very loving face looking at her with complete involvement. She was moved and knew that there were feelings and his feelings were as strong as hers.

Shelby picked up the telephone and dialed. "Richie, it's me, Shelby. I wanted to let you know that I feel fine and I will be at my desk first thing tomorrow morning. Yes, that's all it was. Yeah, a twenty-four-hour virus. Bye."

She hung up and leaving the bathroom door open walked into the shower. Sidney didn't hesitate about jumping in with her.

The alarm clock buzzed and kept on buzzing until Sidney turned it off.

"Well, this was my wake-up call," he said.

"Wake-up?"

"Yes, I didn't want to forget a meeting with Alexandra. Remember her?"

"How can I forget? Your publicist." She was dressed, fixing her hair and eye make-up.

"Good memory," he said, teasing. "But really, she arranges my PAs." To Shelby's questioning look he added, "Public Appearance tours."

"Boyd is dead. I have to tell Pamela." She took a deep breath and looked into his eyes.

"How do you tell an eight-year old that there will be no more weekends with her father? Ever."

Sidney took her hand in his. "You can tell her. I'm sure you can tell her the truth about her father."

"I'm not that strong."

"You're stronger than you think. I am sorry I can't help you. I would if I could."

"You did already," she said. "In many ways."

She went to the refrigerator and poured two glasses of water.

The phone rang. It was George calling regarding the new movie he was starting to work on for Sidney. It sounded as if Sidney was disagreeing with George about something. They arranged a meeting. Sidney would go to George's office at MGM Studios in an hour instead of George coming there. Shelby sensed that Sidney guarded his secret *pied-a-terre* from everyone.

"I have never been on my own," she said but glancing at him she saw that his mind had already moved on, back into his own world. She got her purse and waved goodbye while he was talking on the phone. He waved back. She closed the door behind herself.

"Looks like I'm on my own," she said to no one. She stretched her neck up toward the sky, took a deep breath, started counting to ten and regained her full height by the time she reached her car.

The drive back on Sunset Boulevard was, as always, revitalizing. With each mile the surrounding beauty replenished Shelby's energy. Even better, she was proud of herself for taking care of her needs first. She had never been selfish before. *I used a man,* she thought. *I didn't think I could ever do this, or would do this. I must be getting jaded and calloused.* After a long moment of a mental blank, she spoke out laud. "I feel no guilt! How sweet."

Once again, the school was emptying out and the kids were on the playground while waiting for their rides. Shelby saw Pamela run over to say her Kiss-kiss-hug-hug goodbye to Lorraine. Shelby also waved in that general direction while Pamela ran to the car.

"Surprise," said Pamela. "The vette!" Shelby drove both cars. She liked to rotate the *Mach 1* and the *Chevette* that Pamela called the *vette,* which always made them laugh.

At home they ran through their normal routine. It wasn't until they were sitting at the patio table, finishing dinner that Shelby decided to face the music and have the discussion.

"I have to tell you something very important and very sad," she said. Pamela's eyes widened as she had grasped her mother's tone of voice. "Come here," said Shelby.

Pamela slid close to her mother. Shelby put her arm around her.

"You know when your dad moved in with the other lady. They went on a safari."

"Like a wild safari in Africa?" asked Pamela. "Kenya?"

"Exactly, honey. And some of those are not very safe," Shelby drew her closer.

"Your father had an accident. He died." Pamela slowly pulled away from her mother, turned on her heels and ran off. Shelby stayed on the patio for a while, then took the dishes and cleaned up the kitchen. Later she looked in on Pamela and was surprised to find her pacing up and down in her room, a poem in hand, memorizing it with pent-up fury. Shelby stood in the doorway until Pamela noticed her. The child ran to her mother, held her tight, and let her tears burst out in full force. They stayed like that for a long time.

Hours later, Pamela awoke on her bed in the arms of her mother. Shelby stayed with the crying child, giving her the needed love, warmth, and security. She could use some of that herself.

Pamela got up and, as if she had been thinking about it, took a large photo album from her bookshelf. Shelby leaned on the backboard, waiting and watching. Pamela started to turn the pages.

"Look, there's dad and me on the monkey bar. He used to lift me up with one arm. He was so strong."

She kept paging and remembering. "And that's on his movie set." She wore no expression; she just kept turning the pages. "Look, Mommy. He could lift both of us at the same time. Look at that one. See?"

Pamela was slowing down with the pictures and moving closer to Shelby until she found the nook under her mother's arm. It was the perfect fit.

"Daddy was never home. Not much, anyway." Her eyes closed. She went back to sleep.

# CHAPTER 12

Rummaging in the walk-in closet, Shelby was separating outfits, dress with jacket, complete suit, dress without jacket, trying to make a decision. Pamela and Thelma came in.

"Mommy, what are you doing? Thelma wants to know when you will be back."

Shelby sat down on the king size bed. Thelma positioned herself on the settee across from her, and Pamela immediately settled next to her mother.

"I'll need a second job. Part time.

"What happened?" asked Thelma.

"You're looking pale, Thelma. You want to go home and I'll do this another night?"

"No," said Thelma. "Just tell me what's going on."

"The real estate agent discovered a lien against this house. They would not forgive the debt. They want it paid."

"They're not like you who forgives everything," said Pamela bringing an affectionate smile to Shelby's face.

"Did you try to negotiate?"

"Yes. I got it down to half but my paycheck won't be enough for all that."

"I'm so sorry," said Thelma.

"I was thinking of going to a few restaurants on Ventura Boulevard. If I go in person instead of telephoning it might work. I will try to get a part time job as a cocktail waitress."

"Do you know how to do that?" said Thelma. "What makes you think you can?"

"I'm a quick study. That's one thing I know for sure. Everyone has told me that for years. No dampers, please. I don't need anything negative."

She talked while trying to decide what to wear for something like this.

"I have to do this. I have to do something, Thelma. I will save up and pay everything off. I can't take Pamela out of Pinecrest." She selected an outfit and put it on. "She's doing so well there."

Pamela studied her and nodded. "Someone will hire you. You look really nice."

"Not too nice, I hope." Thelma and Pamela went to the patio. Shelby got her purse and joined them.

"Thank you for staying later, Thelma. I really appreciate it," she said and sat down next to the woman. Pamela, as usual, squeezed herself in between the two.

"Shelby, you know I love you and Pamela and I'd do anything to help out. Doing a few hours in the afternoons and early evenings was fine but I can't spend weekend nights here while you are at work. Arnie is pretty high maintenance," said Thelma.

"You really love him, don't you?" said Shelby.

"He came into my life late and he is changing for the worse but I guess maybe I'm changing too. Aging is a tough, tough process. But I don't think I would marry him the way he is now."

"Why did you marry him in the first place?"

Thelma smirked. "You know, he was easy to love; he had money, he was thin, had hair, teeth all those little things that old people often don't have."

They laughed a hearty laugh.

"Those little things make sense to me, too," said Shelby.

"Now, we both have to keep adjusting every day but, to answer your question, yes. As hard as it is to love a man at my age, he is the one for me."

Pamela looked worried. "You won't be here?" She reached for Thelma's hand and gave her a pleading puppy look which was emphasized by a hopeful smile. All this made Thelma laugh.

"Oh, honey, I love you like my own but put yourself in my shoes. Would you give up your family to be with mine?"

"Yes, yes, I would!" shrieked Pamela.

"You're a big girl, Pamela. Do you mean that?" Thelma's eyes smiled. "First things first. Let's see how soon your mother finds that part time job. Right now, we have homework to do, am I correct?"

She took Pamela by the hand and Shelby kissed her good night as she headed to the garage.

"Thank you, Thelma. Thank you."

She got in the Chevette and drove to the first restaurant on her list. She planned to be there during the dinner hour when all managers are usually on hand and would take time to talk with her. She introduced herself, handed them her *résumé* and honestly told them that she needed the second job part-time because her husband died and there were unexpected bills to handle. She tried to quickly pass through her lack of recent experience by inserting a little white lie about having waitressed before getting married.

As she was cruising down Ventura Boulevard, she recognized a few eateries that she and Boyd had frequented. There was s quiche house, a fancy ribs barbecue place, a Chinese Mandarin that was inside a hotel, and continuing south she thought of the famous transvestite restaurant in Studio City. She grinned. She knew she could not handle that sophisticated environment with its great food and entertainment. "No, not ready for that," she said out loud.

A corner restaurant called the All-American Steakhouse was serving up steaks and baked potatoes as fast as they could be eaten. Cocktails flowed and the old-timer waitresses were speeding around with their carts of steaks sizzling over the slow-burning hotplates all the way to the patrons. The variety of sides and condiments were lined up on the lower level in easy reach. The manager looked at Shelby and without hesitation hired her.

"We need a cocktail waitress on the weekends. How soon can you start?" he asked.

"Friday? Is that soon enough?" Selby said.

"I tell you what," he looked at her *résumé*. "I will start you on the payroll tomorrow just for coming in and learning the ropes. Then you can come back Friday and be ready."

"Great," she said. "I'll be here tomorrow. Is around 6:30 OK?"

"Yes," he replied. "See you then, and wear your plaid shirt and denim skirt." He turned and left her flabbergasted in the midst of the ever-moving crowd, patrons, workers and drinkers.

At home she was exuberant in telling Thelma about the job and Thelma agreed to stay a little longer again the next day while she was getting orientation. But what about the plaid and denim? She never owned any plaid and denim. Just not her style.

"Oh, there is a shirtdress somewhere," she remembered suddenly. Thelma and Pamela followed her to the guest bedroom closet where she spotted a short above the knee shirtdress made of light denim. She pulled it off the hanger.

"I remember getting this at an I. Magnin Special offering." Shelby looked on the shoe rack and took out the blue mid-heel Capezio pumps with decorative shoe laces.

"I remember now. And look, the Capezios that I bought with the dress!" She put them on and turned around to show them.

"I wouldn't worry about calling these clothes by designer names. It might not go down too well in that place," Thelma warned gently and prepared to go home.

After Thelma was gone, Pamela got ready for bed. Shelby sat down at her desk and tried desperately to juggle her bills and follow the carefully planned budget she had designed. She was not good with numbers and kept checking and double-checking the income-expense calculations. Then, of course, she wanted to find some *how to* information about cocktails in order to maybe sound knowledgeable.

The telephone rang. It was the restaurant with some added questions. Pamela made an angry face as she watched her mother's congenial response to the caller. Pamela felt that the intrusion was on her time.

Shelby smiled wanting to make sure that her smile came through in her phone conversation.

Pamela was more concerned with her own needs. "Mommy, how many chapters can we read before you call it a night?"

"Oh, I suppose two."

"Three?"

"Let's not bargain, OK?"

"OK."

Pamela grinned as her mother closed the accounting book. She happily followed her into the bedroom, got the story book ready for Shelby and jumped into bed. "You know, Mommy, even though I'm a pretty good reader, it's more fun when you read to me."

Shelby settled on the bed next to her favorite person and smiled. She knew she had just been had. She knew she would read more than two chapters. She hugged and kissed her baby, and began reading.

# CHAPTER 13

Shelby pressed the down elevator button. The door opened, she entered. The door started to close. A hand reached in re-opening it. Jeremy jumped in. He grinned. The elevator door closed. They were alone.

"Lunch?" he said.

She was instantly trembling. No words came from her mouth.

"I'll drive," he said as the elevator doors opened in the garage. She followed him to the Mercedes, got in and they rolled out to the street. Not far away, on Pico Boulevard, Jeremy pulled into a small motel. He went to the office. She was immobile, still trembling. Moments later he appeared with a key.

They parked in front of a room. She was overpowered with confusion; speechless. He moved around with experienced ease. She followed him inside. She had never been in a road-side motel room and on entry the word *seedy* seemed to leap into her mind as she suddenly understood its full meaning.

Jeremy withheld nothing. Not his excitement, his desire nor his yearning for her. He kissed her with urgency commanding her body to melt in his arms, commanding her knees to give out as she fell across the bed. She was not thinking of Boyd. She was not confused. She wanted him, wanted to satiate her sexual hunger. He effortlessly undid her clothes and the pieces came off one-by-one. His hot full-mouth kisses sent her reeling in a sea of desire. She never noticed as he meticulously hung his jacket and slacks in the closet, carefully laid his shirt on the chair. She didn't know if there was supposed to be some kind of order to sex in a motel and uninhibitedly went with the flow. He devoured every inch of her body and his touch, those magic fingers, kept elevating her excitement, her need to taste every part of him as he was overwhelming her. Little involuntary moans repeatedly escaped her, firing him up for the umpteenth time. Lost in his arms, lost in his lust, she could not believe all the physical wonders coming her way. What a difference between sex with her husband and the forbidden moments in an illicit setting.

Then it was done. He invited her to save time by showering together since the lunch hour was just that, an hour. They dressed. They got into his car. She was silent; still trembling; still in the afterglow.

"I'll get you something to eat," he said. "OK?"

She nodded and he drove to the In-N-Out Burger behind the Wilshire Boulevard office building and ordered a burger and a coke at the drive-up window. He handed the food to her, drove to the side entrance of the building.

"You'd better get out here, if you know what I mean. Don't forget your lunch."

She didn't really know what he meant but nodded and did what she was told.

"I'll see you tomorrow. I have to go to court now."

Shelby stood there for a moment. Walked around to the front of the building, tossed the food into the trash container and continued through the lobby to the elevator.

In the office she got some coffee and sat down at her desk. Mr. Ross, the attorney was not around. Only the sound of the paralegals busily typing away in the back cubicle could be heard. Richie was probably out to lunch, too. *What was he doing for lunch?* Shelby thought of Sidney and his gentle lovemaking. Then she thought about Jeremy and his impatient, youthful, urgent, hot, burning lovemaking. She thought about herself and a tear came to her eyes. She wrote down the word *slut* several times on the legal pad in front of her. "*Slut slut slut slut*," ten times across and twenty-eight times down.

"Two hundred and eighty," she said. "That's enough punishment."

She returned to the break room and found her little brown bag in the refrigerator with the sandwich and apple, the lunch from home. She placed the food neatly on a paper plate and headed back to her desk. As she passed by the wall mirror and looked at herself, she muttered, "You slut. You slut." She grinned.

# CHAPTER 14

*I*t was Shelby's second weekend at the All-American Steakhouse and she was still struggling at the bottom of her learning curve. She did not feel welcomed by the other waitresses and was hesitant about asking questions. At first they laughed at her for not knowing what calling a drink meant, or how to call the drinks to the bartender because she had no idea how to abbreviate those names and she actually wrote down each order verbatim. The experienced waitresses, who seemed to have been there for a hundred years, knew everything by heart, and they did not like that the boss hired someone who was different from them. Shelby was determined to work through it and learn what she needed to know. The fact that no one revealed on the income tax reports the cash tips they were getting tickled her. She watched the waitresses do their job and was amazed at the ease with which they could push a double-decker cart that held the steaks on top sizzling in a hot platter and the accompaniments lined up in the bottom. Those women were fast, accurate, and clearly from a few decades ago.

The bartenders, who liked the new young blood, helped her with the order shorthand abbreviations. They also laughed at her but she naively thought it was with her. She had to get better sooner than later. She was certain she could. But at that point the owner decided that she was being wasted by doing only cocktails. He proposed that she do food also, just like the other *girls*. She had to call in the drinks first, then to hang the orders on a clip for the cooks, then serve the salads. By the time the salads were on the table she could take her place in the line of waitresses and find her order, fill the cart and serve.

Somehow, this was tougher than she expected. She knew what customers wanted or didn't want. After all, she had been a customer all her life. Shelby knew that customers did not like being informed when a waitress was new. She remembered how Boyd would become impatient with a server-in-training. He did not attempt to be kind or understanding. No matter how much she hoped to get the supportive type guests, she did not. Shelby was always late with her deliveries, had difficulty handling the heavy cart, made mistakes and the customers complained. Not even her winning smile gained her any friends.

The dinner hour was not yet over when, in the back of the kitchen, the owner took the serving cart from her, pulled some cash from his pocket and said, "Shelby, this will cover your hours, OK?"

She wondered at first what he was talking about. "Is this payday? I didn't know."

"It is, for you," he said. "You don't have to come back. Ever. Thank you."

He turned his back on her, walked away and did not see the tears rush to her eyes.

She got fired. She was crushed. She had never been fired before and it hurt. But she never had a job before. She was crying into the night. She felt inadequate. She hated feeling helpless. *What will become of me?* She had to get the money to pay off the lien and time was running out. What kind of job can she do part-time? She had to find another one and not be fired. She kept talking to herself looking for the optimist somewhere inside. No one was there.

Going to her day job without fail she was trying to figure out her next step. She saw some ads in the legal trade-paper about working part-time for a typing service. A few hours at night transcribing dictation tapes. She wished so hard that she could type. Type better and be able to work in such a place. They were looking for 80 words per minute. *Hah!* she thought. Even though she had gotten better by now and was typing at least 50-55 she couldn't possibly in good faith deliver a whopper of a lie to an employer and apply for a typist job.

Two days later a ray of sunshine broke through her dark clouds. Another restaurant called. They had also interviewed her previously at the time when she was initially driving to several eateries, but then they did not need a cocktail waitress. The place called *David and Ingrid's on the Boulevard,* had been a quiche and omelet specialty house since the beginning about two years ago. It was owned by two brothers and their wives.

Shelby thought the initial interview there was strange. Ingrid, of the *David and Ingrid's* marquee, did all the talking. Her chubby neck ended in a chest of ample bosoms displayed by a deep décolletage. One eyebrow raised, her eyes were piercing as she squinted at Shelby in an attempt to impress. Ingrid pointed toward a soft looking pudgy man, her husband, David, standing behind the bar with another bartender. He was unmistakably drooling at Shelby. No doubt, Ingrid was the boss.

Shelby was informed that the two brothers had recently finished bartender school and passed their tests. This allowed them to start serving alcohol. When they called her about coming to work for them she was already more experienced bar-wise than they. No one there knew how to call drinks, not even the regular food waitresses. Since the popularity of the eatery grew, the waitresses were very busy and they needed someone to handle cocktails at least on busy weekend nights. Shelby was in.

She used the powder blue Chevy Chevette, the good old reliable family car to get her to and from the weekend cocktail waitress job. The precious *Mach 1* was kept in the garage except for special rides and would not be seen at her part-time job. The owners didn't require that Shelby wear some short low cut outfit showing lots of skin. This restaurant had some class and good sense. They had no uniforms so she could wear a long Tee shirt dress that passed for an understated hostess gown. Many of the customers had mistaken her for the owner because her demeanor was several notches above that of the average waitress.

She felt comfortable enough. The crowd was more upscale. They would switch from an aperitif cocktail to wine when their dinner came and wine was something Shelby knew about. She understood wine without ever going to school, and in order to increase her knowledge she researched those labels unfamiliar to her. It turned out that a few of the patrons returned not only for the food but also for Shelby's wine pairings. Further enhancing the dining pleasure, a piano bar was set up. The background music provided by the talented pianist added intimacy and increased the restaurant's good reputation.

Shelby relaxed into the position. She was not making friends with her coworkers but chose not to let that bother her. Time was passing. She was focused on paying that outstanding lien, the light at the end of the tunnel.

The reservations for a birthday celebration required that some tables be pushed together for the party of ten. They were ordering drinks as soon as they arrived. They did not want wine until later. Shelby took the order for their sweet Daiquiris, Sweet-and-Sours, Margaritas and whatever else came to their minds. Nothing simple. A challenge for the new bartenders. She wrote down most of the names with her own newly developed system of abbreviating and the two brothers, the bartenders learned them from her.

Shelby put the ten drinks on the tray and headed for the table. Holding the tray with her left palm she placed the drinks with her right hand from the right side of each customer. The third drink was for a man who was talking vehemently. Shelby was about to put the drink down in front of the guest when the woman across from him pointed to Shelby behind him. She probably meant to alert him that his drink was there. As he reacted to the woman trying to get his attention, he suddenly turned his head directly into Shelby's tray. All the drinks went flying and the gushiest mushiest of them all went down the man's back.

Shelby almost fainted. Her embarrassment knew no end. *Well, there goes another job,* she thought. The owner, Ingrid, orange hair piled on top of her head in an oversized bun and with too much make up was reminiscent of a parakeet. She appeared right away to help the patrons regroup and get comfortable. Her husband, David joined her with the apologies. Shelby didn't think much of his body rubbing against hers in all the commotion. The owners washed or wiped the outer garments of those who were the most damaged and told them that they would pay for the dry cleaning.

Shelby stood there, flabbergasted, frozen to the ground. She thought she heard Ingrid tell her to continue with other orders but Shelby couldn't move until the woman gave her a nudge bringing her back to the now. Shelby saw Ingrid get one of the food serving waitresses to take Shelby's place and handle that *table of disaster.*

Customers at another table came to her aid. She remembered them. They were returning guests who tried to assure her that everything would be OK. She should not worry. Everyone survived. Then they ordered a bottle of wine and proceeded to tell Shelby that they had just come back from Rio de Janeiro from a sailing holiday. Shelby found she had a lot in common with them. It felt as if she were talking to old friends. Finally, a good moment in her evening.

The place was clearing out. The birthday celebrants ended up with a free evening, paying nothing for their meals and drinks and the food waitress got a huge tip. All Shelby got was some dirty looks as they were leaving. Shelby kept smiling and saying "I'm sorry" but none of those people gave her an inch. She could not understand why anyone would be that angry.

Eyebrows raised, Ingrid walked around with a high and mighty attitude and spoke with an uppity tone attempting to impress everyone that she was a better person than all the others especially Shelby. Shelby could not warm up to

Ingrid and now, following the costly mishap, she dreaded to speak to her. Finally, she pulled herself together, hid the *small me* and faced the music.

"Excuse me, Ingrid."

"Yes, what?"

"Are you going to deduct the cleaning bills from my paycheck?"

Ingrid's pitying smile deeply disturbed Shelby.

"No, that won't be necessary. But one more costly accident and you're out."

Shelby counted to ten instead of choking the woman.

There were a few tables still occupied. Everyone was on dessert, coffee, or after dinner drinks. The evening turned gentle backed up by the mellow music. When it was Shelby's turn to eat a bite, she sat down at a table by herself. The three other waitresses were at their own table. The two couples who had just returned from Brazil were also on dessert. They noticed Shelby by herself.

Shelby placed the attractive serving of the *Ratatouille* in front of her. That was one of two cheaper items allowed for the staff to eat free. One of the foursome came over to ask her what wine she would like. Sipping on a glass of water Shelby jokingly told him that a Mouton Cadet would go best with her meal.

In just seconds he came back with a napkin on his arm and the bottle of Mouton Cadet for her. He uncorked the bottle, poured Shelby a taster and waited. Shelby looked at his wife who totally enjoyed what was going on as did their tablemates. Shelby didn't notice when a few other people came in for dessert and drinks.

Shelby tasted and nodded and he poured her a glass. Everyone in the restaurant, starting with the owners and the waitresses watched all this and were curious as to who these generous people were. No one knew their names they only remembered seeing them in the restaurant before. As they were leaving, Shelby thanked them and told them that next time their wine would be on her. The two women hugged Shelby as if they had known her a long, long time.

She was busy pouring glasses of wine for the other waitresses. They accepted it.

Ingrid turned to the waitresses. "I'm done for the night. Just ask David if you need anything. Good night."

She left. David could not keep his eyes off Shelby as he stood behind the bar, licking his chops.

Shelby sat back to continue her dinner, which was just as good lukewarm as when she first brought it out hot. A man stood at her table. She looked up.

"Shelby, is that you?" the man asked.

"Marc?"

"Yes, Marc Gramercy."

"Where's Judy?

"Definitely not here. We are divorced." He sat down. "May I sit down?"

"Of course," she said to him, already sitting.

"Yes, it was final a few months ago. The whole thing just wasn't getting any better," he said.

"Would you like some wine? There may still be some in the bottle."

"No, thanks. I'm with my buddy. Just came in for drinks at the piano bar. Someone told us the guy was pretty good. By the way, I heard about Boyd. Terrible way to go. I am so sorry."

"Yes, me too. We were also divorced, but still it hurts."

He got up and kissed her on the cheek. He went a few steps then turned around. "Would you like to have dinner with me some night?"

"Yes. It would be nice to catch up. Why don't you come on over? Pamela and I moved out of the Laurel Canyon house," she said and wrote down the address.

"How is little Pamela?"

"By now she's a wise old eight-year old."

"I'll take care of the food, OK?"

Shelby was surprised. "I work here part-time that's true, but you don't have to bring the food."

"Don't misunderstand me. A friend of mine has started her catering business and I want to support her. She's very good. You'll like her food. That's all."

"I'm sure we'll like it."

Shelby was finished for the night and got ready to leave.

"I'll see you Wednesday, Marc. Good night," she said. She was wondering *what could have happened to that marriage. Shelby and Boyd had spent fun times with Judy and Marc and Shelby was positive that theirs was a wonderful marriage. Oh, well.*

She lived a short distance from the Encino restaurant. When she arrived home, she saw the lights on in the living room but no one was around. She went to Pamela's room and there she was her little angel fast asleep and on the couch that was way too short for her big body, was Lorraine also in dreamland.

Shelby bent down and whispered in Lorraine's ear. "Lorraine, wake up."

Lorraine opened her eyes and looked at Shelby. Lorraine herself appeared to be a child in a grown-up body. *Strange how the night changes people*, Shelby thought.

"Isn't your family waiting for you?"

"There's no one waiting for me," Lorraine said. "Could I sleep here?" Shelby had never heard that one before from a babysitter she didn't even know.

"Can I stay?" Lorraine looked at her, with eyes pleading.

"Of course. Sure you can stay. Do you want to sleep in the guest room?" asked Shelby. Shelby realized she knew nothing about Lorraine except she was moved by the young woman's childlike hopeful pleading.

"I like it right here, if that's OK?" said Lorraine.

Neither of them noticed that Pamela opened her eyes and listened.

"Would you like a tooth brush?" asked Shelby.

"Pamela gave me one. She's really a great kid."

"Yes." Shelby switched off the light. "Well, then, see you in the morning," she said. "Sleep tight." Leaving the door open she headed to her bedroom.

Shelby heard the shower running in the guest bathroom and sat up in bed. It was eight in the morning and her eyes were reluctant to stay fully open. Pamela came in and stood by the bed, watching Shelby. Finally, Shelby had to acknowledge her.

"I know you're here."

"You always know, Mommy." Pamela, dressed in jeans and a sweater, crawled into bed with her. "You don't have to get up. Lorraine is taking me to the art show. She said we have to go when it starts because she'll show someone her *travel time mirror box*."

"Really?" said Shelby, sitting up.

"Really, really. She said someone there wants to buy and sell it and distur—" Pamela stumbled.

"Distribute," said Shelby.

Shelby got out of bed, went to her bathroom to splash some water on her face and brush her teeth. Pamela followed her around all the way to the kitchen. The shower stopped running. In the kitchen, the automatic coffeemaker's red light indicated that coffee was ready. The rich aroma filled the whole house. She poured some and sat down at the table. Pamela got herself a bowl of cereal and started munching when Lorraine appeared hair wet from the shower, tied up on top of her head in pony tail.

"Thank you for letting me stay," she said. She was far from the soft person she appeared during the night.

"We had the best time last night," said Pamela. "Thelma called and told me that she is sending another babysitter because she wasn't feeling well."

"I know you weren't expecting me," said Lorraine. "And I didn't really want to come."

"I just don't know you," said Shelby. "It feels strange but I trust Thelma."

"You know me from the school, you know me from the times I brought the kid home."

"Yeah, yeah and gave me a lecture on motherhood."

"I'm sorry."

"It's OK. I was just remembering," said Shelby almost smiling. "It's OK."

"May I?" said Lorraine, pointing at the coffee.

"Oh, help yourself. I'm not much of a hostess at this hour," said Shelby. "By the way, do I pay you?"

"No. Thelma will. And I am sorry if we woke you but I had to get up early to meet an artist at the art show and show her the *mirror box. The travel time mirror box.*"

"Can I go, Mommy? Please?"

"How long do you plan to be out there?"

"They also have a fresh market on Saturdays so we could bring you some fruits and vegetables," said Lorraine. "We'll be back by noon."

Shelby looked puzzled. "I can be nice," said Lorraine.

"Well, all right," said Shelby.

"Thank you, Mommy. Kiss-kiss-hug-hug."

"Be careful out there, OK?"

Pamela jumped with joy and ran to get her shoes and jacket.

"I'm a responsible person," said Lorraine convincingly. She stood up, put her coffee cup in the dishwasher and got her purse. Pamela returned, kissed Shelby and they were off.

Outside, they got into Lorraine's car. Pamela was bending down carefully pushing the precious *mirror box* package into safety on the floor of the passenger seat. Lorraine backed out of the driveway and as she turned her head she saw a Bentley pull into Shelby's driveway. She watched as the tall handsome older man got out, carrying a Brentano tote bag and hurried to the front door. She looked at Pamela who was unaware of her mother's early morning visitor.

Lorraine stepped on the gas and they were on their way to the art show.

Shelby could not imagine who would be ringing the doorbell at that hour. Her surprise was beyond words on seeing Sidney. Sidney rushed in and grabbed her tight, held her close to him for a long moment.

"I needed my Shelby fix," he said and buried his face in her hair, inhaling her scent, soaking in the feelings she gave him. "We are leaving tonight. We'll be gone a few months."

He opened the Brentano's bag and handed her two books. "I think," he said, "that going through all the changes in your life, reading these might give you some help."

Shelby looked at the titles. *The Silva Mind Control Method of Mental Dynamics* by Jose Silva and Burt Goldman and *How to Be Your Own Best Friend* by Mildred Newman and Bernard Berkowitz.

"Thank you, Sidney. I need all the help I can get."

She walked around for a moment. He was standing in the foyer. She returned to him.

"I really appreciate your friendship, Sidney. How you worry about me." She kissed him. "I'm not much of a mistress and yet you still care."

"I'm hopeful that you'll surprise me once more in this lifetime," he joked. "I really am, you know."

He reached for the door. She didn't move. She smiled, puzzled.

"Growing up is a very serious business, Shelby. It cannot be avoided. Must not be avoided." Sidney knew he would never forget the look on her face as he closed the door behind himself.

# CHAPTER 15

Wednesday night came fast. Shelby and Pamela arrived home and within minutes the caterer was knocking on the front door. Pamela looked through the peep hole.

"Mommy, there's a big lady here. Can I open the door?"

Shelby came to the foyer. "Yes, go ahead."

The big lady had a warm smile on her face and a rolling tray full of stuff.

"Mama Pearl is the name, fine food is the game," she said. "May I?" She headed into the house before Shelby could answer. Within seconds, Marc appeared, carrying a gift of an Umbrella Plant in full bloom inside a decorative basket. Shelby was practically run over by Mama Pearl, who pushed her cart into the kitchen and went back outside. "When we unload everything, I'll put on my chef's hat and finalize your meal."

"Then she will put on her maid apron and serve some amazing dishes," said Marc. "Am I right?"

"You bet," said Mama Pearl.

Marc placed the plant on the floor. Mama Pearl and her helper were bringing in a variety of containers and spreading all the things out in the kitchen. Marc turned to Pamela.

"Well, Pamela, you don't remember me because you were too young back then," he said.

Pamela walked around him and studied him. "I have a good memory, just ask anyone," she said.

"Where is anyone?" asked Marc.

Shelby came out of the kitchen. "Here I am, and yes, Pamela has a good memory." Shelby shook hands with Marc. "But the last few times we were all together you had a serious beard, Marc."

"Oh yes. I was going through my college professorial phase. The scholarly look." This brought some laughs.

Pamela disappeared in her room and returned shortly.

"I know who you are," she said and handed him a book. Marc took it from her.

"*The Wind in the Willows*," he read the title. "By Kenneth Grahame, first published in 1908," he said. He looked at Pamela's victorious face.

"You gave it to me on my birthday," she said.

"And you are right. You do have a good memory."

"The beard helped. As soon as Mommy said you had a beard I knew because it was my birthday party and I have the picture you're in and I am using it as a marker."

"Let's set the table," said Shelby.

"That'll be the last thing you are doing tonight," said Marc. "Mama Pearl will do everything else."

As they covered the table with a bright floral tablecloth, set out the matching napkins, the silver and all the necessary settings, Marc proceeded to tell them about Mama Pearl. It seemed that she was the live-in housekeeper for a friend of Marc and his wife. Apparently when the friend did not need her any more, she thought she would work for Marc and Judy. But that's when they got divorced. It was Marc's idea that she take the catering course and go into business for herself.

"And the rest is history, as they say," said Marc. "I fixed her up with all my friends and Mama Pearl is making a nice living. It feels good."

"Amen," they heard Mama Pearl's quiet voice.

Sure enough, the dinner was amazing and healthy. Shelby wondered *why he would be divorced?* She thought *maybe because he was not all that good looking but he seemed fit, sharply dressed and very entertaining.*

"Marc, it's strange that you came into that restaurant on a night when I was working."

"Are you looking for an underlying message?" he said. "I was also thinking that the timing of the coincidence had to be meaningful."

"Well, I don't think we should make more of it than it was. Yes, a coincidence but nothing more," Shelby said.

When Pamela finished, she excused herself and disappeared into her room. Shelby and Marc went out on the patio with their wine, giving Mama Pearl and the helper a chance to pack up and go. They never bothered them again, just disappeared.

"It's like a Palm Springs sky," said Marc, looking up at the blanket of stars. "Beautiful."

They were silent for a while then Marc spoke. "I've always thought you were gorgeous. I don't understand why Boyd would be such a runaround." He looked at Shelby. She said nothing. She was still looking at the stars as if she didn't hear a word he was saying.

"Beautiful," she said again.

Marc turned to Shelby again and started to say something but stopped. Shelby didn't notice that he was nervous.

"Shelby, more wine?"

"No. It was quite enough. I am a working woman now, you know," she said with a little chuckle.

"Well, perhaps we can do this again sometime?"

"That would be too much trouble," she said.

"Well, then let's just go out. I mean to dinner." He waited a moment and blurted out, "You and I. Just us." He inhaled slowly and deeply as if it was his first breath all day. It took a long time to gather his courage to ask Shelby out. Now he had done it. "Well, what do you say?"

"Sure, Marc. One day."

He got up and she followed him to the door. "That's not enough," he said, turning to her. "When. Tell me when." He grinned with relief. "There, I've said it. When, is the KEY," he emphasized. "Tomorrow? Friday? When?"

"Friday and Saturday nights I work. So, next Wednesday would be good. Let me see about a sitter."

He kissed her on the cheek and left.

Shelby looked in on Pamela. She was fast asleep. Then she went to the kitchen and it was in perfect order. Mama Pearl did it all. The lights were low and the dishwasher was humming. The only thing left for Shelby to do were the wine glasses on the patio.

She headed to bed.

When Shelby went out with Marc on Wednesday she had a really easy time. She didn't think about his looks not being anywhere near that of Boyd. She laughed at his abstract humor and admired his quick wit. Another time she went to a screening of a new film with him and when his Writers Guild Film Society group was showing any children's movies, he invited Pamela along.

Shelby was glad to have no time to think about missing Sidney or to remember about her time with Boyd. But she was bothered by thoughts of Jeremy. She had not seen him since that heated impromptu quickie in the motel but she knew she was doomed. The man was so desirable, so sweet and hot at the same time that her skin was on fire from just thinking about him. Somehow, deep down in her inner raw animal core she knew that should another opportunity arise, she could not control her sexual hunger.

One evening Marc called. "May I stop by?" he asked. "I have some news. Good news."

"Sure, Marc. Come on over. Pamela is about to go to bed. We'll be reading a couple of chapters but we should be finished by the time you get here."

Marc arrived just as Pamela was nodding off. She didn't hear the doorbell nor her mother's greeting. Marc picked Shelby up and twirled around with her feet off the ground, then put her down and kissed her. There was an awkward moment. They let it pass.

"Sit down," he said.

She sat. He sat down across from her. "Shelby, I've been nominated."

As she looked and listened, the smile on her face grew bigger and bigger.

"Best original motion picture screenplay," he stood up as he announced the honor. "Best, original motion picture screenplay," he repeated. Shelby went over to him, put her arms around him and kissed him. He held on to her and kissed her. This time there were feelings in play. The kiss took on a life of its own. Neither of them moved away.

"So now that I'm somebody," he said, "now that I'll be famous," he looked at her. She was puzzled. *Where is he going with this?*

"Now I know that my talent does not depend on anyone. It is mine. Fully."

She was relieved. "Did you ever doubt it?"

He followed her to the wine rack and accepted the glass of wine she put in his hand.

"Yes. I was in doubt. I didn't know what the divorce would do to my work. I knew that not being happily married did not destroy my writing but I didn't know what being divorced would do."

"Yes, I suppose that could be tough. A surprise either way, right?" she said.

Marc lifted his glass to touch hers and they sipped on the wine and Shelby watched him relaxing into his reality. "You came to my mind the minute they called me," he said. "I had to tell you first. I was sure you would care."

Shelby stepped closer to him and studied his joyous face mixed with so much pride, and his arms around her made him seem stronger, manlier than before. They stayed like that for a few minutes. Motionless. Shelby felt that perhaps they were thinking the same thing at that moment, they were happy together for the same thing and she felt the purity of it all.

Finally, they separated. He gulped up his wine. "I know you have to go to work tomorrow. I'll call you after," he said. "Oh, almost forgot." A wicked grin came to his eyes. "The awards dinner will be in about six weeks. Would you honor me by being my date?"

"I thought you'd never ask," she said and watched him as he practically danced out of the house.

# CHAPTER 16

The annual awards dinner was always a swanky, black-tie affair. The writers, their wives, husbands, or dates, dressed in their finest, making sure that at least once a year they got together and told each other how good they were. The rest of the world wasn't concerned with anyone other than the stars of the TV shows and films, or with the bestseller novels with their juicy plots. Never with the people behind the scenes. Never the ones who created those adorable stars and those juicy stories. Never the writer, the one who faces the blank page.

Marc was obviously proud of being with Shelby at the elegant happening. She was beautiful and had the air of refinement that is not acquired. Either you have it or you don't. Shelby was delighted to be there, especially since Marc, as one of the nominated screen writers, received a lot of accolades on the way to their table.

Seated at the round table for twelve were the stars, the director and some crafts people of the film Marc wrote. There were other members of the company at the next table. Shortly after the introductions the drinking, socializing and congratulating became boring to her.

"I'm going for a walk," she said. Marc seemed to understand. This was his work group and she should be free to do whatever she wanted, even if she wished to be alone. They had been friends before, and now they were starting to be more than that, and later, well, much later, they would always be friends. Pushiness was not his nature.

The hotel corridor was cool and quiet. Shelby automatically strolled toward the ladies lounge. She had at least twenty minutes before the event would formally begin and she decided to walk out to the large balcony just beyond the lounge.

She noticed a group of people, couples, coming toward her, heading in the general direction of the banquet room. She didn't really pay attention to them, staring ahead vacantly, deep in thought.

"Hello." She turned on hearing a familiar voice and was surprised by seeing Jeremy Blue Eyes. Jeremy in person.

"Hi," she said quickly as the parade passed by.

She entered the lounge feeling her adrenalin rise. *What happened?* She found herself pleasantly excited and also foolishly surprised, especially since he was not alone, he must have been with one of the women in the group. She shook her head as if to rid herself of the entire involuntary reflex. Then she looked in the mirror, liked the radiance and knew it was more than likely that whatever was happening to her went beyond sex. In time she would know what. Right now, Jeremy had gained a strangely new importance in her psyche. *Can there be a balance between sex and friendship?* She was surprised by the two concepts popping into her mind together. *Another never before moment.*

She returned to the affair just as the lights were dimmed. She saw Jeremy sitting on the dais next to the officers and other luminaries. He was introduced by Joe Swaan, president of the organization as their counsel. Jeremy Kiery.

*Well,* Shelby thought to herself *if he is such a young attorney, he must be married. All law students marry before the bar exams. After all, I saw the movie "Paper Chase," I've read enough books to know how those things go.*

She gave Marc's hand an involuntary little squeeze. She didn't know where that came from. *Yes, maybe Marc could evolve into something terrific in the long run even if he wasn't the most handsome of men. But he had such a warm, mischievous smile. He seemed to be really together. He was not demanding. She could never again handle someone constantly wanting to know where she was and what she was doing. That kind of jealousy meant love when she was young and thought that was how marriage worked. Now she was wiser, knew a lot of things better.*

Marc didn't win the award but being nominated for something that prestigious meant his career was on the upturn. The party, following dinner, turned into an enjoyable time for everyone. Marc and Shelby danced well together. She was comfortable in his arms. She liked being seen with him among his peers. No one mentioned his ex-wife while Shelby was received with respect.

Walking off the dance floor, someone tapped Shelby on her shoulder. She turned to see George Eckert, the producer and his date, Marci.

"Ah, George," said Shelby as she reached back for Marc to come over. "Meet Marc Gramercy. Marc, George Eckert."

"And this is Marci," said George.

As Marc and George shook hands, and before they could talk, Marc and Shelby were swept away by Joe Swaan, the Guild president.

"Marc, I want you to say Hello to our counsel, Jeremy Kiery and his wife. Excuse us, George," Joe added. "They wanted to meet all the nominees," he continued

Shelby didn't notice that George and Marci moved on to chat with other people while she and Marc were left with Jeremy. He seemed to be knowledgeable about writing and writers, about Marc and his background and the two men hit it off. Anyway, that's how Shelby felt about it. Jeremy's wife didn't talk. She was either too shy, or too young, or too uninterested. *She was very youthful and pretty*, thought Shelby.

Jeremy's eyes were on Shelby as he talked to Marc. Marc was aware of that. Did Jeremy's wife see it? Was she too smart, or too dumb to notice it?

Shelby thought that somehow she was betraying Marc. In reality, she knew she wasn't, but she felt too smitten by Jeremy for her own good. She was trying to be nonchalant and was relieved when Joe Swaan returned to take Jeremy and his wife to meet other famous people. Shelby quickly grabbed Marc's hand. "Let's dance."

He looked into her eyes and gently whispered "Let's go home."

*He knew*, she thought to herself. *But what did he know? Ah, forget the whole thing. But she couldn't forget the whole thing.* In the car she turned to Marc and being her normal, outspoken self, calmly said, "I met Jeremy in the hallway of my office building some weeks ago. We talked. It was just unexpected to see him here. That's all."

At home, Lorraine was ready to leave. She was not shy about accepting the cash Marc put in her hand. She thanked him without any facial expression and headed out of the house. Marc went to get the wine and Shelby stepped into the den to check for messages on the answering machine. As Marc was coming back with two glasses of wine, he overheard the messages. One of them was strange.

"Hi. It's *Brutus 22-17*."

The voice was distinctive, soft-spoken, and precise in enunciation. Marc saw her face light up, her eyes taking a quick glance at the wall calendar. She was not aware of Marc. He stood for a beat and then turned quickly. He was embarrassed for listening and he didn't want her to be embarrassed. He sat the wine glasses on the coffee table and picked up a magazine. When Shelby returned from the den he stood up, handed her the glass. He noticed her flushed, glowing face.

"Oh, wine!" She took the glass from him.

"It's a beautiful evening," she said.

"Yes. Almost perfect."

She caught a wicked gleam in his eyes. They kissed with care and passion. His feelings for her were clear. Her feelings? She didn't want to think about that.

# CHAPTER 17

Lorraine closed the front door behind herself. She was slow moving toward her car and slow getting in. Her feet, as if filled with lead, weighed her down. Why was she jealous? She tried to remind herself that she got heavy for good reason, to keep men away. She didn't want to be popular. It was too much work with too many pitfalls, too many lies. She also tried to convince herself that she did not care about Shelby's romantic life but the thought kept reverberating in her head. She knew she loved Pamela and knew that Shelby appreciated her work but she could not get past the male attention Shelby had. She assumed that Shelby had to be promiscuous because that's what men wanted. Girls who put out. But how could she do it with so many men? Why were tears rolling down her face? Lorraine was in a bad place in an emotional black hole as she drove through the manned gate at the golf and tennis community where her mother lived with her third husband.

The grounds were beautifully maintained, the single family homes were freshly painted, the trees were just the right height and the quiet of the night was magical. She turned the corner and saw an ambulance in front of the house. She saw the attendants rolling Thelma out and into the emergency vehicle. By the time Lorraine reached them, they were rapidly sliding the door closed and turning on the flashing lights without the sirens they quietly drove out of the community. Lorraine recognized Arnie's car following the ambulance and she drove behind him all the way to the hospital emergency room.

Inside, she found Arnie sitting nervously. She sat down next to him. They did not speak. Finally, Arnie said "She fainted. Thelma went to the bathroom and I heard this thump. She didn't answer." Arnie was having a hard time describing what happened. He was not looking at Lorraine. Arnie kept his eyes on the door that was ajar and where attendants were working on Thelma. Fifteen minutes seemed like an endless hour. One of the nurses told them that the doctor was on his way and they were bringing Thelma's vitals to balance. The nurse said Thelma was alert and they could go in if they wanted to. They did.

A faint smile came to Thelma's face on seeing Arnie and Lorraine. She nodded toward them and dozed off into a light sleep.

"I hope the doctor will tell us what's going on with her," said Arnie.

"I'm sure," said Lorraine. Dr. Bajas entered and introduced himself. He had a slight foreign accent but everything else about him seemed just like a doctor. One of the nurses was right behind him, answering his questions, pointing to the monitoring equipment, both IV tubes with fluids dripping slowly.

We are going to hydrate your wife and keep an eye on her for a while. When those two bags drip through, we will see a marked recovery." He pointed at the IV bags and the various tubes carrying the essential fluids to Thelma's arm.

"Sodium is the main electrolyte found in extracellular fluid and is involved in fluid balance and blood pressure control. She will have to get a little stronger before the MRIs are taken to see the results of her fall. I'll be back," he said and headed out of the small hospital room. The nurse followed him.

"Your mother is a strong person," Arnie said mostly to himself.

"Dehydration does not seem to be such a big deal. But why the fall?" said Lorraine.

"She fainted. It wasn't anything like how old people slip and fall in the shower or in the tub or at the supermarket. It wasn't a balance issue," said Arnie.

"She's always had good balance."

"Yes, always," said Arnie.

They sat quietly for a while watching the IVs, looking at the heart monitor, the blood pressure numbers changing, wondering what was good, what was bad. Arnie tried to time the dripping fluids which made Lorraine smile.

"You've no idea what you're doing," she said.

"I thought I'd time the rate of speed of this liquid dripping into your mother," he said.

"Why?"

He looked at her, looked at the IV, looked at Thelma. "I don't know," he said.

Thelma opened and closed her eyes. They did not notice it. The nurse came in with medications which Thelma took and then went back into her light nap.

"I'm going to San Diego as soon as Mom is well," she said.

"Why?"

"Because the Culinary Institute accepted me," she said. She spoke fast. She was afraid of being questioned about it by Arnie.

"You're not heavy enough? You have to get into the cooking business," he said.

"I've had enough of your insults, Arnie. Why do you do this?"

"It's for your well being. Someone has to tell you the truth."

"Well, I like cooking and all the kids at school love my sandwiches and the different tide-me-over small snacks. I have a talent," she said.

"Yeah. Talent for getting fat."

Thelma opened her eyes but did not have the energy to speak

"You're hurtful," Lorraine said. "I'll be outside." She started for the door.

"You don't have to go. I'll leave you alone."

"I've been decent to you because you make my mother happy. But I can't stay around with you picking on me. Why not pick on Shelby?" Lorraine was talking on a low but very agitated voice. "It's always Shelby this and Shelby that. The little rich bitch." She looked at Arnie. "The only good thing about her is the kid."

"I don't like kids," said Arnie.

"You guys have to stop this," said Thelma in a weak tone. "Lorraine will lose the weight when she's ready and she'll do what she wants. And Lorraine, Shelby is working two jobs to make sure they will continue having everything they need. No rich bitch, OK?"

"OK, OK," they both replied.

"Try to rest," said Arnie.

"Shelby is my second daughter, Lorraine. I hope she'll marry again. Some people should not be alone." Thelma's voice trailed off into a whisper.

"I'll be back in a minute," said Lorraine, going out to the telephone bank. She dialed.

"Hi. It's Lorraine. Thelma's in the hospital. In the emergency room. We're waiting for results. I thought you'd want to know."

Lorraine was not surprised when in a short while Shelby and Pamela showed up. Shelby threw on a sweat suit while Pamela was in pajamas and a robe.

Thelma smiled and went back to sleep. The nurse checked the monitors. Pamela hugged Lorraine then climbed on the bed and settled down at Thelma's feet. She was asleep in minutes.

Shelby whispered into Thelma's ear. "We're here," she said and saw a faint smile appear on Thelma's face.

"I'm the husband, Arnie," he said. "I recognize you from the pictures. And you know her daughter," Arnie pointed to Lorraine.

"No, I don't. Daughter? I mean, I know Lorraine." She stopped for a beat. "Daughter? I didn't know."

"Would it have made any difference?" said Lorraine.

Shelby frowned, pushing away a chuckle. "No, I guess not." She was pensive for a moment. "Maybe, yes. I'm not sure."

"Are you telling me that you had no inkling?" Lorrain was cocky and pleased with herself.

Thelma smiled. "Lorraine does things her way."

"I noticed," said Shelby. "But really now, Thelma, you're really scaring us."

"The doctors will tell me what I'm doing wrong and then we all go home."

Just as Thelma said that, the nurse entered with a gurney and with another aide they rolled Thelma off her bed and onto the gurney. "We'll need the imaging to see about any concussion from the fall. You can stay here. We won't be long," said the nurse as they proceeded to push Thelma and the IV apparatus out of the room leaving Pamela asleep at the foot of the bed.

Shelby, Arnie and Lorraine sat around.

"I'm going to the coffee machine," said Lorraine. "Would you like some?"

"Here, let me take care of that," said Arnie, handing Lorraine some money.

"Thank you, Lorraine," said Shelby. "I'll have a black one."

Lorraine took the money from Arnie and looked at him. "Me, too. Black," he said.

Shelby sat on the bed, gently caressing her sleeping daughter. "What happened?"

Arnie shrugged his shoulder. "I have no idea. The doctors still haven't said anything, in fact, the one Hospitalist who came in didn't know *bupkes*."

"*Bupkes*?" said Shelby.

Arnie grinned. "We live in a primarily Jewish subdivision. I pick up some Yiddish here and there. *Bupkes* means something like little or less than little."

Shelby nodded as Arnie continued. "The nurses keep saying they want more tests and we should relax and keep the blood pressure normal. I've never seen her like this. I don't think I know how to handle it."

"None of us do. Thelma has always been the rock," she said.

Arnie didn't answer. He appeared to be at a loss or maybe just thinking. "Lorraine wants to leave," he said.

"Leave?"

"San Diego. I think I chased her away," he said.

"How can you do that?"

"Calling her fat."

Shelby looked at him in disbelief. "Yup, that would do it."

Lorraine returned with the coffees and the change for Arnie. Arnie took the change and put it in his pocket without a word.

"Thank you, Lorraine," said Shelby removing the cover of the coffee cup and sipping it. "Maybe one of these days you'll come to our house for a visit, a chat, a little meal. Pamela and I would like that."

Lorraine didn't answer. "Well, it would be nice," said Shelby. "Just let me know when."

Lorraine gave her a facetious grimace. "You mean you could fit me in?"

Shelby was not about to dignify the brazen attitude and took it in stride. "Yes. I could fit you in."

The door opened wide and Thelma was rolled in and transferred back to her bed.

"Don't wake the child," she said to the attendants. They worked around Pamela.

"The doctor will be in after he has reviewed the results," said the nurse.

"You mean the Hospitalist? Isn't a real doctor around?" said Arnie.

Thelma closed her eyes in an effort to stay calm. "The Hospitalist is a real doctor, Mr. Moss. Actually, because they have no private practice they can fully take care of the hospital patients. You don't have to worry about anything," said the nurse.

Shelby smiled at Thelma. They understood each other.

Just then a young doctor entered and sitting on the edge of Thelma's bed, he began to tell her everything he had learned about her condition. He pointed out how the various tests are so advanced that he was able to send some of the information to her primary doctor and they had arranged an appointment for her late the next morning.

"Thank God," said Thelma. "I'll have a chance to shower."

"Yes, your doctor emailed us that he knew you would like to clean up before seeing him." The doctor put everyone at ease. He assured them that she could go home with the prescribed medications and that she would be all right after some uninterrupted rest.

The doctor did not miss Shelby's beauty but only Lorraine noticed as he was leaving the room he had an extra smile for Shelby, trying his casual best to catch her eyes.

# CHAPTER 18

The next morning came in with vicious rain pounding the entire city. Shelby bundled Pamela in her rain gear for school. The traffic was slow and it took Shelby longer to get to her job. She was late. Richie's office door was open. He waived to her when she arrived and continued talking on the telephone. She hurried to her desk, checked all the assignments Mr. Ross had lined up for her to do. She needed the cup of coffee to kick start her after the rough night in the hospital.

She heard Richie on the phone. "Let me know if you can get at least one more carload," he said. "Two would be better. OK? Get going." He hung up the telephone and went through the double-door to the boss' office. Shelby did not see him for a long time. He and Mr. Ross were answering the calls in the big corner office. It was all very private.

Shelby didn't pay much attention to what they were doing until late in the day when a husky, bearded man, Jorge Villanova came to the reception window.

"Buzz me in sweetie," he said to Shelby.

"Excuse me? Who are you?"

"Tell him Jorge is here."

Richie heard his voice and came to the front to let Jorge in. They bumped fists and disappeared into Mr. Ross' office.

Shelby finished her work and left for the day, along with her colleagues. The door locked behind them. Shelby waited with the others at the elevator bank. When the bell rang, everyone got in.

"Oh, great. I left my umbrella," said Shelby. "Gotta go back."

She searched for the office key in her purse. The elevator left. She returned to the office and went to her desk drawer just as Jorge was coming out. All three men were talking.

"The two buses were in different parts of town. You know I wouldn't screw up," said Jorge.

"What about the Cadillac? How many people?" asked Richie.

"We got five and two toddlers," he answered.

Jorge was walking to the front exit the same time with Shelby.

"After you, pretty lady," he said, stuffing some cash in his wallet.

"Richie, trust me. I know what I'm doing," he said. Waving with his fingers he followed Shelby out the door.

"A drink?" he said to Shelby while waiting for the elevator. "You're awfully pretty. Hope you don't mind my saying so."

Shelby took it in stride. "No, I don't mind. Thank you." They got into the elevator that was almost full. "But I'm afraid I have to hurry to pick up my daughter from school."

"Some other time," said Jorge, walking away.

The rain had settled into a slow steady downpour. Shelby's commute back to the Valley was slow. She got stuck behind a city bus that was in an accident. By the time she managed to pull around and pass it, she saw everyone involved in the accident. The police were sorting a carload of several people including a baby, questioning the bus driver that ran into them. The driver claimed they stopped short in front of him. Ambulance sirens were heard as they tried to get through the traffic to reach the injured passengers.

Shelby did not add two and two together until much later that evening.

She arrived at the school but the gate was closed. There was no one around. She drove home and was happy to find Lorraine's car in the driveway.

Shelby went inside. Lorraine came out of Pamela's room.

"She was about to fall asleep while waiting for you," Lorraine said. "I thought I should bring her home. Last night was rough on her."

Shelby caught Lorraine's accusatory tone. She wanted to put an end to it.

"You know, you're critical of me and that's OK. But you don't have the facts. You're running away with your imagination," Shelby said. She didn't wait for a discussion. "How's Thelma?"

"Better. I went to her doctor with her. They rearranged her medications and made her promise to take more time for herself and rest. She can't be running around for you."

"Fine," Shelby said. "I'll take care of us."

Lorraine headed to the front door. "Pamela was very tired when we got home. She went right to bed. She didn't want to eat," said Lorraine.

"And you? Can you handle a sandwich?" said Shelby. "I know you make some killer sandwiches but I have a few tricks of my own. What do you say?"

Lorraine stood at the door. Clearly, she was undecided. Shelby went to the kitchen and started to prepare a couple of panini. Lorraine slowly turned and went back to the kitchen. Without looking at her, Shelby brought out some Focaccia bread, a jar of pesto, cooked chicken breast, bell peppers, and red onion.

"Looks a little fancier than what I make," said Lorraine.

"Different age group," said Shelby with a grin. "When you publish your recipe book you will have to break them down by age group for both the making and consuming." Shelby put some placemats on the breakfast bar with napkins and silver.

"Publish? You know who you're talking to?"

"No but maybe you'll tell me," said Shelby.

"Why?"

"I'm not sure. Maybe because you remind me of Thelma."

Lorraine laughed out loud. "Not funny," she said.

"No," said Shelby and went over to the wine rack. "I have some red open."

"I'll get the glasses," said Lorraine as she headed to the open shelving in the kitchen that housed the various drinking glasses.

Within minutes the chicken pesto panini were ready. She served them on dinner plates so that they could add pickles, olives, shredded red onions, and other accoutrements.

"I hear you're leaving for San Diego?"

Lorraine bit into the sandwich and made an approving sound. "Not a bad combination," she said. "But you're right. A little too elaborate for children. Yes, the Culinary Institute accepted me," she said without looking at Shelby.

"That's great but isn't it dangerous to be a chef and surrounded by food when apparently you can hardly resist food?"

"Recovering alcoholics do the same. They're around others who drink."

"How do you know about that?"

"My dad tried that route once. The recovery. It didn't take. He's still a drunk. The sloppy but loveable kind," she added.

They ate silently for a while then Shelby raised her wine glass. "Let's drink to your success at school and in life."

"Lorraine, I don't know exactly how much Thelma is paying you for taking care of Pamela, but I would like to take over." Shelby went to her purse and took out some cash.

"Tell your mother not to worry. I can handle it," she said. "Now, Lorraine, are we OK? Do you want to tell me anything before you leave town?"

"It's the men. It's the pretty woman syndrome."

"The what?"

"The perks. The attention, the smiles, and all that shit. I hate it. All the men. You have a lot of them."

"A lot?"

"I saw one here one morning when Pamela and I were leaving. Then I saw the other one who took you to the formal. Then I saw the doctor in the hospital giving you the look. I'm sure there are more."

"Friends and acquaintances. That's all I am interested in, Lorraine, friends. Not that it's any of your business, but being a mother has its perks and those are the only perks for me."

"And Thelma. You know she's my mother and she keeps saying you're like a second daughter to her, but I don't feel like I have a sister or that I'm the first daughter. The good news is that she'll be OK, so I can go live my own life."

"When are you leaving?" asked Shelby.

"I have some choices about the classes. I want to make sure mother is well." Once again, she was not looking into Shelby's eyes. Her face took on a snide grimace. "Don't worry. I'll be here for Pamela until then. I'm not going to let her down."

"I wasn't worried."

Shelby went about clearing the table. Lorraine watched her.

"Any news about the *travel time mirror box*?" asked Shelby.

"I told Pamela not to mention it."

"Lorraine, Pamela is my daughter. She does not keep secrets from me. Ever."

"Well, I have no news. It's really none of your business."

"Fine. Forget it," said Shelby.

"It's too soon anyway," said Lorraine, as if she didn't hear Shelby. "The artist gave me a list of places where she was taking it and I guess everyone keeps it for some time before they make a decision."

"I'm sure it'll work out. You're young but you're very smart and very creative. You'll go far."

"Don't patronize me, OK. I don't need a Pollyanna."

Lorraine got up to leave.

"Everyone needs their mother's love," said Shelby and continued cleaning up. Lorraine left.

# CHAPTER 19

*T*he insurance company letter came by overnight mail. It instructed Shelby to go to the insurance company to receive the check from Boyd's travel insurance covering accidental death.

Yes, he left some money for them. She wondered how much? She was concerned about securing Pamela's education. She called Richie and told him she didn't know when she would get to work. She had important business to take care of. Richie didn't care about how much time she was taking off. He was happy that she was not quitting. He dreaded the hiring process and always hated when Shelby called. *What now?* was the question on his mind every time she called in.

Shelby was bursting with excitement when she left the insurance building. Check in hand, she headed over to the branch of her bank just a few blocks away. Banking done, she called Marc.

"You'll never believe this," she said to him.

"Good or bad? Should I sit or stand?"

"I'll tell you when I see you," she said.

"Unexpected pleasure. When?"

"I'm on my way. Where is your office?"

"In my house. Are you coming over? Really? I'm in Sherman Oaks. 3538 Alana," he said. "Just off Sepulveda."

"Is it hard to find?" she said.

"Why don't I meet you at Frascati's? At Doheny and Sunset?"

"I don't want to deal with restaurants and waiters and all that, you know? I'll find you. Let me jot down the directions," she said.

All the way to Marc's house she was wondering to herself why she would think of calling Marc first with the good news. *Why she really had no one to call her friend? Why the sudden reliance on Marc? How did that happen?*

By the time she arrived at his rustic home with a modest exterior, she was ready for the salad he had prepared. The interior of the house was a contrast to the unassuming front, as it seemed to stretch into the hills. He walked her through to the backyard where the view from the terrace was beautiful.

She told him about the money and how she could now give up the second job. He was happy for her. They sat silently for a while enjoying the surrounding. Then he turned to face her.

"I'm surprised, no touched, that you called me. I'm not questioning my good fortune but it's wonderful that you feel you can trust me and obviously know how I feel about you." He took a deep breath and reached for her hand. "You've made me happy."

"I'm pretty surprised, too. But I just go with my impulses usually."

"I'm itching to tell you something in confidence," he said.

"Come this way." He walked her to his office which was a wide open, book-filled loft and ceremoniously pointed to his In-box on a large table-like desk.

"Look, the galleys of Sidney Marshall's new book. Full of romance and adventure, the usual intrigue that keeps his readers hooked. Don't ask me how I got it but here it is."

"*Galleys*? What are they," she asked, moving closer to the desk, studying the weird looking pile of printed pages. "Aren't they some ships or kitchens?"

"In publishing, *galley proofs* are the preliminary versions of publications," said Marc and proceeded to pick up some pages to demonstrate for her. "These are used for previews by authors' editors, professional reviewers, some film producers. See the extra-wide margins? That's for the proofreaders. That's for notes and all that."

"Interesting. There's a whole other business, among others, that I know nothing about," she said. "Why would you want these galleys?"

"Because the early bird catches the worm."

Her bewilderment was obvious.

"I want to do this screenplay adaptation more than I have ever wanted to do anything in my life, professionally. I'm hoping that my agent will get me a meeting."

"Why? Meet the author?"

"No, the producer. I've never met him."

"Yes, you did. We said *Hello* to him at the Writers Guild dinner, remember?"

"I was so busy enjoying that nomination I only remember you."

"Well, I have met him before. Let's see what I can do," she said. "I'm sure you have the studio phone directory. I think he has offices on the MGM lot."

Marc dialed MGM and handed her the phone as it was ringing. She asked for George Eckert. His secretary said he was expected shortly. Shelby left her name and Marc's number.

They went back to their unfinished lunch on the terrace.

"I've read it twice already. I don't know whether it's just me or what, but one of the lead characters reminds me of you a lot," he said in between bites of salad. "I really liked her."

"Really? I thought I was unique." She laughed.

"I could see you from his description and your movements and even hear your voice. Everything. He even gives you, her, some of your gestures."

The phone rang before she could answer him. Marc pointed to it and signaled her to pick it up.

"Marc Gramercy's office," said Shelby, causing Marc to smile.

"George, how are you? Thank you for calling me right back." She took a deep breath as she listened. "Yes, thank you. It was a terrible accident. What about Nancy?" She stuck out her tongue and made a snide face. "Yes. I'm sure you're glad she has recovered." She made a *boring* gesture with her hands for Marc's benefit as she listened.

"Yes, it was good to see you and Marci at the dinner. Pretty fancy. Now, why I called, besides catching up, of course, is Sidney's new novel. Are you making the movie? Do you remember Marc Gramercy? Yes, he was the nominee. You think he should've won?" She looked to Marc giving him the thumbs up.

"I'm glad you feel that way. He wants to do the screenplay for you." She took a deep breath, relieved. I'm not supposed to ask how he got the galleys. He'll never tell."

"Dinner? You and Marci and Marc and I?" Marc nodded rapidly. "Just say when, George. Great. Will do. Say *Hi* to Marci. Bye."

Shelby hung up and Marc collapsed on the couch. "I don't believe it. You're amazing," he said. "I could kiss you," he said but did not make a move.

They sat quietly. There was a peaceful aura in the air. Shelby looked at her watch. "Well, my work here's done."

"Do you have a little more time?"

"I pick up Pamela at four," she said.

"Well, then, let me show you a video I taped a few nights ago. I missed the interview show on KMRTV. The one Marla Hayes does once-in-a-while. I think once a month? I'm not sure. Anyway, I like it and usually tape it and guess what; Sidney Marshall was her last guest."

"I'd love to see it. But I have some errands to run." She was wondering whether or not Sidney has been back in town without letting her know or was the interview taped before he left for Europe.

She prepared to leave. "You know what's funny, George also mentioned that there is a character in the book that reminded him of me but, he said, since he only met me superficially, he couldn't be sure." She laughed. "No one can be sure. It's a creation of the imagination," she said and headed for the door.

The following Friday was Shelby's last night as a cocktail waitress. She had called to tell them that she was quitting and this was her final weekend.

"Kiss-kiss-hug-hug," said Pamela as Shelby was leaving

Pamela and Lorraine went to have dinner at Thelma's house.

Shelby arrived at the restaurant on her own pink cloud. The piano player came in a few minutes later and the smooth melodious notes set the dinner mood. The waitresses were happy to see her go as was Ingrid, owner David's wife. As midnight rolled around there was no reason for Shelby to stay longer. She didn't even try to have her free dinner just wanted to get out of there, however, the guests at one of the tables were lingering and to the delight of the owners they were ordering more drinks and singing along with the familiar melodies. Shelby hoped that one of the waitresses would stay to handle the group. She was wrong. The place had emptied out. Ingrid had already left for the night. Unbeknownst to Shelby, David was eyeing her. Shelby said *last call* to the tableful of guests and was getting her things to go home as well. She also said goodbye to Steve, behind the bar and went to the ladies' room at the end of a long hallway before leaving. When she stepped up to the sink, her deep breath of relief was curtailed by heavy breathing and grunting. David sneaked in. Her shock was numbing. He tore at her skirt as he tried to pull it up and she could feel his weapon hardening against her body pushing and searching to find his way into her. Before she could react, he stuffed a towel in her mouth and forced her down to the floor. She was gasping for air. She tried to kick him but his weight on top of her rendered her helpless. Bang! The door slammed open with a loud crash. Shelby used the split second opportunity to produce a full force high-heel kick into his groin. He fell onto his screaming wife. Ingrid started beating him and punching him in the face amidst a nasty stream of cuss words.

Shelby, still trying to catch her breath, her clothes torn, her face and hair a mess, ran out of the bathroom and left the restaurant behind forever.

She didn't remember the drive home. She was slow getting out of the car, slow walking into the house. She passed by Lorraine and headed directly to her bathroom. Lorraine did a double take on Shelby.

"What happened? Can I get you anything?" said Lorraine.

"You don't have to be so nice. I'm OK. Just go."

Shelby closed the bathroom door and started to run the hot shower.

Lorraine did not want to deal with any problems; not hers nor anyone else's. She stood still for a couple of minutes then left.

Sometime later, could have been five minutes, a half hour or an hour, Shelby had lost all sense of time. She turned off the running water and wrapped herself in a terry robe. As if sleepwalking, she mindlessly marched around and around the house until she collapsed on the couch from exhaustion. Eyes wide open, she stared into nothing. *What do you do when you have been violated? But nothing really happened, people would say. You haven't really been violated. What's next? Do you get over it? Ever? Will you trust again? Ever? What's next?*

Shelby sat and stared. The sun rose. She walked out to the backyard, inhaled the roses and attacked the gym set with all her might. She swung and swayed and stretched until the sun warmed her soul. Healing began.

# CHAPTER 20

Restaurant Le Dome hit the ground running and became an instant success the minute it opened on the famed Sunset Strip. The fact that Elton John was one of its founders back in 1977, may have generated its initial popularity but without the best food, the service and ambiance, continuous growth would not have sustained it throughout the years. Expensive cars pulled up at the valet depositing famous and infamous personalities, a wide range of new and old stars, new and old would-be stars, and there were always the stargazers whose entire lives were spent on idolizing celebrities. Last, but not least, were the every-day rich who just ate there because they liked it. Before Le Dome came to town nobody ever messed with the French recipes, honoring them as classics. But now, the French cuisine was hit with bold Americana twists, it was all new, beautifully and tastefully executed. A trendsetter, it was one of the first expensive places where eating at the bar was welcomed. The fireplace gained fame as a frequent photo op backdrop and it was prestigious to dine on the outdoor patio for those who wanted to be the objects of people watchers.

Shelby had never been at Le Dome before but had heard a lot about it. The idea of meeting George and Marci there tickled her. Marc announced himself at the desk and they were immediately taken to George's table.

Marci remembered meeting Shelby at the Writers' Guild Awards dinner. Shelby told them Marci was so popular at the July Fourth party that George couldn't get close to her. George had to settle for conversation with Sidney and Shelby, herself.

Drinks came and Shelby looked over the mostly French menu. She knew enough words to appreciate it all.

"I know what I'll have," she said. "I think." She put the menu down, picked it up and continued reading.

"Let's start with some caviar and champagne to share," said George.

"I'm in," said Marci.

"How sweet," said Shelby.

"Ditto," said Marc.

All along as George was ordering, he kept an eye on Shelby. She returned to the menu and with squinting eyes she seemed to make a decision.

"Yes." She gave Marc the order so that he could give it to the Maître D' who would hand it to the waiter.

"I'd like the Steak Tartar, the Jonah Crab & Rainbow Watermelon for greens, and could I also have the Roasted Beets?" She looked at Marc who nodded in agreement. "And for the main I'd like the duck."

She put the menu down, sipped her cocktail, and watched as the waiter placed the caviar in front of them and set up the *Cristal* champagne.

George could hardly believe that Shelby would have such an appetite for a woman so slim.

"Slim figure, good metabolism," said Shelby. "Look at Marci, how slim she is."

"Yes, but I have to watch what I eat," she said. "Some days more than others."

George and Marc ordered for the ladies. Marc noticed that George was studying Shelby with extreme curiosity.

"Do you see what I see?" he asked Marc.

"What do you mean?"

"We know that you have read the galleys of Sidney's new book. Don't tell me how you got a hold of it," he said with a negative wave of his hand. "I'm not asking. But the character is just like Shelby. I know Sidney is a genius but how he could capture her every detail from that one meeting, I cannot fathom."

Marci turned to Shelby, "Ladies' room?"

The men rose as both women got up and left the table. In the ladies' room Marci was mock mysterious. "You know we are in the middle of a top secret hush-hush meeting?"

"Marci, all I know is that apparently Sidney wrote about someone like me. Who else would recognize that character? People don't know me."

Marci sat on the ladies' room settee, leaned back and her hand gently touched her chin while her eyes attentively watched Shelby. Then Marci leaned forward, her fingers stretched toward Shelby as she imitated what it would be like if Shelby was the one talking.

"You see, all this is you. George had tried to explain it to me but I didn't get it until just now when I finally had a chance to sit with you. It's quite amazing how Sidney described all your nuances. *How sweet*," she added with a friendly grin.

Shelby walked around, thinking. She sat down next to Marci, leaned forward, rested her fingers on her chin, then stretched her fingers forward and started laughing. "I wanted to say something important to you just now but I can't. This is too funny; don't you think?"

"Your fingers dance a ballet when you sit and talk, but not when you stand," said Marci. "I would be embarrassed or annoyed."

"I think I should be flattered, if it's really me," said Shelby. "Famous author like that?"

"That's your way of looking at it? I'd be mad as hell and sue him."

Shelby's face turned serious. "There are more important things in life to worry about, to get mad about, or complain about or think about revenge."

Marci nodded. "Sometimes I get caught up in George's attitudes. That's all. He's such a fighter."

"I'm ready to go back," said Shelby.

"I'll just be a minute." Marci headed toward the toilet stalls.

On their return, it was clear to see that George and Marc hit it off.

"I told Marc that I like his work so much I hope to produce it one day," said George. "And I said to George here's your chance. Let me do the adaptation of Sidney's novel." "So, what's the outcome?" said Marci. "Don't keep us hanging." She looked to Shelby and they both looked at the men.

"I see no reason not to have Marc on our team. I'll run it by Sidney but he normally let's me do the hiring," said George.

They touched their champagne glasses in a toast.

Plates of delicious food were placed in front of them. The conversation switched to sports. It turned out George and Marci were hockey fans.

"Oy, that reminds me," he said, pulling a Sharp organizer out of his pocket. "I have to make a note to hire Mindy for something. You know, her husband is the hockey star, Mike, Mike Baldwin. Great guy. Yeah, Mike Baldwin." He made his notation and Shelby kept her mouth tightly shut. *As they say, Hollywood is a small town,* she thought to herself.

All in all, the dinner meeting with George was a success. As Marc drove into Shelby's driveway, he was excited. Shelby was happy for him. He leaned over to

Shelby on the passenger seat and they shared a brief goodnight kiss. Then he walked around to open the door for her. Shelby caught a light being switched off in the front room. *Was Lorraine watching her?*

She gave Marc another peck on his cheek and went inside. Marc drove off.

Lorraine got her knapsack and was ready to go.

"Lorraine, I have a feeling you're watching me. Are you?"

"Don't know what you mean."

"I think I saw you at the window. I just don't like feeling that anyone's watching me, OK?"

Shelby kept the front door open for Lorraine. "Everything is all right with Pamela, I assume?"

"Yep. The kid is great."

Lorraine left.

Shelby looked in on Pamela. Spread out on her bed, the angel was in deep slumber. On her desk she saw Pamela's homework pages strewn around. She picked them up and took them to the light of the living room to read. *WHAT I'M TAKING WITH ME by Pamela Carpenter.* There were only three pages but Shelby was deeply moved. She read it a second time. Then she took a Post-It and wrote "I've read it. I love it. Mom" and stuck it to the paper.

Next morning was one of those Saturday mornings when Shelby didn't have to do anything. She had planned on sleeping in, having a slow day, taking Pamela to the movies and generally staying away from the world. But her note on Pamela's paper started a barrage of conversation.

"Yes, indeed. I was impressed," said Shelby. "I didn't know what to expect."

"Well, the class got the perimeters of 1200 words, the subject was open and I chose childhood." She curled up next to Shelby. "You really liked it?"

"I could be biased."

"No, Mommy. I would've noticed that after all these years."

"So you chose *WHAT I'M TAKING WITH ME FROM CHILD-HOOD?*"

"Yes. It could have been anything but my childhood is on my mind a lot."

Shelby crawled out of bed and Pamela followed her to the kitchen. Shelby poured her coffee and they sat down in the breakfast nook.

"I didn't know you had been thinking about childhood," said Shelby. "I'm still thinking of you as a child but then you said *perimeters* and I thought where have I been?"

"I am almost nine, Mommy, so pretty soon I'll be ten and even older."

"I used to think you were precocious and that's supposed to be annoying and you would outgrow it but my goodness, you are really smart," said Shelby.

Pamela laughed. "Am I? Is that because I like how you make everything pretty? Is that what you're taking away?"

"That's only one thing. What about your dad?"

"He gave me a lot, too but it was more like a buddy. You know what I mean?"

"But the Pulitzer Prize?"

"Yes. I will be the best writer. Aiming high is another thing I am taking with me. That's probably from daddy but I think he may have gotten that from you. I know he wanted me in sports."

Shelby was at a loss for words. "I don't know how to talk with you anymore," she said. "It's like something happened overnight and you're a real person."

"I'm still a kid."

"It can't be easy being a perfect kid."

"No. I have to keep it simple around some other kids. I don't want to give them peer pressure," she said with a deadpan expression.

"Come here and give me a super hug," said Shelby. "I love you so much I don't even know how to say the words."

"I'm copying you," she said and picked up a coffee mug, filled it with milk and holding it in her hands the way Shelby held her mug, she drank.

# CHAPTER 21

The following Monday Shelby asked Richie for a couple of days off. She would have to go out of town on the 17th and 18th.

"We'd have to hire a temp and Mr. Ross would deduct it from your salary," said Richie.

"He would do that?"

"Yes, he would Shelby, so if you don't really have to go, don't go."

"Oh, Richie. You know once I make up my mind to do something, I do it."

Richie let out a big sigh. "Yeah. I know. But I'm the one who has to tell Mr. Ross, who has to get the temp and whose schedule gets turned upside down."

"Only if you have a rainy day," she said.

Richie looked at her. He didn't like what she said but he didn't know how to answer without disclosing confidential information.

"What does that mean, Shelby? What's on your mind now?"

Shelby walked close to him as he was leaning back at his desk. She looked at him, her eyes piercing through his.

"Rain, Jorge," she slowed down for emphasis. "Carloads. Personal injury cases."

"OK, OK," said Richie, raising his right palm up as if he needed to protect himself. "I've got it." He walked around, scratched his head.

"OK. Don't bring that up ever again. I'll handle your days off."

"Then we're good?" said Shelby.

"Roger," said Richie.

The phone rang. "Law Offices of Mr. Ross," she answered. Richie waited to see whether or not it was for him but Shelby signaled that it was not.

"Shelby," she heard Jeremy's voice. "Come over to my office at about 12:30. Can you?"

"All right," said Shelby and hung up.

She returned to her work but became quite restless. Her mind was everywhere but the *To Do* pile on her desk. She was ill at ease about seeing Jeremy again. She told herself that she was too smart to go along with Jeremy's idea of her.

At 12:30 she got her purse, switched the telephones to automatic answering machine and left for lunch. She walked around the corner to the oversized frosted glass double door marked Marx, Kiery and Corvin, LLC.

She entered. The place was intimidating. She didn't see anyone around since it was lunch time. She heard typing coming from one of the secretarial cubicles. The hush of rich reddish mahogany dictated the noise level and dominated the color scheme, the shelving, the furniture, and the cabinet doors. As she stood there, the secretary stuck her head out of the cubicle. Just then Jeremy appeared from a long hallway.

"Never mind, Ms. Mason. I've got it," he said. The secretary stuck her head back into her work and the typing sounds continued.

"This way, please," said Jeremy to Shelby. She followed him down the hallway. Through some of the open doors she caught a glimpse into the executive offices that were lavishly furnished and had large windows unlike the interior work pool. Jeremy stopped, ushered her into his office, closed the door behind them and turned on his conference light. By doing that he turned off the ring of his telephone and also let the outside know that he did not want to be disturbed.

He grabbed her in his arms and kissed her with all the passion she remembered. He cupped her breasts in his hands and kissed them through her clothes. He started to pull off her blouse. She was pinned to the wall. Her mind and body were at war. His kisses awoke her erogenous zones which at this moment seemed to be her entire body. Her skin was burning hot. One hand seemed to be pushing him away while the other one pulled him toward her. *Why stop?* Although she was sending mixed messages, the brain won. She managed to slip out of his hold. She didn't know why she pulled out. It was involuntary. Even as she was trying to catch her breath, her body didn't want to stop. *Slut. Slut,* she heard her brain speak. That did it.

"Jeremy," she said, her hoarse voice barely escaping her throat. She was re-buttoning her blouse while looking at him staring him down as if he were a dog. "You stop that."

She pointed her index finger at him. "You stop that and forget you ever even thought about lurid sex in your office."

Jeremy brought on his tried and true blue eye smile, "But Shelby,"

She kept her index finger pointed at him and her other hand held up as to *stop* him from advancing any closer. "Don't but Shelby me."

"I thought you liked it. I thought you were into it."

"Yes. I believe you would think that. I believe I was into it that day, that half hour, that moment. But the next moment reality hit. I felt cheap. I did not like feeling cheap. I never want to feel that way again. I will never allow you to do that to me again."

She turned her back to him and walked out the door. She needed fresh air. She went to the garage, got in her car and sat. *Oh, why?* She thought. "Shake it off," she said. Stepping on the gas she drove to the drive-up window of the familiar In-N-Out and ordered a burger through her tears.

# CHAPTER 22

Marc arrived right behind Mama Pearl just as he did the previous time. Pamela was excited even before the woman showed up and she wanted to help bring in the food and all the things. Mama Pearl was delighted to oblige. Marc walked over to a smiling Shelby who had just finished setting the dinner table. She embraced Marc and their kiss lasted longer than the previous quick Hello-s. She felt comfortable lingering in his arms that extra moment.

"This is so great. I loved Mama Pearl's before."

"Then we celebrated my finding you," said Marc. "Now we celebrate my getting the dream screenwriting assignment deal signed and sealed. You know, the one with Sidney Marshall and George Eckert."

"Wow! That is fantastic," she said.

Marc proceeded to open the bottle of wine he brought. She went to get the glasses.

"How long does it have to breathe?"

"Oh, forget it. Let's just drink."

"Works for me."

Shelby took a sip and looked in on Mama Pearl and Pamela in the kitchen.

"Is Pamela helpful, Mama Pearl?"

"She's very knowledgeable," came the answer.

"See, Mommy? I'm good," boasted Pamela.

Marc and Shelby settled on the patio. The garden of flowers sweetened the air and the setting sun gave it a mysterious hue.

"There's one downside, though," said Marc.

"No, Marc. I don't want any bad news."

"Not bad only inconvenient. My agent told me that the author would be in town in the middle of the month and I am supposed to meet with him. But now I am told Mr. Marshall's calendar is too full during the few days that he is back here. Besides, he likes his screenwriters to know the locales as well as he does. So, I have to go to Europe and meet him and he will drive me or fly me or whatever, around to have a firsthand sense of the locations he uses in the story. So, I can't see you for a few days but not for long," he said. Reaching for her hand they sat quietly.

"I don't know what to say. I think I am very happy for you. But I also think I'll miss you," she said.

"Thank you. That's all I wanted to hear. You've made me feel very good."

"When are you going?"

"Sometimes toward the end of this month. George will let me know."

They looked at each other their eyes scrutinizing the other. Two people who have been hurt, afraid of feelings, maybe even afraid of trust.

"Dinner is served!" hollered Pamela and rang the little crystal bell as loud as she could while laughing hard. "Mommy, Marc, Mama Pearl would like you to come in."

They had a wonderful evening. When Mama Pearl left and Pamela fell asleep, Shelby took Marc's hand and walked him into her bedroom. There, she kissed him lightly. Once he got over his surprise, he returned her kiss much more than lightly. They kissed with enormous passion. Both of them were moved by feelings, emotions and yes, the wine.

"There's more where that comes from," said Shelby. "Wanted you to know what's waiting for you when you come back."

"In the book Sidney calls it *life juices*. Sounds so rich and full and complete," he said. "I admire his wonderful expressions. So positive. As if he knew about life."

Shelby looked at him and then looked away, far away into nothing. "Yes, Marc. As if he knew."

# CHAPTER 23

*T*he 17th came and Shelby loaded her car for an overnight trip. Lorraine and Pamela didn't mind being alone for one night. They made their own plans of arts and crafts. Pamela wanted to surprise her mother with something she would make. She told Lorraine that her mother didn't make things with her hands. She mostly reads to her and takes her to theater and museums. So, the two of them were fine without Shelby. Shelby kissed Pamela goodbye told her she would call to say goodnight, besides, she won't be gone for long.

She smiled, sang along with the radio and thought about Sidney. She had missed him. His clever conversation proved to be guidance that she had not had since her parents died. He became many things to her and seeing him even for a short period of time would elevate her spirit. She didn't think of their brief sexual encounter as an ongoing romantic affair. Now that she knew his wife, she had an entirely different viewpoint of the worldly man and she was sure there would not be any lascivious approaches on his part.

The five-hour drive flew by. She checked into a small, unobtrusive motel on the outskirts of Las Vegas.

She bathed, had a refreshing nap and dressed. The simple, full length sheath dress moved with her body, enhancing her leggy walk. She knew she was looking good. Her steps took on an extra added air of self-confidence. She didn't notice a young man in western garb getting into his car at the same time she got into hers and following her. She didn't think that there would be anything unusual about an attractive woman in Las Vegas and that no one would pay any particular attention to her. The plan was working fine. She self-parked and elegantly walked into the casino of Caesars Palace. Her eyes gleaming, she was filled with anticipation as she beheld the surrounding glitz and glamour, the sounds, the smells, the activities everywhere. It was nine-thirty. She had plenty of time for a tall, cool drink. It would make her feel even better, if that was possible.

"Champagne," she said to the bartender, knowing that was something she could handle.

"California or French?"

"California Chandon, please."

She carried the drink as she walked around. Stopped at some of the gambling tables, watched the players. Some men talked to her, invited her to play. She politely refused. When she finished the drink a pretty waitress in a scanty outfit appeared from nowhere and took the empty glass. *How sweet.*

"Would you like another one?" said the waitress.

"Oh, why not."

Shelby was so involved with observing the casino life that it seemed only seconds when the waitress returned with a fresh drink.

"Would you like to sign for it?" she asked.

"No. It's cash," said Shelby pulling some money from her purse.

The young man in the cowboy outfit materialized and handed some money to the waitress. "I'll take care of the little lady," he said.

"No, you will not." Shelby put her money on the waitress' tray and handed his money back to him.

"Just thought we could work together," he said.

"No thank you. I said that before and I say it again."

"You look like you're looking for a little action. Are you?"

"No, thanks." She smiled and moved along, but he followed.

"Working girl?"

"Who isn't?" Her reply was simple. She actually hated to be reminded of the fact that she was a working woman who, within twenty-four hours, would be back at her desk.

"Maybe I can be of service?" The cowboy insisted.

"No. I'd really like to stay on my own, OK?" She was growing irritated.

"That's what I call independence!" He cockily walked off. She could finally relax. Gosh, some men just can't take *no* for an answer.

Her thoughts quickly traveled back to her own reason for being there. She looked at her watch. In international language the 22:00-hour mark was rapidly approaching. It was time for her secret *rendezvous* and she moved close to the bust sculpture of Brutus.

Sipping on the champagne, she waited patiently. She knew that Sidney could be held up in traffic, or anywhere. She had faith.

The minutes passed. She trained her eyes in the direction of the main entrance.

The young cowboy appeared from nowhere with two plainclothes detectives. He pointed at her and she was quickly picked up. Calmly and elegantly, they ushered her out of the casino, into the security offices.

A yellow cab pulled up in front of the hotel and the tall, grey haired, expensively dressed man, Sidney, practically abandoned it. He rushed into the casino with a travel bag on his shoulder.

He went directly to the bust sculpture of Brutus and looked around. It was ten-twenty in the evening.

Jeremy was doodling, daydreaming. This was no day to work. Why couldn't he just call Shelby and say, "I'm sorry I didn't mean to hurt you." He knew that his eagerness got the best of him. He knew that Shelby was not that kind of a girl. He thought he should have said "Hey, this is it. I'm ready. Let's run away. Let's be together."

Maybe he could fall in love like never before. After their intimate lunchtime misadventure in his office he could not believe the new feelings rushing him. He would never do anything demeaning to her. She was a good thing in his life. He was positive that anything he would ever do with Shelby would be like never before, and lasting. That woman had all the qualities he found himself needing. How easy it was to be ignorant and how difficult it was to be learning. Yet, it was happening. His life took on a new direction. A romantic direction. He was soaking it up. Would he be so preoccupied with her if he were under more pressure at work? Would he be able to get her out of his mind? He thought he knew the answer to that but he was too preoccupied with her to define it.

The buzzing of the intercom rudely interrupted his thoughts. His grouchy answer let his secretary know just how he felt about calls right then.

"Yeah, I'll talk to him." Damned *Caesars Palace*, he thought to himself. Why does he have to handle all the damn hookers threatening to sue? Why can't Stanley Marx do it? Is that what senior partner means? The junior has to do all the trash? He hated Vegas and hated Caesars. But he did not hate the money.

"Yeah, Sam. Who? Beverly Canyon? You've got to be kidding. Why not call herself Candy Stripper, or Sweet Beat? Beverly Canyon. Wow!" He was so bored, he was halfheartedly listening, nodding and definitely continuing his doodling. Then he abruptly stopped.

"Say that again. Her real name. Say that again! Shelby Carpenter. All right. I'm listening. Start from the beginning. Let me tape this."

Nearly an hour later Jeremy walked into Shelby's office to find a temporary receptionist filling her place. Richie walked by and saw Jeremy.

"Hey, Jeremy. Can I help you?"

"Yes. Where's Shelby?"

"Took the day off and then a second day. I had to hire a temp but no one can do this job the way Shelby can. She's a gem."

"Well, nice talking to you," said Jeremy. Richie's mouth was still in mid-sentence as the door closed behind Jeremy.

Jeremy walked back to his office, called Shelby's house.

Shelby answered softly, pleasantly. "Hello, Jeremy? Yes, of course I'm OK. No, I'm not sick. But wait a minute. I need your services. No, none of that, please. As an attorney. I want to sue Caesars Palace for slander, or libel, or false arrest, or something—something drastic! You'll have to give it a name. A legal name. "

"Can I come over to see you?"

"You want to come here? Fine. Sure."

She carefully gave him her address. When she hung up the phone she victoriously uttered, "Fuck you, Caesars. Jeremy'll get you!"

Not much later the Mercedes pulled up in front of Shelby's home in Encino. Shelby saw him arrive, smiled at the flawless lawyer look he favored and displayed with grandeur.

She was wearing shorts and a Tee shirt, but Jeremy thought that she looked special even in that. As he closed the door behind himself, he kissed her hard. For a long moment they both felt that no business was going to be done.

"All right, all right," Shelby whispered. She pushed him away and turned to walk into the living room. Jeremy did not follow. His attention was caught by a large picture on the wall of the den, adjacent to the entry hall. It was a blown-up photo of a baby's face, next to the hand of the mother holding her. Through her softly flowing hair, Shelby's face was barely visible. But it was the hand, gently holding the small being that captured him. That hand told a story and Jeremy had to go into the den to look at the other walls. He felt as if he were in the midst of riches never before known to him. Emotions on record. Photos, poems, sketches and memorabilia. A framed article about the Ocean Avenue Seafood restaurant. Riches that filled him with good feelings.

"Do you want your coffee in the living room?" came Shelby's voice.

"Yes. Let's have coffee in the living room." He went in, took off his jacket, placed it carefully on the back of a chair and sat down. She returned with the coffee. He let her serve it.

"Tell me about Caesars."

"Well, it's really simple. I was there two nights ago waiting in the casino for a friend and was picked up for soliciting. Do you think that's fair? Can't a woman go to Vegas alone without being called a whore?"

"Who bailed you out? Marc?"

"God, no! He can't know about this. He may be my future," she trailed off as she said that, realizing that she was talking to someone who might have different ideas.

"Well, I don't want him to know about it, but I want you to sue Caesars."

"Can your friend, the one you were waiting for, verify your story?"

"No. His name has to be left out completely. That's why they held me in jail overnight, don't you see? I wouldn't tell them who it was and he is probably pretty annoyed with me for not showing up for our date."

"Who is it?"

"I can't tell you even if you are my attorney."

"I'm not. I am Caesars'."

"No!"

"Yes Shelby. We're on a retainer. The case is assigned to me."

"This is hilarious. Three months ago I didn't even know you. Then finally I landed my first job which turns out to be in the same building with your office. I can't even go to the ladies' room to change for work, for my second job, without running into you. You're everywhere. You're in my life and everything about you is all wrong. I don't believe this is happening to me."

"Change for work? What work? What second job?"

"Oh, just a little odd job I hold to maintain my luxurious lifestyle. I cocktail waitress on weekends in a gourmet restaurant."

"That's not so good."

"You're telling me? I hate it. But it pays for our groceries and gasoline and I need it."

"What's not so good is the general concept of cocktail waitresses. And the fact that you went to Las Vegas; the fact that you cannot give the name of your friend; the fact that without that you have a lousy case; the fact that you can't have me for your counsel. And now I can't even handle this case because I'm involved."

"Involved! Ha! Since when is sexual desire synonymous with involvement? I don't care if you do the defense. I will find someone else!"

"I'll give you a couple of names."

"You give me nothing." Her frustration was growing out of control.

"Just get out and I'll see you in court, counselor. Because until you show pictures of me taking money for sex, I am no prostitute and as long as I'm holding two jobs to support myself and my child, I am an even more respectable citizen."  Her hands, her fingers were reaching out and pulling back then clenching in a fist.  She was searching for words. "My rights, my body, no part of me will ever be violated again.  Understand?"

"It's about the jurors who won't like the idea of your taking the trip alone. Your kind of individualism and proud independence is, in this day, more dangerous than respectable."

"Go. Just go away. I have to think."

He somehow felt that the total frustration she was experiencing was his fault. He also felt that there must be something he could do for her.

"You'll have to disclose the name of the person you're trying to protect. Under oath it'll all come out."

"What about the Fifth Amendment?"

"That's there to protect you, not for you to protect the only person who could get you off."

She became defiant. "That's my choice, counselor for the defense. And I'd never divulge his name. He's too . . . Oh, forget it. Just go away."

Jeremy stood and silently walked to the door. He was torn.

She was in the living room, looking after him. He stopped at the door, turned back for another glance into the den. That picture again.

He went inside and jotted down something on a pad next to the telephone. Then he left.

Shelby, very angry, muttered under her breath, "Hope your car won't start." She didn't know if he heard her. He probably wouldn't have laughed anyway.

As Jeremy was backing out of the driveway, Lorraine was pulling in with Pamela. Jeremy didn't pay attention to the other car but Lorraine saw the handsome young man.

Pamela ran into the house. "Mommy, Mommy, you're home!"

"Yes, honey. I came home early and was going to pick you up. What happened?"

"I ate a sandwich that Lorraine didn't make. So, I'm sick to my stomach."

"That's what it is," said Lorraine. "Something she ate."

"Thank you, again for bringing her home. Can you stay?"

"No, I'll go back to school and cover for the afternoon."

"I appreciate your help. I do," said Shelby.

"I wanted to say goodbye to Pamela. I'm leaving."

"Well, we're a package. Goodbye to her is goodbye to me," said Shelby.

"Yeah," said Lorraine. "Yeah."

Lorraine started for the door. Pamela put her arms around her. "Kiss-kiss-hug-hug."

"Call us sometime," said Shelby.

"You're too busy for me with all your men," Lorraine said with a snide smirk.

"I'm not going to dignify that."

"Dignify, schmignify, my ass. Can't you just come out and tell me I piss you off."

"I'm not good at fighting," said Shelby.

"Yeah, sure. You're just an angel," said Lorraine. She walked out the door without another word.

Shelby looked in on Pamela. The stomachache changed her back to *little girl* who let her mother bundle her up and baby her. They settled down to watch television. It was much later in the evening when Shelby found Jeremy's note in the den.

# CHAPTER 24

Marc was ready when George arrived in the limousine transporting them to the airport. The uniformed driver placed Marc's bag in the trunk and drove them to the international terminal at Los Angeles airport. They were first to board the overseas flight, accepting cocktails, ignoring the rest of the passengers still getting situated. During the long flight George and Marc shared a lot of good drinks, good food and good conversation.

"Getting back to my theory," George continued with their interrupted conversation. "Marci and I met a couple of days before I took her as my date to a July Fourth party. I wasn't even supposed to go but once I had a date especially one that looked like her, I had to show her off."

He was visibly enjoying himself reliving that afternoon. Marc didn't know exactly why George even got into this but a good writer listens. There is never anything that should not be heard, should not be learned and could not be re-used by an open-minded listener.

"Now get this," George continued. "I wasn't supposed to be there and Sidney wasn't supposed to be there. Then to top it all, Sidney's wife brought my ex, Nancy to the party. So, true to herself, Nancy took over, picked up Shelby's husband and off they went. Poor man didn't have a chance. No one knew, of course, how terrible that would turn out. Beautiful Shelby has never harmed anyone in her life and she is still doing good things for others. That's what she did when she called me from your office."

George took a deep breath. "This probably sounds weird but sometimes I get a little spiritual and I start to believe that things happen for a reason."

"Sometimes I think about believing that," said Marc, "but I really don't. And what about Marci?"

"I'm not sure," said George. "I think she is fantastic. I don't know why she is with me. I really don't. But I love it."

"This is where we have to fall back on the old *time will tell* adage,'" said Marc.

"I think we may have had too much to drink to get this deep, hm? Don't you agree?"

Marc started laughing. "I do. I agree. Let's take a nap."

"Together?"

"Together, yes."

With a smile on their faces, they both put on sleep masks, made themselves comfortable and dozed off.

The morning arrival at Milan Malpensa airport was on schedule. At the baggage carousel George spotted Sidney and Alexandra. The introductions were brief since everyone knew everything about each other. Except for Marc who did not know anything about Alexandra. He never asked. The unspoken *male rules* dictated that whether the girl is a groupie, a fling, a mistress, a colleague, one does not ask.

Sidney's driver located their luggage and they got into the limo. Sidney opened the bar and started pouring wine for everyone. No one asked what time it was.

"You know, somehow living in Europe makes me drink more," Sidney announced. "People are less uptight here."

"Sidney, you don't need an excuse," said George. "Writers are notorious drinkers. But as long as you can handle it, why not?"

"Marc," said Sidney. "I'm glad you came on board with our movie. I like your work."

"Thank you. I'm glad too."

Sidney continued. "I asked the driver to take the long road to the house because I wanted you to get a sense of this area. Milan is one of the locations in the story."

"Yes. I'm familiar."

"That's right. I'm not supposed to ask you how you got hold of the galleys. Who betrayed me?"

"It's nothing that dramatic."

Sidney stopped to give it another thought, and then shrugged.

"Spilt milk," he said with a dismissive gesture of his hand. "Tomorrow, you and I will use the convertible and really see the places I need. Details, details. George has to review another binder that I have compiled."

Marc just nodded. "I'm here for the ride," he said. But he was thinking. He had a feeling that he had heard that voice before.

Alexandra laughed out. "We're all here for the ride," she said. She patted Marc, sitting next to her, on his thigh. Sidney and George were across from them talking busily. Neither of them noticed the familiarity expressed by Alexandra who was looking at Marc, waiting for a reaction. It came. Marc measured up Alexandra. He was clearly amused.

"Appears to be a promising ride," said Marc.

"Count on that," said Alexandra, letting her foot slide close enough to Marc's so that they touched.

"We'll stop at a couple of locations now," said Sidney. The limo rolled into the circular driveway of a true castle. Marc made a notation for himself and continued to pay close attention to Sidney. Several stops later, as the sun was setting, they arrived to their destination. The car slowed and pulled into the narrow driveway of the villa coming to a stop. Sidney instructed the driver where to put the luggage while they entered the main house.

Alexandra followed Marc who politely slowed to let her in front of him. "If Sidney is busy tomorrow morning maybe I can show you some of the spots," she said.

"Fine, if that's OK with everyone," said Marc.

"Excuse me, Sidney," said Alexandra, catching up with him and George.

"You and George can attend to the business and I will take Marc around in the morning if that'd save time."

Sidney nodded in agreement.

"Besides, I'm taking the convertible back to my place tonight so I will have it," said Alexandra.

"Good idea," said Sidney. "I will have a list of the stops for you in the morning. Good night. See you at eight, hm?"

Alexandra left and the men were greeted inside by Moira who had a refreshment service set up for them. George and Moira hugged.

"Great to see you. You always light up the day."

"George, you have to stop flattering me. I've passed that age," said Moira embracing him with a delighted smile.

"Never," said George.

"Moira, this is Marc Gramercy," said Sidney.

"I've read about you and am thrilled that you're doing Sidney's screenplay."

They shook hands. "Happy to meet you, Ma'am."

"Moira. Please call me Moira."

Marc met Moira for the first time. Moira looked pale but once a great beauty, she walked with regal elegance, her aloof smile commanded a protective distance and it was not possible to know what she was thinking. Marc studied her. Could that be a veneer of a lonely person? Why? Or just status distinction?

Shortly after their refreshments, Sidney took Marc and George to their quarters. The guest cottage in the back of a private mansion sounded cozy until they arrived. It was once the pool house built for the aristocratic family who owned it and all the land and everything around it. Later, as the fame and the funds of the family shrunk and their aristocratic presence meant less and less to the new generation, the pool house became a luxurious guest house. People like Sidney Marshall and other *nouveau riche* of the world found the mini-mansion with its private redecorated guest accommodations to be perfect for a few months. Not too demanding and not intrusive. The predictable remarks about the entire property were *quaint, old world, charming, unusual* and the likes. These words were bandied about often.

The rooms were not large but felt spacious and comfortable due to high ceilings. A common living room separated the two sides. Off the center was a spiral staircase for walking up to the flat top of the house which overlooked the pool. This rooftop deck was decorated as a sitting or sunning spot where numerous attractive umbrellas created as much shade as was desired. Quaint. Indeed. George and Marc each got a private bedroom and bath. Apparently Alexandra had a separate apartment nearby. It was explained that since she was structuring and implementing the publicity and public relations build-up for Sidney and the new novel, she was working practically all hours.

Alexandra came to pick Marc up but before they took off, she would have a cup of coffee. She acted as if she belonged there and was unashamed of moving around the house as part of the family. She took two green apples out of the fruit basket.

"Thank you for the rations for the road," she said. "Marc, ready?"

They waved goodbye and walked to the car. Sidney's list was taped to the dashboard and Marc was impressed with her efficient work ethics.

"We're on the clock and Sidney knows exactly how long this will take. So, if you don't mind," she said with an inviting wink, "I wrote down some descriptive words about these spots in case we run out of time."

"I trust your judgment," said Marc. Unaware that he was getting Alexandra's interpretation of the location list, the tour turned out to be a lot of driving-by, circling around, stopping and taking pictures from the car. Not enough time for capturing the flavors. Before he knew it, Alexandra was getting out of the car at her apartment."

"Mi casa," she said. "A refresher for the road weary."

Marc was interested in finding out what exactly she wanted to accomplish. The bright one-bedroom apartment looked attractive in a simple way. She closed the door behind them and eagerly kissed him slipping her tongue inside his mouth while her hand squeezed his balls just the right way. He lost his footing and Alexandra easily pushed him down on the couch. She started to unzip the fly of his pants but Marc put his hand on hers to stop her. He sat upright and waited for her to collect herself.

"You're moving too fast," he said.

"We don't have much time."

"We should get to know each other first."

"My sentiments exactly."

"You call this getting to know each other first?" he said.

"Well, what do you call this?" she said placing the emphasis on YOU. Then she slid so close to him that he could feel her skin on his.

He got up. "We must be coming from different planets. You're hard to resist but this is not my speed."

Neither of them spoke on the way back to the house. Alexandra looked angry and Marc chose not to start a dialogue thus not giving her a chance to continue her game. When she pulled into the driveway, she gave it one more try.

"Are you sure this is what you want?"

"I'm not much good at quickies. Sorry."

"I tell you what. When you're ready, just give me a sign. You know, just whistle. You do know how to whistle?"

"You're no Bacall," he said.

"And you're no Bogie, for sure." She marched into the house without looking back at Marc.

The early dinner setting indicated that this would be a short evening for everyone. They washed up and surrounded the long table.

"Welcome back," said Moira as everyone sat down. Sidney was across from her at the head of the table, Alexandra on the left of Sidney, George and Marc on the right of Sidney. Moira introduced Marissa, the cook and housekeeper and a genuine gem. Marissa's attitude reflected her self-pride as she openly smiled and tried to chat in broken English.

"Marissa is also a friend, a wise woman," said Moira. "She tells me that we are a welcomed change of pace for them. After we leave and the owners return, they lead a very ceremonial life full of rules and traditions."

"Yes. This is nice, different," Marissa said. "Vacation."

"I forgot to mention that her husband is also our driver and our houseman and we want for nothing," said Sidney."

Marc felt a special connection with Moira and wished he could spend some time with her. He had hoped there would be an opportunity for a chat in the near future. Over dinner everyone was in a good mood. Moira apparently liked the simple Italian country cooking which she whimsically contrasted with more formal table setting. This was considered American creativity.

Alexandra handed Sidney the schedule.

"We have developed the timetable for the whole week so that we can accomplish everything in the shortest amount of time. Here is a copy for each of you," Sidney said in his precise speech pattern and handed one to both men.

"Brutus 22-17." Marc blurted out the words. His brain seemed to have been taking a nap. Shocked, he looked at Sidney. Sidney looked back at him. Actually stared. "Not funny," he said. They sipped on wine, George and Alexandra talked across the table. Moira got up.

"Excuse me, everyone. I'm a little tired today. I must go." She left the room. Marissa followed her.

Sidney got up quickly. "I'll be a minute," he said and stepped out to follow Moira.

"Moira has not been feeling well," said Alexandra. "Sidney can't figure out what's wrong. He said she was fine all along. But I tell you, since I got here I have not seen her at her best. Could it be me, who knows," she said laughing at her own joke and washing it down with wine.

Marc had no comment while George felt it was his duty to remain conversational until Sidney returned. He picked up his glass of wine.

"Shall we go upstairs?" he said starting for the path through the pool-garden and up the stairs. They followed him with their wine and settled down on the deck. Sidney returned.

"Looks like I'm the hostess now," said Alexandra. "Does anyone need anything?"

"No, thank you," said George then turned to Sidney. "What is the matter with Moira? Is she sick? When I saw her just before you left she was in great spirits and great form."

Sidney took a deep breath. "I really don't know. We have been back and forth and up and down this half of Europe for weeks and she was the best trooper, as always. Alexandra just arrived about two weeks ago after setting up the worldwide book campaign. I showed it to Moira. She was impressed."

No one spoke for a while. "I'll have the doctor come around tomorrow morning to check her out. See what he has to say," said Sidney. "I may take her home to UCLA Medical."

"Maybe we should skip the location survey tomorrow. Or not go until after the doctor," said George.

"I agree. But we have to adhere to the schedule as closely as possible the rest of the time," said Sidney.

"I'm pretty beat," said George. "It's been a long two-in-one. Days."

"OK, guys," said Sidney. "I'll drop Alexandra at her place. We'll need the convertible for tomorrow."

"The VW is over at my place," she said.

"I'll be back in a few minutes," said Sidney. "In case you want to—"

"Forget it, Sidney. I'm done for the day," said George. "Good night all."

Sidney got up and letting Alexandra go down the staircase in front of him, they left.

Marc was not comfortable. He loved the book so much, he had wanted to meet Sidney so badly but now he was sensing peculiar vibes. He had mixed feelings. Very mixed.

Marc could not fall asleep. Staring at the ceiling, he kept sorting the effects of meeting the author and watching his interactions with others, especially Alexandra. Marc sensed that he was better off before he was one of the boys. Better off before he heard *Brutus 22-17*. Better off before he fell for Shelby. Well, maybe not that. As soon as Marc heard Sidney's voice he recognized it from the telephone message. But what in the world made him blurt it out? He felt foolish about blurting it out. He didn't make any points and possibly created a wall of hindrance between him and the author. Marc already knew from George that Sidney had met Shelby and must have been so impressed with her to use her characteristics and capture some wonderful details about her. She is interesting, a little flaky but beautiful and kind. Why wouldn't every man go for her? But somewhere under his skin Marc's intuition put him on alert. What if there was more going on between Sidney and Shelby than met the eyes? An instinct. How much more? Was any of it his business?

As a writer himself, he was keenly aware of character development and he had drawn frequently from people he knew firsthand. *Just let go*, he told himself.

# CHAPTER 25

Lorraine was ready to go. She and Thelma lingered over a cup of coffee in the kitchen reflecting. The passing moments were indescribable because of the unexpected overflow of emotions. Some stood still. Some rushed. Neither of them wanted to let go or let go first.

"You know you're always welcome here," said Thelma. Lorraine's smirk expressed doubt.

"No, thanks. This man is changing you. You're not the feisty person I grew up with. You're bending every which way to please everyone but it used to be just the opposite. We had to bend to please you. You were self-important. Look at you now."

"Is that why you went ahead and chose your dad? You could've talked it over with me."

Lorraine thought for a moment. "No, I couldn't talk with you. You were over mothering me."

"I didn't know that."

"I couldn't live up to your expectations," said Lorraine.

"And now? What about now? Is it different? Why can't you stay?"

"Your life is different. Everything's changed."

"Not my love for you."

Lorraine got up, zipped her purse and was ready to go.

"You keep saying that."

"Because it's true." Thelma was about to raise her voice but stopped herself. "You don't understand the mother's love. There is no love like that. Nothing like that." She reached for a tissue.

"Well, you have too many people."

"You mean Arnie? Never mind about him. He's a good man. He cares. He just has a hard time explaining his feelings, you know."

"And Shelby, and Pamela and the toddlers at the daycare. Too many."

Thelma put her hand on Lorraine's. "Arnie's a good man. He cares," she repeated. "The others are like family, but *not* family."

"I don't know anything right now, Mother. Nothing," said Lorraine. "So I have to go away."

"Aren't you leaving for school?"

"Oh, yeah. That's what I'm doing," said Lorraine. "The Institute. The culinary school."

"Well, honey, I hope it will be everything you've imagined and it will make you happy," said Thelma.

"Happy?" Lorraine looked away. The word sounded strange. "Happy?"

"You can be happy. Think about it. You have a long drive." Thelma leaned close to her. "You think about it on the road. What it'll take for you to be happy."

"Yeah, you always have the words."

"I'm glad you've noticed. I don't want to sound preachy but you know I've never smothered or knowingly over mothered you, as you said. I'll just tell you that you are always welcome here. My home is your home. No matter what, we can make it work. We didn't do so badly this past year, did we?" They got up from the breakfast nook and started for the garage.

Arnie was running around, trying to be helpful. He was awkward around Lorraine. She made him feel insecure and wanted to prove himself. He made sure the Pinto was loaded with her two suitcases and oversized duffle. He checked the tires once again, the gasoline gauge and waited for Lorraine to come out. She and Thelma appeared. Lorraine had a halfhearted smile for Arnie but said nothing.

"Does Pamela know you are leaving?" said Thelma.

"Yes. Just not *when*."

"Who will tell her?"

"I'll give her a call. Soon."

Arnie started to say something but Thelma stopped him.

"You have a safe drive, hear?" Call us when you arrive." They kissed and Lorraine rolled out of the driveway.

The early morning traffic was easy to handle and Lorraine shortly reached the San Diego Freeway heading south. Crisscrossing thoughts raced each other in her mind, baffling her. She hated admitting that she was confused but she could not lie to herself. She always got around her helplessness by being mean and nasty to anybody and everybody. She was surprised when she recognized that she wanted to be happy. She had never thought of that before. She had to change something. What? How?

Lorraine was unaware of the passing scenery as she left all of Los Angeles behind driving through the beach cities, the ports, San Clemente and further down. She found herself inadvertently following Thelma's advice, using the long drive for sorting her feelings. She lied to everyone about a culinary school in San Diego. She had not applied. She was far short of having saved up the tuition. She was sure she could get a good-tipping waitress job in San Diego while living at her father's house free. She knew that she had to make enough money to actually be able to attend Le Cordon Bleu. She had her eye on San Francisco. She was sipping on the ice water Arnie had put in the car while her mind was jumping around and often returning to thoughts of how everyone around her was happy except her.

She barely noticed when she reached Interstate – 5 and merged into it continuing south. She lovingly patted her car. "There, there, good little Pinto," she said and laughed out loud.

It had been almost a year since she moved away from San Diego. Once Nick, her father, actually married Bea, his live-in woman, Lorraine had to get out. Bea was always jealous of Nick's relationship with his daughter and she wanted Lorraine out of the way. Lorraine knew the only way she could piss Bea off was to stay in and watch television in their family room, drink their beer, and eat their food. As a result, she grew heavy and miserable. She ran with a low-brow crowd, thinking that was the only place into which she could fit. She participated in malicious acts and thought nothing of it. Unbeknownst to Nick (or anyone) she had had close brushes with the law, but managed to get away without a police record.

She often felt sorry for herself. Moving in with her seedy friends seemed to be a solution, before the fact that her life was going downhill became painfully obvious. When she got into a fistfight with the pretty gang leader, she walked out. She left San Diego to live with her mother, but only until she was on her own two feet again. Her mother frightened her. They had not had a relationship for years, and instead of opening up to Thelma, Lorraine locked up her feelings and continued eating.

Two and a half hours later Lorraine took the cutoff exit to Pacific Beach in Mission Bay on the outside of San Diego. Procrastination. How sweet. She chose to procrastinate. She didn't want to arrive to her dad's house too early and have too much time to talk. She was not looking forward to seeing her dad's wife and her three-year old toddler from some unprotected teenage sex.

Lorraine parked, walked down to the edge of the Bay and sat in the sand, her toes cooling in the velvety water. The sun was dropping fast, lower and lower, closer and closer to the horizon. Finally, she had no excuse left. The idea of going to the house did not seem as inviting as when it first came to her mind.

She pulled into the driveway of a two-story home on west Briarfield Drive. It was early evening. She dragged her bags up to the front door before ringing the doorbell. A wiry man, Nick Hunter, her father, carrying a can of Coors in one hand, cigarette dangling from the corner of his mouth, opened the door wide. She was greeted by his fogged up hazel eyes and deep hoarse voice.

"Hey, kiddo. You made it."

He put the beer down on the entry step, gave her a hug, picked up the bags and they went inside. His wife, Bea, was standing in the foyer, nearly smiling.

"Hello," said Bea.

Bea didn't move. Lorraine nodded toward her and said "Hey." Nick headed up the stairs with Lorraine right behind.

The upstairs of the contemporary red brick home had two small bedrooms. One clearly belonged to Bea's kid and the other one served as the guest room. Lorraine had to share the bathroom with the little boy. She knew she also would have to keep it clean.

"Dad," she said as he placed the luggage on the floor near the closets. "Thank you for letting me stay for a while."

"How long?"

"The shortest course is four months." She was lying without batting an eye.

"Four months?" he said with no enthusiasm and took a deep disappointed breath. More like a sigh. "Well, dinner will be ready in a bit. Come on down. Bea made something simple, I think meatballs."

Before Nick left the room Lorraine asked him if it would be OK to use their telephone to call her mother.

"Sure you can," said Nick. "It's in the living room."

Lorraine finished unpacking quickly but didn't go downstairs until she heard the little boy arriving home. He was dropped off by the colorful van displaying the name of the preschool. He noisily charged into the house.

Lorraine went downstairs to the telephone and dialed Thelma. "Hey," she said. "I'm here. Yes, no problems."

The noisy little boy was screaming, "I'm home!" several times as he ran through the living room, his shoes pounding the hardwood floor. "I can't talk now. Bye."

Lorraine hung up, crossed the family room and saw the three of them outside on the deck overlooking Mission Bay. Bea was grilling vegetables. She made a *gagging* face as she witnessed the warm and fuzzy family moment. Both Nick and Bea were talking with little Wally who excitedly told them the events of his day. Lorraine, having lived there before, knew that it was expected of her *to pull her weight*. She automatically started to help with the table. She brought Nick another beer and a bottle of wine for the dinner table.

"I'm drinking beer," said Bea.

There wasn't much age difference between the two women. The main contrast was their weight. Lorraine's big, buxom figure overshadowed everything about Bea. She was rail thin, flat-chested, and boney. Bea's face already showed the premature aging lines of an overly scrawny person.

Without a word, Lorraine picked up the wine glasses from the table, went back to the kitchen, poured herself a glass of wine, and put the other glasses and the bottle back in place. She returned to the deck with Bea's beer and some chilled beer mugs. Bea ignored the mug and drank the Coors from the can.

The evening wore on with little conversation. It was the view that made it worthwhile. Once, a few years back, the beach in front of the property was private as were the boat launch and the short pier. When a new city ordinance declared everything outside the house public, the owners did not want to deal with strangers walking around at all hours. They were annoyed and sold. Nick bought it. He didn't care about what was going on outside. The house was off the beaten track and while it sat close to the beach not many people walked around it or used it.

Lorraine had nothing to talk about with Bea and didn't even try. Nick had one beer after the other. That was all he needed.

Wally came over to Lorraine, climbed up in her lap and started to open her mouth with his little hands. Lorraine pulled her face away.

"What's up, little guy?"

"Mommy cleans your teeth, see?" He tried to get into Lorraine's mouth.

"Not mine, kid," she said.

Nick and Bea laughed at the cuteness of the *darling* child. How hard is it to be cute at that age?

"He thinks Bea's a dentist," said Nick.

"He likes to tell people about what I do in the dentist office."

"Well, if you don't mind, I'll get myself ready for school tomorrow. I don't know how long I'll be so don't hold dinner for me."

"We won't," said Bea. She got up and leaving the table of dishes behind she took Wally and they went inside to watch TV. Lorraine looked at the mess.

"Yes, I'll be happy to help you clear the table, Bea," said Lorraine to no one there. Nick went to the bathroom and Lorraine did the dishes.

Bea stepped out on the deck. "I told your father that I don't want you to stay here," she said to Lorraine. "He knows."

Lorraine, carrying several plates, walked by her without a word.

"I'll take Lorraine out for a welcome home drink," said Nick. Lorraine's face tightened when she heard that. But since she had just arrived she thought she should be agreeable.

Nick drove a short distance to a strip mall where a series of small shops were mixed with fast food restaurants and her father's favorite watering hole. The lettering of the *PETE'S* sign was loose and the "*S*" looked like it was about to fall off but *PETE'S* was still standing. Nobody inside cared how the outside looked.

"Lot of the guys hang out here. I bet they'll remember you. Big surprise," he said.

"What guys?"

"The other cameramen, some grips, even one of the broads from the TV station. She's a floozy. Anyone can have her."

"Don't people spend the evening with their families?"

"I just did. When that's done I come out here, that's all."

They went inside and sure enough the long bar in the dark place had not one empty seat.

"Standing room only," said Nick, shaking hands, high five-ing, and reaching for the beer the bartender was handing to him. "The best place in town, hm guys?" He looked around at the laughing faces of his drinking buddies.

"This is Lorraine. You remember my daughter? She's back."

There was general merriment and Lorraine knew she was the only sober person around. The small cocktail tables lining the walls were busy and she stood next to Nick.

"And what will the little lady have?" asked the bartender. "A Coors? Keep it in the family?"

"Little?" said Nick laughing. "Nothing little here that's for sure." Lorraine was ready to kill him.

"Dewars, please. Rocks," she said. She knew not to ask these people for a decent wine.

The crowd grew deeper and rowdier. But as the boom hour was thinning out Nick got a seat at the bar and was immediately holding court. Nick knew everything and was showing off for Lorraine. Finally, *last call* came.

"I guess I'm ready for some drunken driving," said Nick appreciating the approving laughter of the few remaining patrons. They all agreed that so were they.

In the parked car Nick suddenly turned to Lorraine and grabbed her breasts. "There now. Did you miss me? Is this what you came back for?" He rapidly reached for her crotch and she punched him in the face with a tight fist.

"You stop it," said Lorraine and got out of the car. "What the hell is wrong with you?"

She went around to the driver side, opened the door and put her hand out.

"The key," she said. Nick looked at her cockily.

"No way, Missy."

Lorraine made a fist again. "You want more of this?"

She looked foreboding to the drunken man. He obeyed. Handed her the key while crawling over to the passenger seat and letting Lorraine drive.

Morning couldn't come fast enough for Lorraine. She was all packed. She waited for everyone to leave before going downstairs. There was no coffee left in the coffee pot. She took an apple, went back upstairs and dragged her suitcases down to the front door.

She was out of there. She needed to breathe. Her car seemed to automatically drive back to the beach, back to the exact spot where she sat the day before. Unexpectedly the dam broke and an uncontrollable flood of tears rolled down her face forming a thick veil between her and the world. Gradually the wet flow slowed and she could encounter an amazing emotional release.

The question was how to start fresh. The words *how, start, fresh*, were new in her thinking. It would be natural to return to her old stomping grounds on the wrong side of town where she knew everyone. She also knew that it was a dead end. All along she found herself battling with unfamiliar forces. New positive stuff. Curious. Was this the subconscious influence of Shelby the self-reliant? *Subconscious*? *Influence*? What's going on? Lorraine's mind was reeling with images of the recent few months in which Shelby and Pamela enriched her life and where her mother's reality was comforting, not confusing.

She walked over to the food hut by the parking lot, bought a cup of coffee and realized that the mere thought of Pamela and Shelby put a smile on her tearstained face.

# CHAPTER 26

Lorraine drove around aimlessly. She felt like a loser. She wanted to go home. The word home created even greater anxiety in her mind and was followed by new tears. Damn it, she thought. What's with the tears? I was never a crybaby why now? She started to look for an exit from the highway before she would let her car go all the way back to Los Angeles. She realized her car had already reached La Jolla, The Jewel of the Pacific, north of San Diego. She used to know some girls from her childhood who lived there, or used to live there. She drove around until she found a parking strip on a cliff that was an official look-out point. She stopped. The view was beyond amazing. She stared at the endless ocean. Simply stared. She was the loneliest person in the world. Why is it getting dark? Why is it evening? What happened to the day? She didn't notice how her eyes grew heavy and she fell asleep.

Harsh banging on her window woke her. It was the City Patrol checking all the municipal parking lots.

"You have to leave, Miss," said the uniformed man. He was large and could be scary if not taken seriously. "Nice nap? There's no sleeping here. Go home. Or go to a shelter downtown."

He waited until Lorraine started the engine and watched her roll out of the small parking lot. Purposeless once again, she headed south back toward town and somewhere between La Jolla and Mission Valley she stopped at a small hotel on the highway. It was on the inland side of the road with no view of any kind. *THE INN* said the fading sign. "Forget about curb appeal, ha!" said Lorraine as she parked in the open area in the front of the one-story building.

She took her duffle bag from the back seat, passed a few rusty garden tables and chairs as she went inside. A middle-aged woman was keeping busy dusting and wiping the desk that displayed a sign in fancy lettering: *Mrs. Barkley,*

*Proprietor.* Nothing else was going on. It looked to Lorraine like a cheap operation catering to the budget-conscious poor travelers, people on their way to and from the expensive attractions and events of San Diego. There was a small cocktail lounge off the side of the lobby. She went inside and took a seat at the end of the bar. She ordered a Dewars and put down a ten dollar bill, indicating that she would have more than one and hoping that would cover it. Glancing around she noticed a young couple at one of the three small booths very busy with each other. Beside them she saw a few lonely men sitting on the bar stools skipping one in between them. They looked at her but she didn't have to worry about being accosted. She was not their cup of tea.

*Thank Goodness for peanuts and pretzels*, she thought and munched away on the stale snack.

"Is there a kitchen here?" she asked the bartender.

He stared at her. "Yeah," he said, pointing to the nowhere direction in the back. "It's closed."

"That's the way I like it," she said. She walked around the bar and went through the swinging double door.

Lorraine turned on the lights and found herself in a smallish standard commercial kitchen. The bright lights illuminated every corner of the seemingly clean place. She stood still studying the equipment. Moving over to the refrigerator, she opened the door, viewed the contents and after a few minutes of thinking, she proceeded to take out things. She turned on the built-in stovetop grill to pre-heat it and started to concoct a variation of Shelby's *Panini.*

The bartender went out to the lobby. "Hey Maw' this woman is in the kitchen."

"What woman? What kitchen?"

"A drunken woman. A big drunken woman."

Mrs. Barkley left the front desk and went to the kitchen. She looked at Lorraine. "Hey, what's going on?"

"Oh, T.G. Thank god you're here. I can't find the focaccia," said Lorraine.

The old woman was at a loss. "What's focaccia?"

"Bread. It's the kind of bread that you make *panini* with."

"You're not drunk," said Mrs. Barkley.

"Did that big ape call me a drunk? No tip for him," Lorraine said.

"Big ape is my son. Matthew. Why are you making a piganini—whatever you call it—in my kitchen?"

"It's good," said Lorraine. "You'll see." She buzzed around, gathering ingredients. "I saw some sour dough in the bread box. That'll do. It'll be different, but OK."

Before long she had the mix of chicken, pesto, veggies and cheese all melded together on flavorful sour dough bread. In place of the *Panini Press* she used the hot grill pressing with a metal spatula. She cut the finished product into bite-size servings and laid them out on medium size plates.

"This way we can spread it around to the customers," she said, handing a plate to Mrs. Barkley and gesturing her to take it out to the bar.

The rich aroma seeping through the one-story hotel brought out some of the overnight guests who eagerly ordered drinks to go with the tasty finger foods. Thinly shredded Vidalia onions mixed with radishes became another platter and the party was going. The bartender, Matthew, had not been this busy in years.

A huge explosion rattled the building. Except for the young lovebird couple everyone in the bar rushed outside to see. A van's tire blew in front of *THE INN* and flipped on its side. The two men inside were shaken up as the bar patrons helped them climb out. No one attempted to turn the van right side up. They all went back into the bar.

"Could've been worse," said the older of the two men.

"You can say that again," said another man.

The younger of the two men locked the door of the van that was on the topside before following everyone into the building.

"You shouldn't be touching that thing, Bobby," said the older man. "It can blow up, set on fire."

"Nah, Walt it would've blown already if it was to blow."

"Not gonna blow if your tank is empty," said one of the bar guests.

"What's smelling so good?" said Walt.

"Panyanas," said Matthew.

"You asshole," said Lorraine coming out of the kitchen. "Sell them a drink. Do your job."

"Don't boss me around."

"Maybe since you almost got killed and all, the first drink should be on the house," said Lorraine.

"Is that OK, Maw?"

"The girl is right," said Mrs. Barkley.

"Your mother is smart," said Lorraine.

"You sound like my wife, Missy," said Walt to Lorraine.

"I'm an original. I don't sound like anyone. Now, which one of you will call the police to get that van out of here?" asked Lorraine.

Walt didn't move.

"Guess I'd better," said Bobby and went to the front desk where the phone was. He turned to Mrs. Barkley. "Is it OK, Ma'am for me to call?"

"Yes. Just do it."

Then looking at Lorraine he said, "Will you save some sandwiches for me, Miss?"

"You do your job and I'll do mine," said Lorraine, returning to the kitchen.

By the time Lorraine was bringing out the next platter of food Bobby had brought in the camera equipment.

"Pretty fancy," she said then playfully leaned her arm on Matthew's shoulder and posed.

"C'mon barkeep. Say *cheese* to the camera," she said while making a wide *cheese* smile herself.

Bobby went along and took some pictures of the people, the place, but especially of the interesting food. The police came. The tow truck came. Bobby and Walt got ready to leave.

"There's no charge," said Mrs. Barkley. "You're good people."

"Maybe you can see yourselves on TV tomorrow. If they have time. Maybe on the 4:30 news," said Bobby, putting his business card on the counter. "You too, people. You'll be in it."

"Thank you for coming," said Mrs. Barkley.

"We didn't mean to," said Walt, "but glad we did."

He followed Bobby to the door.

"Now come back, you hear? My son Matthew and the girl will fix you up."

Mrs. Barkley turned to the other customers preparing to leave.

"You come back, too. Simple, fast, and very tasty—a nice change," said Mrs. Barkley. "We'll make sure everyone is happy."

"What are you serving up tomorrow?" asked the young husband from the booth.

"We're here for three more days," said another woman pointing to her husband. "We'll be back early. What time do you do this?"

Bobby, Walt, Mrs. Barkley, and the others were looking at Lorraine, waiting for an answer. Lorraine got her duffle bag.

"Five thirty," said Mrs. Barkley.

"We'll be back," said another guest.

The place was emptying out. It was getting late.

Mrs. Barkley saw Lorraine heading for the exit and stopped her. "Why did you do this?"

"I was hungry."

"Do you want to eat again tomorrow?"

They looked at each other. Finally, Lorraine said, "Five thirty?"

"I make the breakfast for the guests so your shift can start at five in the afternoon." Then the woman turned to the bartender. "Come here, Matthew." He stopped cleaning up and stepped next to his mother. "This is my son. What is your name?"

"Lorraine. It's Lorraine Hunter." Lorraine was surprised to see the large young man and the thin elderly woman as mother and son.

"Matthew, meet Lorraine. Lorraine, meet Matthew. And I'm Mrs. Barkley."

"Good to meet both of you."

"Now, where are you staying," asked Mrs. Barkley. She watched Lorraine freeze up, not looking in her eyes, acting strange.

"Oh, just down the road. Down toward San Diego."

"Well, it's late. You shouldn't be driving. Here, come with me. We have an extra room."

Lorraine followed the woman through a dimly lit hallway of what seemed to be an endless ranch style structure: door after door, room after room. It was surprisingly immense toward the back.

"I'll pay you tomorrow," she said as she entered the small room with a single bed and held the door open for Lorraine. "We'll talk then. Leave the key at the front desk when you go out. That's the rule."

"Aren't you worried that I'm not coming back?"

"That's the rule. That's what I said." Mrs. Barkley left Lorraine to close the door.

Lorraine could hear Mrs. Barkley's shuffling footsteps disappearing into the night. She collapsed on the bed and had her first restful sleep since she left Los Angeles.

Lorraine was awakened by the hotel guests nosily getting ready to go on their various sightseeing tours. She heard them tell Mrs. Barkley that they were looking forward to getting back in the evening and having drinks and hors d'oeuvres.

"Yes, the girl will be here to make them," said Mrs. Barkley. "How was the breakfast?"

"Almost five-star," said one customer.

Lorraine smiled. She felt refreshed. She dug deep into her bag to see how much cash was in her possession. Not much. The lights came on in her mind. She felt like one of those old *Ford* or some car commercials with the light bulb bringing a bright idea. Something had to be done. Being at this dumpy hotel would only do for the short term. How could she get money from Nick was the next challenge she had to meet.

She brought in her two suitcases. The smaller one had wheels on it but the larger one had to be dragged by its sides. Mrs. Barkley was nowhere in sight. Neither was there a luggage dolly in sight. Lorraine caught a glimpse of Matthew cleaning the bar. She thought he purposely turned away when he saw her struggle.

"Hey, you," she called to him. "Matthew or whatever. I need help."

He came to the entrance of the bar, leaned to one side of the door frame and hands in his pocket, eyes squinting, he looked at her.

"Did you call me a big ape? Did you?"

"So what. You called me a drunkard."

"Now you need a man."

"No. I need you."

She continued pulling and dragging the two suitcases toward the hallway, turning her back on him. "But never mind."

Mrs. Barkley appeared from the kitchen. "Help the girl, Matthew," she yelled to him.

He jumped to attention, picked up Lorraine's large suitcase as if it weighed nothing and marched down the hallway to Lorraine's room. He was clearly pissed as he stood while she opened the door. He put the suitcase on the stand and left.

"Thank you," said Lorraine but he was gone.

Lorraine showered, got a clean pair of jeans and a flowing top. She felt feminine. Put on open-toe sandals and walked to the lobby where she placed the room key on its hook.

She drove to the heart of town, to the TV station where Nick was a cameraman. The gate guard took her identification and gave her directions to the sound stage. She parked in the visitor parking and walked over to the studio. She waited until the red light went off then entered quietly. The regular local news announcers were in rotation with the network news and the programming. Everyone, the on-camera announcers, the crew, the director and his assistant had to be at the ready in just moments when the signal came and the camera rolled. One of the men who saw Lorraine at the bar with Nick two nights ago recognized her. He came over and although he seemed to have a nasty smirk on his face, he told her where to sit and wait for Nick.

When the break came, Nick saw her and lighting his cigarette he ushered her out of the sound stage. He reached to hug her but she pulled away. He walked around the corner of the building where there were patio tables and chairs in a sitting area.

"Looking good," he said plopping down on a chair.

"I'm not staying," she said standing over him.

"What the fuck is the matter with you?"

"You are the matter."

"What, the other night? Is that what's bothering you?"

"That was not the first time. Do you think I'm stupid and I don't know where your hands went when you thought I was asleep? Perv."

"Don't you go talking to me like that," he said raising his voice then looking around and lowering it.

"If you're not staying, then go. What are you waiting for?"

"Five-thousand dollars," she said.

"Joking?"

"Telling your wife."

"Your word against mine."

"I saw you go into Wally's room. I stood by the door," she said. "Perv."

Nick was visibly disturbed. He got up and paced around the tables without looking at her. Sat back down again. She knew she got to him. She remained standing, looking down.

"Come to the bar tonight. I'll bring the money."

"Cash."

"All right, cash."

"I'm not going to that bar ever again. I'll come back tomorrow. Here. Same time. Right here. Leave a pass for me."

She turned around and headed toward her car by the main drive-in gate. She was deep in thought, got in and turned the key. As she rolled out of the TV station she felt sweat beads on her forehead. Her heart was beating fast. *That was tough*, she thought. *Once more I'll have to face Nick. Tomorrow. Once more.*

She filled up with gasoline and stopped at a Ralph's market which was on her way. After going to the ladies' room she bought a couple of Pippin apples and counted her change. She looked at her watch and determined that Pamela would be home but Shelby would still be at work. Lorraine went to the phone booth, dropped some coins and listened for the number of rings.

"Pamela," she said enthusiastically. "How are you, buddy?"

"Lorraine, oh, ohho, it's you!" shrieked the little girl. "I just got home. The school bus dropped me off. Thelma didn't have to. I'm a big girl now, I can be home alone."

"Do you have a snack to eat?" said Lorraine.

"Yes, mommy left me a granola yogurt," she said. "I miss you. When are you coming back?"

"I'm not sure yet, Pamela. I can't come back until I belong."

"What does that mean?"

Pamela heard Lorraine's laughter. "Sorry, kid. I was really talking to myself."

"That's silly. You can talk to yourself any time. You called me so you talk to me now. I want you to come back."

"I will come back when I can. I will call you again. I miss you, too. You take care," said Lorraine and hung up. There was a frog in her throat. She didn't wait for their usual *kiss-kiss-hug-hug* sign-off. She really loved that little girl.

# CHAPTER 27

*P*amela could hardly wait for her mother to get home. As soon as she heard the car in the garage, she rushed to see her.

"Mommy, mommy! Guess what! You'll never guess who called," she hollered.

Shelby came inside carrying a Trader Joe's bag of fresh bread and dairies. She placed them on the kitchen counter. "Do I get a kiss hello?" she said.

Pamela threw her a little air kiss and continued excitedly. "You'll never guess, never guess."

"OK, I give up."

"Lorraine. It was Lorraine! Would you have guessed?"

Shelby looked at Pamela. "Really? Lorraine?"

"Really, mommy. She said she missed me and I said I missed her."

"What else did she say?"

"Nothing. Oh yeah, she wanted to know if I had a snack. I told her you had a granola yogurt for me."

"Anything else?"

"Very funny talking to herself. She will want to *belong*. Something like that. I don't remember. I was so happy."

"Belong?"

"Yeah, pretty funny. Then she laughed. I didn't understand any of that," said Pamela.

"Did she say how she was doing?" said Shelby. "A job? School?"

"No."

"Anything about school?"

Pamela walked toward the kitchen. "No."

"Anything else?"

"I saw the red light blink. You have a message.

While Pamela went to the kitchen to unpack the tote bag of food, Shelby looked for her messages in the den. She forgot all about the Las Vegas Caesars Palace incident but the message was from an attorney. The one she chose to represent her. She had to go see him. Over dinner Shelby explained to Pamela that she had a legal matter that she had to take care of and that she would ask Thelma to give them a hand.

Shelby's attorney was a short, pudgy guy. Donald I. Barnaby. A shifty look in his eyes, he wore mediocre clothes and used a lot of long words. Shelby had no idea why Jeremy would have given his name to her, among the others. He must be good. But no, maybe Jeremy wants her to lose. *Would he do something like that?* She was having a constant dialogue with herself, getting in and out of conclusions. She generally felt like a yo-yo in unskilled hands. Now, with the case going, she had to save her name but not at the expense of Sidney and certainly not of Marc, whom she started to miss. Strangely, however, her attachment to Sidney was very real. Wrong but real. Marc was sweet, respectful and appeared to be happy with himself. She kept pushing the idea about her and Marc together out of her mind because, after all . . . what? Well, maybe it's not too good to make plans like that.

The legalities dragged on. Caesars was moving toward trial. A sensational event that would bring them controversy which in turn would translate to more business. They demanded and got a date for Shelby's deposition. This was it. She would have to testify under oath and there was no one to console her. No one. Marc didn't even know about the situation and shouldn't know. He was out of the country with Sidney and George! How ironic. Even in case she would have a sudden urge to tell Marc this sordid story based on a series of mishaps, she really couldn't. She couldn't reach him. She was on her own. A big girl.

# CHAPTER 28

Sidney made sure that he was never alone with Marc. Ever since Marc blurted out the words Brutus-22-17 on the day of his arrival, Sidney was wondering about it. He tried to add two and two together. However, he knew better than to make a scene that would go public and hurt the book-to-film image. Finding a reason for hiring another screenwriter could create a problem and bold as he was in his thinking he did not believe in advantageous controversy. Alexandra was successful in taking the cliché out of the Three Musketeer concept and building the campaign of the trio of Sidney, George and Marc to such pulsating intensity that breaking it up could be detrimental on many levels. Besides, Sidney sincerely liked Marc's work. It impressed him that Marc instantly captured his characters and the flavor of the many nuances of the story. In the meantime, the discussions between Sidney and Marc became so specific to the work at hand that no other person, not even Alexandra, could understand what they were talking about. Feeling excluded, she would make light of the instantaneous professional shorthand at work between the two talented men.

Marc was motivated to get the first draft ready for Sidney's review before he would leave Italy and return to Los Angeles. Little things in the manuscript reminded him of Shelby and working on the script every day he found himself thinking of her often.

According to the schedule, George would return to Los Angeles to oversee the development of the production schedule with his technical crew. Sidney and Alexandra would travel around Europe to do radio and television interviews and hype the upcoming film while selling the book that was available in several languages. Moira would join them whenever she was interested. Not often. She liked the privacy of the house when everyone was gone. She assured Sidney that she would be all right, she would read and go for walks. Together with Marissa she would go to the fresh market. They would shop and lunch and talk to all kinds of strangers. Foreigners, locals, everyone.

Sidney was mindful of Moira's health and questioned her about her frequent naps. She kept denying that anything was wrong. He loved to see her happy when the two of them spent alone time together. Moira would become her fun loving self seeing the cup half full as before. In spite of being the meticulous writer of exceptional character development, at no time did Sidney realize that around Alexandra his wife was uncharacteristically reserved. He was satisfied with his observation that the two of them had nothing in common and had no need to cultivate anything in common. Sidney promised Moira that their trip to Europe would not be all work and they would have a few weeks to kick back after everyone else had gone.

Throughout the years Moira understood that Sidney wanted to be able to experience more and more realms of life to set his writing apart from that of other authors. Traveling extensively and assimilating into different worlds would assure more success in his creativity. Her faith in him and admiration for him never faltered.

One night Sidney, Moira, Marc and Alexandra were lingering after another fine dinner served up by Marissa and assisted by her husband. Sidney and Alexandra had just returned from a personal appearance jaunt. Alexandra was eager to relate the highlights of their trip.

"Sidney, tell the story. You know, the *Pálinka* and the little secretary."

Sidney smiled his wide grin and proceeded to tell them how it went. He kept pouring wine and laughing about the experience they have had in Budapest the day before. He and Alexandra arrived at the TV station early and were ushered into the waiting area better known worldwide as the *green room.* A secretary rolled in a serving cart of *Pálinka,* a traditional fruit brandy in Hungary and neighboring countries, with a set of schnapps glasses. The secretary who apparently did not speak English served the drink and indicated to them to go ahead and gulp it up.

"Alexandra always researches the local habits and customs," said Sidney. "We always know what behavior is expected of me but drinking shooters at ten in the morning was a surprise."

"Then, not wanting to be the arrogant, thoughtless and ignorant Ugly Americans, Sidney swallowed one shot not knowing what to expect. He sat down quickly," said Alexandra.

"Wanted to save my dignity," said Sidney. "Definitely didn't want to fall down the way that shot hit me."

Marc and Moira were waiting for the punch line.

"I knew exactly what he was thinking," said Alexandra. "I looked at the woman standing there. She was nodding and smiling and encouraging us to drink more. I took a shot and sipped on it. She said *No, Nem, No.* She picked up a glass of the drink, pointed at her eyes telling us to watch her and gulped it down. That woman had no problem with the morning alcohol. Not even close. I guess that's how they get through the day in a Communist country."

Alexandra took a sip of water, chased it with wine and continued. "Just then the show's host came in and saw or maybe even heard the secretary swallow. *Klára, ezt nem lehet csinálni vendégek elött. Inni? Délelött? Hozzon kávét és teát és vizet. Ezek nem magyarok. Espressot hozzak?* said the woman. *Nem. Egyszerü kávét. Ezek nem magyarok.*"

Alexandra was animated as she relayed the story. "It seemed that the woman was reprimanded. Then the host turned to us. *I apologize. This secretary is new and she doesn't know. I told her that Americans are more proper than our every-day interview guests,* he said. *We'll get you some coffee and water however, as a welcoming gesture, let's toast.*

The host poured three fresh glasses of *Pálinka* and since Sidney could not rise, the host sat down next to him to raise his glass and tell us how happy and honored he was," she said.

Alexandra laughed the hardest. "We were a bit giddy. Then the host said *Maybe you're not so proper, Mr. Marshall?* His English was good but by now he was confused. He didn't know whether or not he had insulted us. Or maybe it was Sidney being so famous that made him nervous."

"Anyway, to put him at ease I had another shot of *Pálinka* and I remember nothing after that. Not the interview, not the ride back to the airport only that I went to sleep in the plane for an hour." Sidney was looking at Moira and watching to see if she was entertained by this silly episode. Moira smiled pleasantly and noticed that Sidney poured Alexandra more wine.

"We'll know how the interview did for the business when we get the report from the monitoring agency that has the sales statistics. *Maybe you're not so proper, Mr. Marshall?*" Alexandra said, imitating the Hungarian's accent and washing it down with wine.

"I think Sidney can do an interview in his sleep," said Marc. "I saw the one you did on Marla Hayes before you and Moira came overseas."

"That was charming," said Moira. "Sidney had always had a soft spot for Marla Hayes. That woman brings out the best in him." Moira leaned back in her chair. "I like her, too."

"That's a hard interview to get," said Alexandra. "She is very picky, has read everything, remembers everything. It doesn't matter what a publicist sends her. She makes her own plan."

"Well, children, for your information, I helped her out when she first started. She never forgot it. She's always there for me," said Sidney.

"Loyalty is a dead art," said Moira.

"Spoken like a writer," said Marc. Everyone smiled.

"And there is always the sunset," said Moira. "Always beautiful. Always soothing. They looked toward the horizon burning hot as the sun was moving to illuminate other lands. They were silent.

"Well, it's time for me to say goodnight," said Moira and headed out of the dining room. Sidney jumped to attention but Moira signaled him to stay.

Later, around midnight, Marc finished work and climbed the spiral stairs to the deck with a glass of wine in hand. He stretched, relaxed in the moon glow, soaked up the quiet of the night, the unique sounds of nature, the shiny blue reflections of the pool water. The convertible was quietly creeping up to the driveway on the side of the house without its lights on. Marc saw Sidney exit the car and head toward the pool. Sidney dropped his running shorts and jumped into the pool. The light came on in the master bedroom of the house. Marc saw Moira appear at the open full length French doors, look outside then withdraw and disappear from his sight.

As Marc finished his drink and stood up to go back downstairs, Sidney climbed out of the pool. Instinctively Marc pulled behind the sun umbrella. Sidney never looked up at the deck. He took a bath sheet off a hanger inside the open wardrobe cabinet. Drying himself, he went into the master bedroom through the French doors.

Moira was stretched out on the settee. The softness of the low lights seemed to create a halo around her head. Her smile was angelic. Sidney stood still for a moment. His eyes reflected her love as she looked into them.

"Champagne?" he asked.

"Always."

Sidney went to the wine chiller in the wide hallway on the way to the master bedroom suite. Got the bottle of sparkling wine from Italy's Franciacorta region, popped and poured it. Moira smiled with anticipation as she lifted her glass to Sidney.

"To you, mi amore. Il mio amore, I love you."

"You've never changed."

"My love has never changed," she said.

"We're still here."

"Till death do us part," she said. They both sipped on the light bubbly. Sidney cuddled up next to her on the settee.

"It was a magical ride," he said.

"And the beat goes on."

"You've always trusted me."

"I always knew you," she said.

"You did. Always."

"I always did," she repeated. "I do."

"And now?"

"You need more excitement."

"You know?"

"Your office is a bedroom," she said softly.

"Has a bedroom." The shadow of a smile passed her face as he said that.

"Is a bedroom. I know you know Shelby. I like her. Probably will know Mindy and whoever else.

Sidney was sheepish, hung his head, nodded.

"You're letting Alexandra know you."

"She works for me," he said without force or conviction.

"On you, dear. Her plans are not our plans."

Sidney looked and felt old. There were lines on his face. Not laugh lines. "I can't stop the merry-go-round."

"Now you live the lives of your characters," she sipped on the wine. "They'll get you and you know it."

"I can't get away from them and you know it."

"I know everything, Sidney. Everything. But you forget that you're not the characters."

"After so many of them I don't know who I am."

"You have to find your core again."

"Yes. My core." He was introspective. "You're my core."

"It's a tough job. Getting to be too big. I hurt."

"I can stop your hurt. You're my absolute strength," he said. "Absolute."

She placed the champagne flute on the side table and looked to the starry sky through the open French doors.

"Amen, my dear," she said.

Sidney picked up the decorative throw blanket from the arc of the settee and covered their legs. She leaned back into his arm around her as she has done a thousand times. He held her protectively. They fell asleep.

Only Sidney woke up.

# CHAPTER 29

*T*he morning of her deposition came and Shelby was a nervous wreck for many reasons. She knew from her attorney that Jeremy stayed on the case. According to Donald I., Jeremy informed the court that he had some personal issues and needed to withdraw as attorney for Caesars after the deposition, but she, of course, need not concern herself with who would depose her. Just be there, tell the truth. Donald I. added that it may be a good idea if she would give the name of the man at the heart of the lawsuit. It would bring the case to a large settlement in her favor.

Shelby walked into the cold conference room with her attorney and sat down. She was calm. She knew what she was going to do. No lawyer was going to intimidate her; definitely not Jeremy.

She didn't know whether or not he would show up, but he did. He, too, appeared calm and emotionally removed. The videographer was ready to roll as soon as he was signaled.

Jeremy started the questioning with the boring required basics like name, address, Social Security number, age, so forth. She answered. Then it became more specific regarding the events surrounding her arrest.

"Why did you check into a motel?"

"It's cheaper."

"Why did you use an assumed name at the motel?"

"To avoid any complications, such as these."

"You didn't want to be known?"

"I didn't."

"Were you hiding from anyone or anything?"

"I didn't want to be known by the motel personnel."

"Have you done this sort of thing before?"

"Yes."

"Why?"

Shelby looked at him, not knowing what this particular "why" referred to. He rephrased his question.

"Why the camouflage?"

"To protect my friend?"

"Who?"

"My friend."

"What's his name?"

"You can skip that question."

"You're under oath."

"I cannot divulge his name under any circumstances. Take me back to jail. Do anything you want. I'll quote the Fifth Amendment." She was getting fired up.

"Why can't you give us his name? It is a 'he,' correct?"

She nodded, then was silent. She was weighing the matter once again in her mind.

"Can you answer why not?"

When she remained silent, Jeremy decided to try and ease into a possible answer.

"Can you tell us why you must protect him when your reputation, and possibly your entire future, is at stake?"

"He's a world famous author—married—and he is also a good friend."

"Are you having an affair with him?"

"Not in an ordinary sense."

"In what sense?"

"Do I have to answer that?" she turned to her attorney.

"I don't see why not," came the matter-of-fact reply.

"We're friends. He's my mentor. And I love him."

"Do you see him often?"

"We meet for lunch at his favorite restaurant."

"Then a tryst?"

"Good word," she said to the dismay of her attorney.

"Do you make love to him?"

"I have. But mostly we're friends."

"Do you, are you in love?"

"Without his encouragement I couldn't survive the hardship I'm living."

"Are you in love with him?"

"I just answered that."

"No, you didn't."

"We're not in love in the ordinary sense. But we have a need for each other. He travels a great deal. He lives in Europe a great deal."

"In spite of all that, you can maintain a relationship?" Jeremy was truly amazed.

"We're good friends and we always accommodate each other's needs."

"Mostly his?"

"Any time. As long as it is morally in my power, I will see him."

"What does that mean, 'morally'?"

"When I commit myself to one man, whether in marriage or otherwise, I'll tell my friend that. I'll still want to keep in touch with him, but things will probably change."

"It didn't change his moral, marriage, and ethical standards?"

"No, but it'll change mine."

"There seems to be a contradiction here. If you're such good friends, how come you don't approve of his moral standards, yet you're its object?"

"I'm me. He's he. We're individuals with our own lifestyles. When we met I was married. We weren't lovers, only friends. That's how I wanted it."

"It sounds rather cocky and private."

"It is private. It worked for us."

"Even if it makes you a loose woman? Perhaps a prostitute?"

"It does not." She was indignant and rose to give her words emphasis. "It makes Las Vegas a sick place where a woman cannot appear alone without creating doubt. Where there's no respect for a single female because of its built-in prostitution. Look at all the high-powered money being wasted right here. Why isn't somebody out there picking up the real criminals?"

"Ms. Carpenter. We don't need any of your speeches at this point."

"Well, well . . ." She trailed off, realizing that he was right. She sat back in her chair.

"Is it difficult to be a beautiful single woman?"

"I wouldn't know about that."

"I was referring to you."

"I don't consider myself beautiful and I see no difficulties I cannot over-come in time. But," and she raised her forefinger again, "I will not stand for this kind of slander and invasion of privacy, which, as a citizen and tax-paying . . ."

Jeremy pushed a smile out of his eyes. He sensed that Shelby would make speeches all day long and not divulge the name of her boyfriend.

"I move," he forced a serious face, "that we continue tomorrow. In the meantime, I'll recommend to my clients, Caesars, that they go out and look for some real criminals. Mr. Barnaby, can we meet in my office at two this after-noon and discuss this matter further?"

"What about me?" Shelby asked.

"I'll call you later." Her attorney answered.

Shelby was in a daze. She knew she was guilty of nothing, but why would they just stop the proceedings? Was it because of Jeremy, or was it because of her testimony? She did not understand the whole thing.

Shelby went to pick up Pamela from Thelma's house. They had just arrived from school and Thelma started to prepare dinner. Pamela was happy to see her mother.

"Can we have dinner here, Mommy?"

"No 'hello,' no 'how are you, Mommy?'" asked Shelby. "Guess your stom-ach comes first," she added. "It's up to Thelma, honey. Thelma and Arnie," she said sending a smile toward Arnie.

"Absolutely. It'll be mostly leftovers though," said Thelma.

"I like your leftovers," said Pamela.

"Thelma, Arnie, I just want you to know that I love being part of your fam-ily and I hope we're not a burden," said Shelby.

"Well, honey, it's good both ways. You and Pamela have never been a bur-den and never could be." Thelma squeezed Arnie's hand. "We have seen you grow. Both of you. Watching you take responsibility for yourself and your child was amazing. I never thought you could do it after all that you have been through. We're so proud of you. Your mother used to say it's OK that you're a bit flaky because Boyd was such a strong leader. Well, no more flaky," said Thelma with a big smile.

"I miss being flaky. The good old days," said Shelby. "I was pretty passive. That worked for Boyd."

"You're far from passive. Look at getting a job, two jobs. You've become a regular problem solver. I wish I'd been that smart at your age. Look at you raising Pamela. You should be proud of yourself. I don't know what Lorraine is doing but she has never taken care of herself."

"I like to be fair, but Lorraine was mean to me," said Shelby.

"I think Lorraine is angry. Too many contradictions in her life," said Thelma.

"But why be angry with me?" said Shelby.

"She's nice to me," said Pamela moving over to Thelma and wiggling herself inside the woman's arm. Thelma smiled.

"Lorraine used to be like Pamela," said Thelma. "We had so much fun, did so much together. She always wanted a sister."

"Now she could have one," said Arnie.

"She doesn't make me feel sisterly."

"She's angry. She has to find herself," said Thelma.

"That's a lot of lay psychiatry," said Arnie.

"Parents understand. Each child reacts differently to similar circumstances," said Thelma. "Lorraine got fat. That's her anger."

"I don't think she's that fat," said Pamela. "And her bed smells like flowers."

"She was slim and beautiful like a model. She wanted to model before she moved out of my house. I can't imagine what happened. Something between her and her father or his wife, something she doesn't talk about."

"Mommy says we have to talk about everything. Nothing should be in the bottle," said Pamela.

"Bottled up," said Shelby with a smile. "Yes, I talk. That's what I do. I even asked Lorraine to say what's on her mind."

"When she's ready," said Thelma with the confidence of a loving parent. "And you don't talk very much when something's bothering you," Thelma said to Shelby. "While we're at it, I've asked you about this legal thing and still have no answer."

"You're right. I'm not ready either."

Pamela needed more attention. "I love sleeping in Lorraine's bed, you know. I even dust the *travel time mirror box* she has in the corner of her room."

"I'm sure she'll appreciate it," said Thelma.

"Has anyone heard from the artist that wanted to take it on?" asked Shelby.

"No. I don't even know who that is," said Thelma.

"Pamela, do you remember who it was? You and Lorraine went to see her together," said Shelby.

Pamela thought about it. "I don't remember her name but I think I'd recognize her."

"I can check on the art shows," said Arnie and went to the computer. A few minutes later he returned with the Chamber of Commerce advertisement of the next full outdoor art show in the San Fernando Valley.

"I'm still the computer whiz in this family."

"The only one, dear," said Thelma.

"So let's go to the art show and see if we can find the woman. That could be a challenge," said Arnie.

Shelby and Pamela headed home. Shelby was tired. She had no idea what would happen next about the Caesars Palace thing. All she wanted was to get some sleep. To let go.

At home there was a very excited message on the answering machine from her attorney. He reprimanded her on not being there to take his call and asked that she call him after ten the next morning because he had to attend a court hearing first thing.

Once again Shelby became anxious and knew that she would have another sleepless night. What could the attorney want?

# CHAPTER 30

Next morning after taking Pamela to school, Shelby went to work. There were large piles of To Do-s waiting on her desk. Richie was happy to see her.

"You know, I still don't understand why you didn't use Mr. Ross to represent you," he said.

"Because I didn't want my personal affairs to be on record in this office where I work," she said. "OK?"

"Roger," said Richie. "But he would've saved you money."

She started laughing. "You've been with him too long, Richie if you have this vague sense of trust. Believe me he's not the type of lawyer who goes around saving money for anyone but himself. It's what attorneys do. Boyd said that more than once."

Richie was nodding. "Roger that. I know what you're saying."

Around 10:15 A.M. Shelby went downstairs to the payphone in the lobby. She dialed Donald I. who came right on the line. He told her that he had accepted a settlement for false arrest and invasion of privacy damages in the sum of $89,000.

"Sure, that's fine." She didn't care. She had never expected any money so this was a pleasant surprise. He wanted her to come to his office, sign the settlement papers and get her check. She was curious about how it all came to such an ending and asked him.

"The defense attorney thinks your deposition testimony proved that your principles and moral character are beyond reproach, and the manner in which you put yourself on the line to save your friend also proves that you possess the kind of integrity wherein you are incapable of distorting the truth. Attorney Kiery saw through all that. Sensitive guy."

She smiled. "Guess I'm a really neat lady."

After the phone call she went back to the office.

"Richie, we need to talk," she said. She surprised herself with the positive strength in her voice.

Richie glanced up from his work and reacting to the seriousness of her tone, a worried look appeared on his face.

"What is it, Shelby?"

"You have to start interviewing again."

"No," he said in disbelief.

"Yes. I'm afraid Yes."

"Tell me what makes you think that? Why don't you need this job?" He leaned back in his chair.

"If you must know, I got a nice settlement. I am going over later today to sign the agreement and get the check."

She headed back to her desk and continued working. Richie stopped by.

"You're still here? Not walking?" he said.

"No. I'll finish the week. Don't worry." She got up and started for the exit. "By the way, you don't give typing tests with a one-minute timer. A professional needs at least five minutes on the timer. Look into it."

"Then I'll have to calculate."

"Yes. That's true." She turned back to him. "You can handle it. Be right back. Ladies room."

In the hallway, she saw Jeremy and his partners heading for the elevator. He was in no position to stop and talk with her and she walked past them.

She didn't go to pieces on seeing him and that put a smile on her face. The smile remained shining on her face when she went to pick up Pamela from school.

"Guess what, babe! Mommy doesn't have to work anymore. Not for a long while. So, I've been thinking about taking a vacation. Then we can spend all of your free time together and read, and paint and make things."

They turned onto Bergamo Road. She pulled into the garage.

"I'm thinking that instead of going back to work later on, I should learn about money. I should take some courses."

"Is that hard?" said Pamela.

"I hope not."

"Mommy, can we go away somewhere?"

Shelby gave it a thought. "You know what? Let's go to Catalina. I haven't been there since your father passed away."

"I like places that daddy liked."

"Then it's set. Catalina. A boat ride. The works. Maybe we can splurge and go for a whole week! That's what."

"Goodie, goodie."

When they arrived home, Jeremy's car was parked in front. He was at the door, ringing the bell as Shelby and Pamela pulled into the garage.

"Honey, I saw Dana and the kids down the block playing. Why don't you play with them for a while?"

"Now?"

"Yes. I'll come and get you. I have to talk to this man alone."

"Yeah, lovey-dovey talk."

Shelby smirked. "Not exactly, honey. I think that this time it will be all business."

"But he's so handsome, Mommy."

"Yes. That he is." A deep sigh punctuated her sentence. "You heard about *don't judge a book by its cover*, honey?" Pamela pecked her on the cheek and took off. Shelby unlocked the door, letting Jeremy in.

"Long time no see." Neither of them laughed at her attempted humor.

Jeremy touched her, took her face in his hands and kissed her. Wow! The excitement was beyond belief. As if their bodies had come alive. Nothing had changed. They wanted each other and both knew it.

Jeremy finally let go and pulled away. He went to the den, walked around as if he wanted to absorb the good feelings he sensed in that room. He spotted Sidney's manuscript on a shelf all by itself; then noticed the framed article about the Ocean Avenue Seafood and the restaurant's famous regulars that included Sidney. His eyes rested on the photo he had spotted when he was there the first time. It was the photo of Shelby, or rather her hand gently touching seven-month old baby Pamela.

Shelby watched as Jeremy returned to the living room, switched on the VCR, put in a tape and pressed *play.*

She wondered what he was up to and then realized it was the surveillance tape from Caesars. He sat down but Shelby stood, her feet glued to the floor. There she was on the screen, in front of the Brutus bust sculpture; as was the busy-body cowboy bothering her; her negative body language; his growing annoyance; his marching off and returning with the arresting security guards.

Jeremy stopped the tape. He took a deep breath, glanced at Shelby still frozen in place and pressed *play* again.

The tape continued with Sidney rushing in, running late, finding no one at the sculpture. The tape went to *snow*, then *black*.

They were silent. "When did you get this?" she said.

"It came from Caesars just before your deposition."

She walked out of the room. This was too much to process. Way too much. Jeremy followed.

"You knew all along. Why didn't you use it?"

"Hollywood is a small town. One of your friend's film producers is a client at our office."

"So you're protecting my friend's producer?" she said.

"No, you. I love you."

He stood in front of her like a little boy. "I don't think you're really in love with him."

"You don't?"

"No. It's an infatuation. 'Celebrity worship' is written all over it and you will forget it. Here's what'll happen next: I divorce my wife. I will then marry you. Somebody has to keep you out of trouble. Your friend, Marc, doesn't seem to be able to do it."

"My friend, Marc, gives me my freedom. Lets me be who I am."

"I would, too."

"In case I agree to marry you? Jeremy, can't you see that you are putting the responsibility of your decision on me?"

"No. All I can see is that I want you more than anything else. I'm willing to get divorced and marry you. Doesn't that mean anything?" They were back to arguing.

"Of course it does," she said. "Means a lot."

"I want to be a senator. I could be jeopardizing my running for public office."

"Don't jeopardize, Jeremy. Stick to your plan," she said. "You'll make a fine senator."

Jeremy got up and sat down again.

"I saved you," he said.

"Bull!" she put her hand on her mouth surprised at having said half a cuss word. "You got tired of going around in circles with your questions and my answers. Admit it."

"I wanted to do the right thing. I always do."

"Yes, and that makes you a good attorney. You did the right thing. You trusted your instincts, you listened to your inner voice."

"I did, didn't I?" He was pleased with himself.

"I was so touched when David read your court filing to me praising my impenetrable integrity. You're pretty smart."

"Then you're happy? I did well by you? So why not?"

"Why not what?"

"Be married?"

"Because we don't know each other."

"We'll learn."

"I hear you, but you don't hear me." She walked into the kitchen, took a pitcher of lemonade as she spoke. He automatically followed her and accepted the refreshment without comment. He was listening hard. He needed to learn.

"My good friend, who, as you know, shall remain nameless even though he is on the tape, gave me a book. I can't loan it to you because I need it every day," she said picking up a book from the coffee table. "*How To Be Your Own Best Friend* by Mildred Newman and Bernard Berkowitz," she said. "When we can't have our guardian angel to guard us, we need this book."

"Oh, that's it? A book will take care of everything?"

"If you're going to divorce your wife, it should be because it's not working for the two of you. If you have to have somebody else to replace her, you'll need to look harder at yourself than you have so far."

"But I want you."

"I want you too, but it's all physical. I don't know you. We don't know each other."

"I'm offering to marry you."

"I'm offering to give us a chance to get to know each other. If we fall in love, we may get married. I'm not going into some kind of replacement program."

"Are you refusing me?"

"Only marriage."

"I've never met anyone like you before."

"You mean a thinking woman? There are lots of us around."

"Well," Jeremy lost his footing. "What'll happen now?"

"I think you'll go home and figure out the reason why you and your wife aren't happy together. Once you know that, the answers will come a little easier."

"Will I talk to you again?" A little boy, dressed in man's clothes. She adored him.

"Yes, Jeremy. You'll talk to me again. There's time."

"Lunch?"

"In a restaurant."

This brought a smile to their faces. It was obvious that she had hurt his ego, but she knew that in the long run she had done a great deal of good for him. After all, he may never meet anyone like her again. Maybe there aren't lots of women like her around.

# CHAPTER 31

The Mach 1 was nearly flying on the San Diego Freeway in the early morning hours with two very happy people, Shelby and Pamela, on their way to an adventure. Pamela's singing overpowered the music on the radio. When they reached the exit to the San Pedro harbor they turned off the highway.

As they pulled into the parking lot of the Catalina Express company, they saw the helicopter still sitting on its pad in the next lot, propellers noisily whirling. Shelby quickly turned around to switch to the other parking lot and pulled up at the helicopter transport office.

"Go over there, honey and ask them if they have room for two more?"

Pamela got out of the car and ran to the office window. Shelby parked and followed her.

"We had a cancellation just now. Two people cancelled so there's room for you," said the cute young woman inside the office.

"We're supposed to be on the first Express of the morning," said Shelby.

"We get you there faster. Take the copter! I can call them over there and cancel. Did you have round trip reservations?"

"No, we haven't decided how long we would stay."

The clerk got on the telephone and returned in just moments. "You're all set. Get in. You'll be taking off in a few minutes."

Pamela noticed the two other passengers already in the helicopter, one long-haired, one bearded, clapping.

"Let's go, we're all here!" said the bearded one.

"Finally," said the other, happy that the craft was filled and they would be taking off.

The pilot was equally jolly. "Yup. We're almost on time. The boss is a stickler for sticking to the schedule."

"Say that fast three times," said the bearded man with a loud laugh.

Pamela started to run in the direction of the helicopter.

"Pamela!" she heard her mother's voice. It was stern. It made her stop and turn.

Shelby took the travel bags out of their car. She looked at Pamela who came back, picked up her own duffle bag but did not move before she was allowed.

"OK, honey. Let's go. You stay right next to me," said Shelby.

Pamela understood that her mother wasn't kidding. She walked alongside her, carefully observing the instructions about staying out of range of danger, about handing her luggage to the attendant, about getting on board, fastening her seat harness. As the aircraft was revving up and its noise became louder, Pamela reached for her mother's hand. Once up in the air she forgot about the large blade rotors that spun around above them. She was visibly enthralled by the view. She was even more excited when the pilot showed her some of the tricks the little craft could do; how it could fly vertically and horizontally and before they reached the landing spot on the island, he showed her how it could hover. Pamela was shrieking with joy. No one seemed to mind.

"Was that a good fifteen minutes?" the pilot asked Pamela as he took their bags and pulled them over to the area marked for passengers' safety, away from the helicopter.

"The best, the best!" giggled Pamela, jumping up and down. "I want to do it again."

"We might take it back when we are leaving," said Shelby. "We shall see."

An electric golf cart pulled into the waiting area and the other two passengers from the helicopter hurried toward it. The driver, wearing a large brimmed hat and reflecting aviator sunglasses, seemed to be stretching his neck trying to get a better look at Shelby as she walked behind the two men from the helicopter.

"Shelby?" asked the driver of the golf cart.

Shelby stopped. Holding Pamela's hand, squinting, looking curiously at the man, she stood still.

"It's me, George. George Eckert!" He turned to the equally disguised woman next to him. "Marci, look, it's Shelby!"

Marci took off her sunglasses and laughingly ran over to Shelby.

"What a surprise. George, do you believe this?"

George removed his sunglasses and planted a big kiss on Shelby's cheek. "And this is?"

"This is my daughter Pamela," said Shelby. "Pamela, meet George Eckert and Marci."

There were smiles all round. The two other passengers from the helicopter turned out to be on George's movie staff and came to work with him on the preparations of Sidney's film.

"Are you with anyone? I mean is anyone meeting you?" asked George.

"No, we just took our chances."

"Oh you have to stay with us," said Marci.

"We wouldn't want to . . ."

"C'mon woman. We have plenty of room. I won't take No for an answer," said George.

A *for hire* six-passenger cart pulled up to the group.

"Who needs a ride into town?" yelled out the driver.

George took charge. "Just follow me with those two guys, OK?" he placed Shelby's luggage next to the others then motioned Shelby and Pamela to sit behind him and Marci on his cart. The caravan started the brief drive to town.

Marci, thin, tall, pretty and bright liked Shelby, also thin, tall, pretty and bright, ever since they had dinner with her and Marc. Pamela was instantly one of the girls. When they arrived at George's hillside villa, Pamela heard her mother's stern voice again.

"Pamela."

She hurried to her. She took her duffle bag from the cart and waited for her mother who insisted on carrying her own bag as well. Pamela seemed to sense her mother's tension about doing something like this on her own.

A spectacular panoramic view opened up in front of them as they climbed the narrow flight of stairs to the house. Pamela couldn't get enough of the amazing sights no matter which way she looked. The back of the house had a lap pool that hung over the driveway. It was a smart design bearing dramatic impact. There were no gasoline operated cars—except for the emergency vehicles—allowed on Catalina Island, so the driveway of the house was merely the width of a couple of golf carts. The poles that secured the lap pool to the hillside also shaped a carport for the golf carts when they were not inside the golf cart garage.

The conversation overlapped in many directions. Marci showed Pamela the room for her and her mother. The two crew members were also given their quarters.

George turned to Shelby, "Shelby, can we talk a moment?"

"Of course," she said and followed him to the terrace.

George gestured for her to sit down. Standing against the house, on locked wheels, was a service bar with a wine chiller at its bottom. He poured her some wine. She was gazing at the ocean and felt enormously at peace. He sat down next to her.

"Shelby, did you know that Moira had passed away?"

She looked at him. Her whole body seemed to have stiffened. She tried to swallow but couldn't. She tried to breathe but couldn't. George got up and held her in his arms.

"Take a deep breath now, hear?" He patted her on her back until she started to inhale.

"When? Where? Was she sick? Why didn't he call me?"

"Let's see. It was a few of days ago. In the Milan house. Yes, she had been having minor health problems for some time. That answers those questions. Why he didn't call you? I cannot answer that. Maybe there are too many details to handle. Maybe Alexandra doesn't want it publicized."

"Alexandra? Alexandra?" Shelby's voice became a whisper. "The publicity lady?" She looked at George and then away. "I am not the public," she tried to process the information. "Or am I?"

"They should be home next week, I think. They'll make the announcement of the memorial services."

Shelby sat down. "You know, for some strange reason I thought I was closer to him, them, him and Moira. Close enough that I should be notified." She walked to the railing and turned back to George. "I was wrong."

"I didn't know." Then, to her questioning look, he said, "I didn't know you and Sidney were close. Or you and Moira for that matter. They never mentioned you to me."

Shelby got up and headed inside the house. "No. Guess not," she said slowly, more to herself.

"I thought you and Marc were close."

"That's true, George. We are. Is he over there now?"

"I am not sure when he is coming back. I left them a week ago."

"Well, it's neither here nor there," said Shelby. "I'll go unpack now."

"Later we'll go down to the Marlin Club for a drink or two. Just a local hangout," said George.

"Oh, George, please don't mention this in front of Pamela. She only met Moira once and I hope maybe she has forgotten about her."

George agreed. "Don't worry."

Then he went inside and started the production meeting with his two crew members. When dusk fell they all walked down the hill. Pamela ran ahead of them then ran back on realizing she didn't know where they were going. Her playfulness made everyone feel good.

"Turn left at the next corner," said Marci. Pamela ran ahead to the next street and turning left, disappeared.

"I see it, I see it!" she said enthusiastically as she returned to the group.

Not far into the block the *Marlin Club* sign was prominent. Inside the oldest bar in Avalon the interior was an underwater seascape painted in the popular classic Art Deco style of the early 50s. Central in the establishment was a boat shaped bar, which demanded attention and served as a conversation starter. The flooring, furniture, pool table, darts, two game tables, and foosball table—everything took you back a few decades. Nothing had changed since the club opened in the 1940s. It was clean, noisy, and inviting for locals and visitors alike. The prices were low enough for the locals and welcomed by the tourists and summer guests.

They took a large booth and ordered a round of drinks.

"I don't know when you were here last," said George to Shelby. "But, except for the upgrading of the hotels, maybe not all only some of the hotels, nothing ever changes."

"I was here with Boyd about a year ago. Good memories," said Shelby, unable to hold eye contact with George.

"I actually wanted to show Pamela some favorite spots so that she would have an idea of the things her father liked."

"Did you and Boyd take the Sundown Isthmus Cruise?" asked George.

"Oh, yes. We did. We had a ball."

"My wife hates boats but loved the food and music on that two-hour trip," said the bearded man.

"We have reservations tonight," said Marci.

"Well troops, Marci's right. We're doing it," said George. "We'll be cruising into the sunset shortly, and when the sun drops into the ocean an hour later, the boat will turn around and come back and we'll go dancing."

The plans were made. Shelby and Pamela loved the sunset cruise, ate appetizers of all kinds and sizes being served on the main deck and sang along with the rock band. Pamela watched everything closely. She was intent on finding out whether or not the sun would really drop into the ocean. She could never be sure and no one confirmed it for her. At the end of two hours the boat returned. Shelby and Pamela said goodnight to everyone.

"Just come and look at what they did this year to Solomon's Landing," said Marci. "We hope we'll get in. It's a great restaurant even if we can't eat another bite."

"Speak for yourself, Missy," said the longhaired man. "I'm just about ready for the next feeding."

The always busy Solomon's Landing was situated in El Encanto Market Place. Translated to English, *the enchanted* locale was designed as a Mexican pueblo. One of the featured attractions was an amazing view of Avalon Bay dotted with boats of all sizes, even an overnight cruise ship.

By this time Pamela was slowly fading.

"Well, we've had too much excitement for one day," said Shelby. "We'd better go to bed."

"Tomorrow is a work day for us guys, but you girls can do some fun things," said George.

"Thank you, George. It was very nice. Everything," said Shelby.

George kissed Pamela on the cheek and Shelby and Pamela headed back to George's white villa waving to them from the lush hillside.

Shelby knew the entry code for the security system and they went to their room. Pamela was exhausted. She barely stayed awake for a shower. Shelby went for a swim in the lap pool. After she looked in on the sleeping child, she returned to the living room, and watched the news on TV. She could not get her racing mind off Moira. *Why did all this happen and how did all this happen? While Moira was alive I could accept Sidney and her together. But what now? She's not alive. Sidney is single. But he did not call me. How come? What am I to him?* Swallowing became hard as tears were rushing her. She went to the kitchen for a glass of water. Walking around the living room she saw pictures displayed in whimsical island-style frames on several book shelves. Some formal photos of

George and Sidney at the Oscars alongside casual Catalina pictures of them with Moira and others whom Shelby didn't know. But these were definite signs of Sidney in George's house. Shelby recalled the lawsuit and how she had just spent several days of her life defending Sidney's character and protecting his anonymity. *But why didn't he call me?*

She walked to the terrace, sat down admiring the view, the lit-up Casino building protruding out of the island like a big elephant dressed in fancy whites and golds ready for the *circus* procession.

Shelby witnessed the last boat of the day crossing the channel and pulling into dock. She could hear rowdy passengers who had already started their partying on board, getting off and hitting the island with all its drinking spots. Shelby was entertained by watching the main drag of the Island lined with hotels and restaurants on one side and the strip of sandy beach on the Bay side. The numerous boats and yachts of every size, style, and make were tied up for the night. People were coming and going from and to them on dinghies. Shelby smirked as she watched the colorful parade of wall-to-wall semi-clad revelers going up and down, disappearing in a bar then after a drink returning only to walk over to the next bar. It was a good show. She helped herself to wine and, leaning on the railing, she sipped and watched, trying not to think sad thoughts, to not think of Sidney. Sidney and Moira. Sidney. Do not think. Stop it.

She heard the buzzer of the security system and was surprised because she did not see anyone coming up the hill while she was watching the never-ending show below. She turned to see who was back. She remained hidden on the unlit terrace and looked in the direction of the main entrance through dim illumination of night lights.

The sound of a woman's laughter reached Shelby as she entered ahead of a man. They dropped their overnighter bags in the entry and got lost in an everlasting passionate kiss.

Shelby recognized Sidney and Alexandra.

"Jacuzzi?" said Sidney.

"Oh, by all means," whispered Alexandra.

Sidney tossed their bags through the open door of one of the guest rooms and they headed to their skinny-dipping romp in the outdoor spa.

Shelby went to her room, closed the door, plugged her ears with cotton balls, and laid down. She cried. Silently, all night, she just cried.

Morning followed the sleepless night. Shelby walked through the quiet house to the kitchen and got some orange juice and crackers for Pamela. Soon Shelby's private ray of sunshine appeared, hair messy, eyes squinting, wondering why her mother was so happy. Shelby opened her arms and Pamela let herself be enclosed next to her mother's heart.

"You are the most wonderful thing that ever happened to me, sweetheart. The most exciting, the most beautiful, the most interesting person I ever knew and know." Shelby held her for a minute then said "Let's go for a swim."

After a few laps they sat poolside. Pamela munched on the snack.

"More people arrived last night. I don't think we should stay with George."

"I really like George," said Pamela. "And Marci. I think she likes me, too."

"Yes. The only reason I think we should go on our own is that they will be working on this movie and they don't need to worry about entertaining us." Shelby was not asking she was telling Pamela that they were going.

Back in their room they packed and Shelby wrote a note for George.

"We'll leave them a note so they know that we just didn't want to be under foot—"

"And thank them for their fun hospitality," said Pamela finishing up Shelby's sentence. Another moment of muffled laughter.

They left. As the two of them walked toward town Shelby knew that things had changed, that she had changed and left her old self, the victim, the flake, the sex-toy, the *small me* behind in Catalina. She had no doubt that whoever she became would be better than her younger self was.

# CHAPTER 32

The ticket window at the designated visitor center where the trams and buses lined up for sightseeing tours was already open. Shelby picked up a schedule leaflet from a stand.

"Let's have breakfast and decide what to do," said Shelby.

"I didn't think you'd remember that I am hungry."

"You're always hungry. You're a bottomless pit."

They stored their bags in the luggage lockers on the square near the ticket office and followed the sweet inimitable aroma of pancakes. "Oh, yes," said Pamela. "That's where I want to go."

They were seated by the window and could enjoy the sights. They ordered.

"I've also been thinking about Lorraine's *mirror box*. Maybe we can help without butting in. But how? I keep hoping that if she finds a little success and can build on it, she will be happier," said Shelby.

"Are we going home?" asked Pamela, preparing the Silver Dollar pancakes to her taste.

"No. Not yet but maybe later."

"How much later?"

"Let's see about spending the day and then let's try to figure out how to follow up with the *mirror box*. Is that OK with you?"

Shelby studied the tour schedule. "Here's one we could take. Let's do the Casino then the climb to the airport on top of the mountain. On the road we'll see buffalo and other wildlife. I have always been fascinated by this ride."

Pamela appreciated every bite of her full breakfast. "I think that would make you happy," she said.

"What would make you happy?" asked Shelby. She was having coffee and juice and finishing the yogurt-granola parfait. She sprinkled some dry cranberries on top. She also took one of Pamela's pancakes.

"If you show me everything Daddy liked."

"OK. Deal."

They paid the bill, stepped outside, stretched, ready for the new day. Back to the ticket window. The sightseeing tour they chose turned out to be exciting to both of them for different reasons. Pamela was caught up in all the novelty around her and did not notice her mother looking off to some far-away point with eyes getting moist, pulling out a tissue to wipe her nose. Shelby was deeply disturbed by the Sidney and Alexandra affair. Shelby's confidence was slipping. The strength she gathered from Sidney was eluding her. She looked at Pamela and the sight of her child, the person who depended on her, gave her the intensity she needed. *She had to separate herself from being used, being a victim, being a joke. It's now or never.*

Taking pictures of Pamela pushing her nose close to the buffalo that came up to the open safari-style tram made them laugh out loud. They saw rare birds, Shelby missed a shot of a black antelope that curiously came upon them. The guide warned the tourists about a large snake population and asked everyone to stay inside and keep arms and legs inside. Pamela took.

The driver was explaining everything to the passengers through a loudspeaker. He said that the Airport in the Sky was the nickname for the Santa Catalina Island Airport. The runway was built by blasting away the top of two mountains and using truckloads of rock to fill the gap between them. The weather was also often foggy up there which limited landing times. Stories were told about how hard it was to land there. Because the runway was at the very edge of the steep mountain there was no room for mistakes. If a plane came in too low, it could run into the mountain; if it didn't take off with enough thrust, it could have a hard time staying out of the water. Stories abounded.

They were encouraged to taste buffalo meat at The Runway Café. Since Shelby and Pamela would be leaving the island it was their last opportunity to eat the burger made of the sweet darkish red meat which was only available there. The Catalina Island Conservancy kept tight control over the protected buffalo and other animal inhabitants. The Conservancy also oversaw the vegetation and flowers and everything unique unto their island.

Finally, they had to finish eating, return to their tram as another one arrived and parked next to theirs. Since only one tram was able to navigate the winding narrow mountain road at a time, they had to change places. The drive downhill was pretty scary especially when a delivery truck was coming up. The two drivers had to find a spot on the road that was wide enough for them to pass each other. Pamela was compelled to peek through squinty eyes. When the vehicles had passed each another, everyone on the tram applauded with great relief.

"No tips," said the driver and pointed toward a large bucket. "If you really liked your tour, there is a donation bucket for the Conservancy." On that note, people threw dollar bills into the bucket and felt better about themselves.

Shelby and Pamela slowly walked to the lockers. They were still under the spell of the exciting ride. They got their bags and rolled them down to the harbor.

"Your father never wanted to get back to the mainland in 15 minutes so we didn't take the helicopter. He liked to savor the moments of the island and chose the ferry," said Shelby.

"Gee, let's!" squealed Pamela.

They took their seats on top deck. Pamela held her mother's hand without looking at her and subtly gained security in this strange unfamiliar environment. The wind was blowing their hair. Looking around, Shelby pointed out rainclouds gathering over the island and they could already feel bumpy waters under them. Wearing sunglasses and visors the two of them looked like sisters. Maybe even without sunglasses Shelby's dewy fresh look would qualify as a sister before as a mother.

Ninety minutes later they were docking in San Pedro. As they walked to their car, they took one last look at the island, at the dark clouds changing to heavy rain and washing the town of Avalon.

"Well, we've left the storm behind," said Shelby without realizing the profoundness of the statement.

It was so hot inside that Shelby had to run the air conditioner on high before they could get in. As they reached the Harbor Freeway they started to sing but this time they were too tired and their voices were worthless. Pamela fell asleep. When they arrived home she had just enough energy to walk to her room and fall into bed.

Shelby was also exhausted not only from the fresh sea air, the wind, the sun but from the emotional upheaval she was still experiencing.

She opened the front door to go out to the mail box for the mail. A telegram that was stuck on the door dropped to the ground. She picked it up.

The attached Post-it sticker by her neighbor said "I signed for it." *Why would anyone sign for anyone's telegram without knowing where they are? It made no sense although obviously the neighbor was trying to be helpful.* Shelby got the rest of the mail then and locking up the house for the night, she went to the den to check for messages. In the den her eyes glanced at the photo of her with seven-month old baby Pamela and something made her stop to look again. She remembered the moment when a photographer friend of Boyd took it. Then a few days later when he returned with the blow-up of the picture he told her it brought on *Madonna and Baby*-like feelings in him.

Shelby tore open the telegram. It was from Marc. "I'll be home on the 17th. Please try to be free for dinner at 7 the next day."

She knew she would make herself free for Marc even if she had other plans. But she didn't. Yet, Marc gave her the benefit of the doubt that she may be busy. There was something very comforting about Marc. She pulled out her pocket organizer and entered the dinner date.

Next she turned her attention to the blinking red light on the answering machine. She sat down while pressing the replay button.

*Santa Monica 12-17,* came Sidney's familiar voice. She stopped and stared at the machine. She couldn't tell exactly where and when he placed the call. She had never before looked for the detailed envelope information on her answering machine about any calls. She knew there was a way to do that and now she had a reason. She was really curious about the order of the events. She checked. The message from Sidney came two days earlier from a Los Angeles number. So he was back in town at that point. Why use a code? Was he at home? Was Alexandra with him at his home? The questions were buzzing around in her brain creating a traffic jam with their unprecedented rate of speed. *And what's with the number 17? Is that a number he gave her on his list in the little black book?* She was steaming.

She also had a message from Thelma about Arnie having found the next local art show, and there was another plea from Richie about coming back to work for them.

"That'll be day," she said with a chuckle.

Heading for the bathroom she started to run a bubble bath. Back to the wine rack she got a glass of wine then settled into a leisurely bath. She cried a little, drank a little, laughed a little, drank a little, then showered off the soap and spread out in the wonderful king size bed with all its luxurious frills.

"How sweet," she mumbled and trailed off into dreamland.

The telephone jarred her awake. She sleepily picked it up.

"Good morning."

"Good morning," said Pamela as she came flying into her mother's bed. Cheerful and rested, she cuddled up.

"Good morning," said Thelma. "I was calling to leave you a message about the Renaissance Faire"

"You already did."

"No, that was the art show. Arnie and I want to go over there Saturday but if we don't find the artist we can try the Renaissance Faire a week later."

"Don't you need Pamela to recognize the woman?"

"Yes. That's what I wanted to find out. When you will be back?"

"We're back."

"Oh, yes. Dumb me. I'm calling. You're answering."

"She left Nick. He doesn't know where she went. So you see, I have to do something fast. I have to find her but it would be better if I could bring her good news about her dream."

Shelby sat up in bed.

"I have to think. When is the show? Next Saturday?"

"That's day after tomorrow," said Thelma.

"OK, we'll go. I have to do the wash and the mail today and tomorrow and we will pick you up Saturday morning at 8."

"Good. That'll be good. By the way, did you have a good time?" Thelma said.

"Very good. Very different," said Shelby. "Glad we went."

She hung up and for a few minutes she and Pamela laid quietly in bed. Shelby turned to her. "Well, shall we get this day going?"

Pamela jumped up. "Yes. I'll shower and make cereal."

"And I'll shower and start the wash," said Shelby. "And Saturday we'll find some good news for our sister, Lorraine. That's what."

# CHAPTER 33

*T*he freshly painted façade of THE INN appeared bright and clean and could be seen for some distance. Walking from the parking lot also changed to a refreshing statement accented by flowering hibiscus bushes that lead to a new patio dining space in front of the main entry. The welcoming setting included tablecloths and colorful umbrellas on the garden tables and speakers projected middle-of-the road music from inside the hotel. It was cheery yet simple. A glass double-door that reached the ceiling was the newly installed entrance. While no one could see in through the treated glass, the view was clear to the outside.

As 5:30 in the afternoon arrived, people started to show up. It was rapidly becoming a ritual. The Menu cards gave no choices only stated the one item that was being served on that day. There could be any one of unusual creations like portobello fajitas, fig and cheese stuffed chicken breasts, caprese bites, with or without roasted Cajun potatoes and even a variation on Giada De Laurentiis' chocolate and brie specialty. There would be ample assortments of Tacos and Pita Pockets of every size. What they all had in common was that they had to be *very pretty*.

On the main wall of the Lobby was a framed article from *Food & Wine* magazine entitled "Very Pretty Only." A small picture of Mrs. Barkley, Matthew and Lorraine was in the corner of the page but the entire article was praising the "innovative mind of Lorraine!" The article referenced a local television review of the small eatery with the smallish hotel *serving the best of the roadside*. Another article from the Food section of the local daily paper also found its way to a matching frame and a place on the wall. The words *very pretty* seemed to appear in each write-up. People came even if they were not staying at the hotel.

As *THE INN*'s popularity grew, Mrs. Barkley gave Lorraine a percentage of the sales to use for continuous upgrading of the place. Little-by-little, there seemed to be touches of Shelby's taste all around. The living room style lobby and other interior areas highlighted furniture and furnishings almost identical with the décor of the Encino house. Lorraine hung drapery scarves on the windows. Fabrics and colors started to match. Even through the hotel's hallways there were signs of prosperity. In fact, the television news reporter dubbed *THE INN* a "boutique hotel," a name that was then picked up by *Food & Wine*.

This new notoriety brought in new money. Mrs. Barkley let Matthew handle the money. It turned out that he had a business college MBA. The income was allocated according to need. Ten percent of every dollar went to an interest-earning savings account. There was a new cleaning woman on the staff now, Dorothea Woods, who took over all of Mrs. Barkley's earlier chores of cleaning not only the rooms but also the kitchen and the bar. In fact, on Lorraine's suggestion, the woman would be paid a set figure every week. If she wanted to take all the money she had to do all the cleaning. If she wanted to farm out some of the cleaning chores, she had to hire and pay the person out of her own income. The budget was carved in stone. It worked wonders. There was not one speck of dirt or dust in sight anywhere.

Late one night after last call, Mrs. Barkley and Matthew sat down with Lorraine and had a relaxing glass of Dry Sack Sherry at a table in the bar. Two remaining customers were finishing their drinks.

"Miss Lorraine, good night," said one of them. "Good night," said the other and they started for the hallway to their room.

"Goodnight Mr. and Mrs. Marton," said Lorraine.

Out of the dark of night they heard a car screeching as it came to a sudden stop in front of the hotel. Through the one-way glass door they saw a man stumble out of his car and weaving up the walkway into the hotel.

"Oh, shit," said Lorraine jumping up. "It's my dad. Drunk dad."

She hurried out but was too late. He had already come inside the hotel and pushed the swinging doors of the bar out of his way. Arms wide open he headed for Lorraine.

"Lorraine, my famous daughter," he said and sat down on a bar stool.

"How did you find me?"

"You're on the TV, you're in the magazines, you're fucking famous."

"I didn't know you could read," said Lorraine.

"Don't get smart with your dad."

"We're closed. You have to leave. Right now. This is not an after hours joint."

"Are you being uppity with me, girl? Because I have no hard feelings," he said. "I say forgive and forget." He looked around and nodded as if he knew everything. "Nice place but there's nothing like home."

"This is home. Please leave."

"Looks more like a bordello. Suits you just fine."

"Hey, Mister. I don't like you saying those things," said Matthew. "This is a respectable hotel with respectable guests. You shouldn't talk like that."

"That's my daughter there. I can talk to her any way I want."

Matthew was growing angry.

"I don't care if you are Lorraine's father. You're not welcome here. She doesn't want you here."

When Nick didn't move, Matthew rose to his full height and appeared foreboding next to the wiry drunk. He slowly menacingly moved closer to him until he was in his face.

"Do I have to say it again?" Under Matthew's threatening stare Nick got up.

"Lorraine?" he said.

Lorraine did not move a muscle. "I'm done with you. Go away."

Nick backed out of the bar. Outside, he turned and ran to his car.

Mrs. Barkley dimmed the lights in the bar.

"Well, I'd better turn in. Too much's happening here. Too much for me, anyway," she said. She started for the hallway beyond the lobby. "See you tomorrow."

"Thank you," said Lorraine to Matthew after his mother was gone.

Matthew sat down next to Lorraine and nervously munched on the leftover melon-balls in a bowl on the table.

"It was nothing," said Matthew. "Kinda' fun. I could never scare anyone before even though I am a big ape."

""You are a nice big ape. No one has ever spoken up for me before."

"I'm here," he said and looked away almost shyly.

They heard Nick's car speed away.

"You can call me big ape. It sounds nice the way you say it." Matthew looked at Lorraine from the corner of his eyes, with his head turned slightly on an angle. He didn't appear so big.

"Don't get all soft on me now," said Lorraine. Her face reflected the nice feelings she was experiencing. "I can't give you a good fight this way."

They smiled. They were silent.

"We don't have to fight." He put his hand next to hers and slid his fingers close to touch her. "You know, my mother always had a dream of running a fine establishment. But it was never more than a beer joint and a short-term motel. It made her happy that I got my business degree after dad died. But I had no ambition to do better."

"I've always wanted to be an artist. Make things with my hands. Beautiful things. Hated school and ended up working at a school. How funny is that? But kids are great. I started to make snacks to tide them over in the afternoons. They loved it and my stuff just kept getting more creative," Lorraine was pensive. "I don't like to talk about myself."

"Me neither."

They sat quietly, their fingers touching on the table. After a long silence, Matthew took a deep breath before speaking. "I would like to make this a fine place for my mother. I have some ideas. Want to stay and help?"

He was not looking at her. She was staring into the dark nothingness of the road. "OK."

She got up. "I'll walk you to your door. He got up, took her hand and together they walked down the long hallway to their rooms.

# CHAPTER 34

The periodic Chamber of Commerce sponsored Arts and Crafts Show of the San Fernando Valley spread throughout the city park adjacent to soccer and baseball fields. There was plenty of parking, but with Thelma's disabilities, they parked in a handicapped parking spot close enough that she could walk. The food stands seemed to be getting the first crowds of the morning. It was Pamela's job to walk in front of Shelby and Thelma and check every exhibitor inside his or her tent.

"I love the *Renaissance Faire*," said Shelby "but it takes too much out of me. I'll go once more mostly to show Pamela how much fun it is but after that, I can't keep going back."

"It used to wear me out, too," said Thelma.

They had passed at least a dozen interesting tents but still no luck. The end of the row had a barbecue stand with tables and chairs for the customers. Tantalizing odors rose out of the pit early in the day in preparation for when an hour later, closer to lunch time, people would begin to show interest in the spicy meats. The next row of exhibitors was opposite and facing the first row. The distance between the long rows of tents and stands was wide enough to accommodate large crowds usually walking up and down looking for bargains, looking for unusual items or just looking.

The three of them started back the way they came but this time they concentrated on checking the next row of tents. Not very far down the line Pamela jumped with joy. Hanging on the inside wall of a tent among the artist's own art works, Pamela saw a 10x14 photograph of the *travel time mirror box*. She turned and ran back to Shelby and Thelma.

"Mommy, Thelma, come here!" They followed her. Pamela ran into the tent pointing directly at the bright color photo of the *mirror box*. The slender artist in a long black dress and sparkling white scarf around her neck got up to greet them.

"I knew that one day the owner of the *mirror box* would come back." She reached out for a handshake.

"I'm the mother of the owner," said Thelma.

"I'm the sister," said Pamela.

"I'm her sister, too," said Shelby.

"Nice family," said the artist. "I am Babette. Your daughter and I were so busy talking when we met, that we didn't even introduce ourselves. She was carrying the *mirror box* in her hand, holding it gently with so much love."

"Yes and you called out to her and wanted to know everything about it. I remember you!" said Pamela.

"And I remember you," said Babette. "What is her name anyway?"

"Lorraine," said Thelma.

"I told her that my husband is in advertising and would probably be interested in representing this unique thing and maybe get some distribution. Next thing I know you and Lorraine were so excited you just left. No name, no telephone number, nothing. And that's when I got the idea of displaying it. And here you are!"

"Here we are," said Thelma. "Lorraine is down in San Diego but we really want her to come back and live with us. So we thought if we found you and found out what was going on with it, maybe she would come back home."

"If we give her good news, she'll come back," said Pamela.

The three of them looked at Babette. "Yes, good news it is." She went to a small bench seat in the back of her tent. In the bottom drawer of the bench she had some business cards including her husband's. "Here is my card and here is my husband's. He would like to talk with Lorraine and make an arrangement to put the *mirror box* into specialty boutiques. It is so unique we're sure it will be a hit."

Pamela couldn't stop grinning. "It'll be a big hit. Lorraine gave one to a lady for her trip to Europe. She will be back soon and I will find out how she liked it."

Shelby tightened up. *Looks like Pamela did not forget Moira. Not at all,* she thought.

Thelma took a little notebook from her purse with a pen attached. "Now let me write down her name, Lorraine Hunter and my name and telephone here in the Valley. I'll try to contact her as soon as I can." She reached out to shake Babette's hand. Pamela hugged the artist and Shelby also reached for a handshake.

"Do you have a studio where you work?" asked Shelby. "I'll be decorating our house and we might buy something from you later on."

"Yes, I do. Just give me a call."

They were on their way out of the art fair grounds. Judging by the number of cars already parked all around, the event showed signs of being a successful day for the exhibitors.

Shelby drove to Thelma's house to drop her off. They went inside. Thelma excitedly told Arnie that they had located the artist; a smart woman and how they thought Lorraine would come back and make a success of the *travel time mirror boxes.*

"We have to find her."

"Isn't she at her father's house?" asked Arnie.

"No, Nick said she didn't stay. I'm really worried. What did they do to her? Lorraine was just a perfectly normal youngster when she left me to move in with him and now, I don't know who she is."

"We'll find her," said Arnie.

"Yes, yes," said Pamela.

"We have to get going," said Shelby. "Talk to you tomorrow."

Pamela kissed Thelma and Arnie and followed Shelby to the *vette.*

On the way home Pamela said "Tomorrow is Sunday. Can we go to the movies?"

"We probably can. Is your homework done?"

"Hm," Pamela mumbled.

"That doesn't sound very positive. I'd like to see it before we make any plans."

Pamela grimaced and was quiet for the rest of the drive. She knew her mother was onto her.

They were tired when they arrived home. Shelby stopped to pick up the newspaper from the driveway. She maintained the weekend subscription. She liked the television magazine and the entertainment section but she did not need a whole week's paper cluttering up the house.

Pamela went to her room and reluctantly took out her school work from the sack. She went to work at her desk.

Something was gnawing at Shelby. She poured herself a glass of fruit juice and settled down in the den with the newspaper. The answering machine light was blinking. There was no message. Someone rang and hung up. Nothing Shelby could do. Maybe whoever it was will call back. Her gaze traveled to the wall calendar. Her hand curled into a tight fist. The 17th. The famous 17th in Santa Monica. *What should I do? What does he want from me?* She was ill at ease; afraid of getting hurt. Undecided about facing him now. The fact that the day after that she would see Marc made her feel better. There was no confusion about that. *What should she do about Sidney?* She was hoping that somehow natural instincts would supersede all misgivings and the answers would just come to her.

Lorraine didn't know that Shelby had quit and was no longer working at her day job so she waited until a week day to catch Pamela when she was alone after school before calling her again. Pamela answered.

"Lorraine!" she yelled out. Shelby listened up. "Mommy wants to talk to you. Wait a sec." But Lorraine hung up.

"What's wrong with Lorraine?" said Shelby. "She's carrying some kind of grudge. I can't stand when people don't speak up and say what's on their minds."

Shelby got on the phone. "Thelma, we're going down there and find that daughter, sister person. How soon can you go?" She was quietly listening for a while. "You're right. We can't leave Pamela . . . Friday, after school. It's a date."

"Were you going to leave me? Really?"

"Yes. I wanted to go right now while I was still good an angry for her hanging up," said Shelby. "OK. We're all going on Friday."

# CHAPTER 35

*A*rnie insisted on driving Thelma's station wagon, a very comfortable Ford Woody. She loved that vehicle. Although the women did not ask him to come along, no one stopped him. Perhaps it was natural that he would be part of the team, part of the family. He finally fit in, was needed and everyone was comfortable. Maybe Lorraine will be, too.

Pamela sat next to him in the passenger seat. Thelma and Shelby were in the back. Pamela talked incessantly. She was thrilled about seeing Lorraine again. She was also thrilled about the ride, the sights and everything. She noticed that once they left Los Angeles County the roads became wider, cleaner, with blooming floral landscapes and healthy trees.

"How come the Freeway here is nicer?"

"Orange County has more money or they just spend more money on beautification," said Arnie.

Pamela nodded as she absorbed the information.

Shelby wasn't listening. Thelma and Arnie tried to answer the child's numerous questions.

"You're not listening," said Thelma.

"I have things on my mind."

"Are you worried about Lorraine?"

"No, not really."

"Then what?" asked Thelma.

"Things."

"What things?"

"Grownup things," said Shelby then looked at Thelma whose face was a big question mark.

"That's no way to talk to me, your mother's best friend."

"You're right. I'm sorry. I really don't want to discuss it. It's hard. I have to figure out some stuff."

"You know, when your mother was alive and Nick left me I couldn't have made it without her. She was happily married to your dad and she understood life. She taught me so much. I was all over the place, loose and indiscriminating. A slut on a downhill spiral. I don't think I would have been able to find my happy or happier ending, find the way to settle down and accept life with Arnie without your mother's guidance." She took a deep breath as if ridding herself of all the negatives in her past. "What I am saying is that I understand grownup stuff."

Shelby took her hand and held it. There were no words. She could not find the words to express her confusion. She turned her head away from Thelma and absentmindedly nodded toward the fast moving roadside scenery. Thelma was patient. She identified with Shelby and the mother in her recognized that she would come around in time. When she was ready.

"I've got six days to decide," said Shelby.

"Decide what?"

"How to handle a situation without hurting any more. I am hurting now. The 17th. Deadline."

"You're hurting?"

"There's this man. I like him. He's older but virile, exciting and kind. I could easily spend the rest of my life with him."

"Sounds like you love this man."

"True," said Shelby after a moment thinking.

"How does he feel?"

Shelby's sigh was a little too long. "His wife just died. I saw him with another woman."

Thelma patted Shelby's hand. "Oh dear. That hurts."

"Worse. He left a message. He wants to meet on the 17th."

"Are you going?"

Shelby looked like a little girl. Thelma's eyes were searching into her soul.

"I don't know. What do I say? How do I look into his eyes? He never gave me the courtesy of a phone call about his wife's death. I don't know. I just don't know."

"You be who you are. He knows who you are. You are a work in progress."

They were quiet for the rest of the drive. There was a lot to think about.

It was the dinner hour when they reached the Pacific Beach exit. Turning on to West Briarfield was the call for action. Everybody up. Thelma pointed out the house to Arnie and he pulled into the driveway. Thelma got out of the car. Shelby and Pamela followed a few steps behind her. Thelma rang the doorbell. There was silence. She rang again. She heard movement inside and rang again. She was standing erect, looking straight at the door as it opened.

"Bea?" said Thelma. She could not believe the sight of the prematurely wrinkled skinny woman holding her son on her arm, her mascara running down her face fresh from crying.

"He's out drinking," said Bea. "That's who you want, isn't it."

"No. I'm looking for Lorraine."

"I didn't want her to come back. She was a tease."

"You watch what you say," said Thelma.

"I don't watch anything. I'm too young to be mixed up with the likes of you."

"I'm looking for my daughter."

"I'm sure he knows where he stashed her for his own use."

Bea walked to the kitchen for a moment. When she came back to the door she handed Thelma a *PETE'S* matchbook and closed the door in Thelma's face.

Thelma was furious. "I don't understand how people like this live."

They got back in the car, stunned at the rudeness. Arnie drove a few blocks to be out of visual sight of Bea's house and stopped to check his map for the address on the matchbook. It was a few minutes' drive to the strip mall. They parked away from all the other cars crowding around *PETE'S* entrance at the end of a long walkway.

"If I get out and go with you, I might kill him," said Arnie.

"Just sit tight," said Thelma. "We're glad you're here."

As Thelma started for the bar, Shelby and Pamela lined up by her side. They knew they were being watched through the window as they walked in unison. Before they reached the entrance, Nick appeared, beer in hand, cigarette dangling from the corner of his mouth. Some of his drinking buddies also came out but stayed by the door watching as Nick approached the women. The moment was reminiscent of the old Westerns where the two gunslingers walked toward each other on main-street, ready to draw and shoot. It took an eternity. Slow motion and tense faces focusing on one another.

Nick stopped a few feet from them, looked cockily toward his friends watching. "What kind of a fucking *posse* is this?" he shouted. "Bunch of hysterical broads."

"Where's Lorraine?" said Thelma.

"I don't know."

"What's become of her?"

"A sleep-around. That's what she is. Like mother like daughter." He slugged down the end of the beer and tossed the can high. The clanking sound of the can hitting a car was ignored. "I should report that place, a hotel, my ass. A bordello. That's what."

"I want to know where she is," said Thelma.

"If I show you the whorehouse where she lives will you go away forever?" he yelled.

"I will."

They watched as Nick headed toward his messy old car all scratched up, dented, dirty.

"You still have the old Ford," he said laughing. "The asshole should buy you a new one!"

"Just go. We'll follow," said Thelma. She was stern and unyielding.

They jumped into the car and Arnie took off after Nick. Both Pamela and Shelby sat in the back with Thelma in the middle. They were holding Thelma's hands on each side. Thelma kept her eyes on the road as if she was trying to help Arnie drive. Suddenly, on the highway, Nick hit the break and his car came to an unexpected stop. Arnie almost rammed him.

Nick pointed to *THE INN* by the highway, gave them the *famous finger* and drove off. Arnie slowly pulled into a parking spot. They breathed a sigh of relief. Thelma and the girls got out of the car.

"I'll keep the engine running in case you need a quick getaway," said Arnie. No one smiled.

Once again, the three women, side by side, walked up to the entrance, passing the tastefully decorated tables where people were eating and drinking. Relaxing music filled the air.

"Look, Mommy. It's just like the triangle vase that we have."

"And fresh daisies," said Shelby.

"Like we have."

"And the music is soft," said Shelby.

"It's like your house," said Thelma.

They went inside and there was more of Shelby's good taste in the lobby and in the bar. "It's as if you've set up this place," said Thelma.

Mrs. Barkley came over. "You may sit anywhere you like." Handing them a handwritten menu, she walked away. Thelma looked at the menu and passed it to Shelby. She studied it and handed it to Pamela.

"What do you think?" said Thelma.

"It's Lorraine's handwriting," said Pamela.

"Definitely," said Shelby.

They looked up and standing at their table was Lorraine. "Let's see, now," she said. "There will be a glass of Merlot for the young woman, a Cosmo for the matriarch and," she smiled at Pamela, "you will have a virgin Cadillac. Hm? How did I do?"

There were smiles and hugs. Guests came and went, the environment was relaxing. Mrs. Barkley and Lorraine served the three of them and every chance Lorraine had she sat with them.

"I'm so happy you didn't give up on me," said Lorraine.

"You're our sister-daughter. That's what we call you," said Pamela.

"That sounds great," said Lorraine. "How's Arnie?"

"He's in the car," said Pamela, pointing toward the car.

Lorraine went outside and walked up to the car.

"Arnie," she said. "Come on in."

She stood and waited for him to get out of the car. Neither of them had anything to say. Words were not their way of communicating. Together they walked back into the hotel. Thelma and Shelby smiled but made no comment. Lorraine looked at them. Arnie sat down next to Thelma.

"You're the group. The family," she said. Pamela was eating but Thelma and Shelby were touched. Lorraine continued. "Pretty soon, as the night comes, we will slow down. People will be leaving."

Pamela picked up the menu. "*Light Lorraines?*"

Then a shy smile filled Lorraine's face. "Matthew gave them the name. I just called them The Bites."

Matthew, the big guy with a big grin behind the bar came over.

"This is my mother and my sisters," said Lorraine. "This is Matthew."

She held his hand and the two of them looked like bashful children. Mrs. Barkley stood by the bar, watching. She was touched. The moment generated a lot of delightful vibes in all those witnessing the scene. One could sense the good feelings radiate the entire place. One of the patrons at the bar pulled out his pocket harmonica and started playing *Sweet Lorraine*.

"That's lovely, Mr. Salton. But although I'm a big girl, I have a delicate stomach. I get sick easily," said Lorraine.

He nodded and put away the harmonica. "One day, Miss Lorraine, one day, I'll get the right song for you and you'll let me play it through."

Matthew shook his hand. "I bet you will, Mr. Salton."

Finally the place emptied. Mrs. Barkley came over. "I have a couple of rooms ready for you. Lorraine will show you where they are. I'll say my goodnights and will have breakfast for you any time after 7."

She walked off closing doors and turning off lights for the night. Matthew sat down with them. The changes brought on by his romance with Lorraine filled his heart.

"You can probably imagine how much I care about Lorraine," he said. "She changed my life. Our lives. She changed our business. Everything she suggests turns out to be a success. She has the touch."

Lorraine looked like she was about to cry. "Oh, stop it, Matthew. I just make the sandwiches."

"You also made the *travel time mirror box*," said Shelby. "Don't forget the range of your artistic talents."

"Let me tell it, let me," said Pamela. She looked at Thelma and Shelby waiting for an answer.

"OK," said Thelma. "Go ahead."

Pamela was all smiles. "We went to Babette, you know the painter lady who took the *mirror box* to show it to her husband? Well, guess what," she rattled on. "So now you have to come home because they will do something specially," said Pamela.

Lorraine didn't understand her at all. "What was that?"

Thelma took over. "Babette's husband has a way to distribute the *mirror box* to specialty shops. The small independently owned places that always carry unusual items. So, they want to talk with you, make the arrangements. Make a deal."

Lorraine was stunned. She looked at each of them, back and forth. Flabbergasted.

"I don't know what to say. I forgot all about it."

She got up. "I'll have to think about it. Overnight, OK?"

"I thought you'd jump at the chance of coming back home," said Thelma.

"I thought so, too," said Lorraine. "But now, for the first time I am needed. Somebody, some place, needs me. You know what I mean? I belong."

She got up from the table and started for her room. Turning around and facing her family, she repeated, "You know what I mean?"

Pamela looked at her. Shelby nodded. Thelma got up, put her arm around Lorraine and walked a few steps with her. "I know," she said. "I do."

When Lorraine was out of view, Matthew also got up. "Ladies, nothing wonderful has ever happened to me in my life and it was long ago when it did to my mom. Then Lorraine showed up and it's like the sun came out. Shining. Shining on us."

Thelma and Shelby were touched by his words. "Yes, she is like that. She can make things wonderful," said Thelma.

"I'll see you in the morning," said Matthew. "Let me give you your keys."

They followed him to their rooms. Not knowing what to expect they were surprised at the nicely decorated, color-coordinated, and comfortable, well equipped rooms. Nothing fancy. Everything just right. The windows of both rooms overlooked the pool and spa area. Pamela was asleep in moments. Shelby watched her for a while. She felt old in a way. The idea of being a responsible adult, the parent of a fast growing new person, seemed romantic before Pamela was born. Then the decision of wanting to be a hands-on parent was scary at first but necessary. Clearly the way to go. Her thoughts went back to Boyd. Moist eyes and quiet sniffles brought memories of being a *small me*. The touch of Boyd, the sex of Boyd came into the room, into her bed, into her body. She shivered. She got goose bumps. She felt the moment of conception that very split second when she knew she had been impregnated. Her genitals involuntarily contracted. "Oh, Boyd," she whispered.

Thank goodness for sleep as it overtook her. It was nearly midnight. It has been a long, long day.

# CHAPTER 36

The breakfast aroma crept through THE INN invitingly waking the guests. Matthew was at the desk dialing one wake-up call after the other. "Good morning!" he said cheerily then hung up. Dialing the next one he repeated "Good morning!" even more cheerily. He was in a great mood. Lorraine appeared. They kissed lightly.

"Good morning."

"Good morning!" he said.

"Don't give me your cheery wake-up call stuff," she said. "Give me something you mean. Something I can work with."

"I think when we get married the lovemaking will be fantastic." His eyes never left her. "And I mean it."

This stopped Lorraine in her tracks. "Do you?"

"Yes, Lorraine," he said. "Now that I saw your beautiful mother and sisters I know beauty runs in your family and you'll stay this beautiful forever. So, what do you say?"

"I mean did you just propose?"

"Yes."

Lorraine sat down. She was dazed. Flushed and between deep breaths, she said, "I never thought I'd hear those words."

Matthew walked around the front desk and got down on one knee. "Is this what's missing from the picture?"

She started laughing. Thelma and Arnie appeared in the arc of the hotel hallway. They realized what was happening. Astonished, Thelma put her hand over her mouth and looked from Arnie to Matthew and Lorraine. She could not believe what they were witnessing.

"So what do you say?" said Matthew.

"Yes, yes, yes!" She shouted the third *Yes* so loud that everyone in the lobby and the bar restaurant could hear it. There was applause and congratulating remarks. Mr. Salton and his wife came over to Lorraine. He was about to pull out the harmonica from his pocket but Lorraine stopped him.

"No, Mr. Salton. Just words, OK? Words will be good," said Lorraine and there was general merriment.

"Yes, Miss Lorraine. The wife and I are happy for both of you. You're good people."

They noticed two cars and a news van pulling into the parking area. Several men and women got out of the cars. The local news reporter with her cameraman moved close to the action.

One of the men wearing a crumpled suit and tie went to the front desk holding up his police badge and showed it to Mrs. Barkley. She stepped over to him.

"How can I help you?" said Mrs. Barkley then turned to the guests. "Everyone, please go on with your breakfasts. The buffet is open, help yourselves. You don't want to miss your tours."

No one moved. This was getting interesting. The news camera rolling, preserving every nuance.

The policeman spoke way too loud. "This is a raid."

"A raid?" said Mrs. Barkley.

"Yes. We have to inspect everything and everyone in this house," said the man.

"It's a Saturday morning and I have work to do in the kitchen. So please state your business more clearly."

She looked him in the eyes, waiting for an answer. Matthew and Lorraine stood up and moved behind Mrs. Barkley. Thelma and Arnie noticed that they, too, were surrounded by the cops.

"I am detective Millstone. We were tipped off that a Miss Lorraine is running a house of ill repute here. She is the mastermind."

Mrs. Barkley's eyes opened up, rounder and bigger than ever.

"Which one of you is Miss Lorraine?" he asked.

Mrs. Barkley, Thelma, and Lorraine stepped forward at the same time saying, "I'm Miss Lorraine.

The guests were holding their breaths. One could hear a pin drop.

The detective and his people were grimacing impatiently.

"No games, please," Millstone said.

One of the plainclothes police pulled out a photo and handed it to Millstone.

"Here," he said. "That's the one."

Millstone did not review the photo because something wonderful caught his eyes.

Just at that moment, the beautiful Shelby and equally beautiful Pamela entered from the hallway. They were smiling, looking rested.

"Good morning everyone," said Shelby and was echoed by Pamela.

"You must be Miss Lorraine," said the detective.

"Why?" said Shelby.

"We know that a Madame would be beautiful."

"Haven't you heard about the *dumb blonde*?" said Shelby. Pointing at herself she grinned, pivoted around. Pamela copied her.

"You're not doing a lot of good for the reputation of my hotel," said Mrs. Barkley.

Matthew stepped up. "I'm Matthew Barkley and this is my fiancé."

He looked around. "These are our hotel guests and none of them could pass for a prostitute, if you look closely. Now, can you tell us where this all came from?"

"I can't do that," said the detective.

"I bet my no good ex husband put you up to it. He's the only one mean enough to do something like this," said Thelma.

One of the other policemen came up to detective Millstone. "We should take names and IDs just to be sure," he said.

"Be sure of what?" said Shelby staring down the young cop. "Open your eyes, Mister. This is my mother, my dad, my sisters. That over there is Mr. Salton and his wife. They have a Sea World tour to catch." Shelby walked around the other guests. "This family is heading to the San Diego Zoo. World famous, remember? You live here. This is your town, don't you know?"

Matthew looked toward the TV news reporter. "Since we're all in this video, let's give them something to remember." He picked up some menus from the nearby tables and handed one to the detective and his team. "The bites are called Light Lorraines," he said. "You're welcome to be our guests for breakfast."

The plainclothes police looked at one another. Millstone looked at the rolling camera and the newswoman. She pulled the camera operator to a close-up of the detective.

"This will be all for now," said Millstone. "Thank you for your attention."

The camera was turned off. The newswoman went up to Matthew.

"Is this the boutique hotel that was written up in *Food & Wine* a few weeks ago?"

"Yes. If you please find a place to sit, we will get some tastes ready for you," said Matthew. He was unrecognizably in charge.

"I missed seeing you on our local news so I only saw the national magazine. Did that article increase your business?"

Lorraine headed for the kitchen and Mrs. Barkley followed.

"Miss, if you give us a few minutes we'll serve you the Light Lorraines prepared by none other than Miss Lorraine."

Lorraine waved to them through the pass-through from the kitchen to the bar. Like children, everyone waved back to her.

"After breakfast, we can give you an interview," said Matthew, starting to serve coffee and water.

Thelma and Arnie were still standing by the hotel's front desk when they heard a car screeching into the parking lot, stopping next to the news van. Nick got out and swaggered up to the open front door. As he looked inside, he saw a bunch of happy people, police and guests, together talking and eating. He spotted Thelma and at the same time Arnie's furious look came into his face. Nick started to back away as Arnie was apparently about to take him down. Nick was out of there.

Satisfied with himself, Arnie looked for approval from Thelma.

"Done like a man," she said. "Let's eat."

Shelby and Pamela were at one of the small cocktail tables enjoying the *Light Lorraines*. Thelma and Arnie helped themselves to a small sampler and sat with Shelby.

"What a great day," said Thelma. "I miss Lorraine but look at how happy she is."

Lorraine joined them. She was all smiles. "I don't know what came first, you or the proposal but I am glad you were here. You made it perfect. Just as I began to wonder what else could I do around here to remind myself of home, of Shelby's tasteful decorating touches, of mom's organized refrigerator, of making a place for myself? I knew I had to stop envying Shelby's beauty and life. I wanted to remind myself of all those things that made me comfortable. And here you are. All those things."

"And you belong. Don't forget that you belong," said Shelby.

"I'll call Babette and her husband. I hope they will accept that I will make the *mirror boxes* down here and ship them to wherever they want me to."

"That's a good idea," said Thelma. She got up, took Lorraine's hand.

"I'm standing here and I can see the growth. I'm so happy."

Shelby came over and held Thelma's hand. "I'm standing here and I can see the growth in you, Thelma."

"And I'm standing here and see the growth in you, Shelby."

"I want to stand here, too" said Pamela and taking their hands she completed the circle.

Mrs. Barkley and Matthew watched with great appreciation. As the place was emptying out Dorothea arrived and was introduced. She was always on time and somehow always kept the entire establishment clean and neat.

Shelby went up to the bar to talk with Matthew.

"I am really glad for the two of you for many reasons. People who can make each others' lives better and stronger, should be together, should be married."

Matthew came around from the bar and with general hugging and well-wishing, they were ready to leave. The waving continued from the car as Arnie drove out to the highway.

Minutes later Pamela became her chatty self. "Are we leaving because we need a change of clothes?"

# CHAPTER 37

Shelby was in front of the full-length mirror studying every detail of her outfit. She wanted to look drop-dead gorgeous. She wanted to be able to look into his eyes and not falter. She wanted to be able to tell him what she thought of him. She wanted to show him that she was strong, not the helpless pretty thing.

Finally, this was it. She had to get going to reach Santa Monica shortly after he does.

The *Mach 1*. Definitely, this event called for the *Mach 1*, the muscle she needed. It seemed as if she arrived to Ocean Avenue Seafood in only minutes because her overactive mind was scattering every-which-way. She still was not sure she should be there or should she have ignored his message? In the end she had to follow her gut instinct and go.

She circled the block a few times and decided against giving her car to the valet. Instead, she parked in the public lot, the same place where she left her car the very first time she went to see Sidney. She was angry and lost then. It seemed like ages ago. Now she was angry again but not lost. *Oh,* she thought to herself. *The light came on. I am not lost.* This boost of confidence was immediately visible on her face. *Large me. That's what,* she thought.

She walked in. She was anticipating the friendly Maître D' who always remembered her. As she entered, however, she was disappointed on seeing a different although polite Maître D' who escorted her to Sidney's table. Sidney looked better than ever. He got up to greet her. Good manners as always. She did not fly into his open arms. He gestured to the waiter for the chair. She sat down.

"Hello," she said.

"How are you," he said? "Are you all right?"

"Just fine, thank you."

"I finally got back," he said. She didn't reply. The waiter poured the wine for Shelby. She lifted the glass for a quick sip.

"I didn't call because of Moira."

She still didn't reply. She studied his eyes.

"Moira has passed away. I was not up to calling."

Sadness shadowed his face. He paused to give her time to speak but she remained silent.

"The services will be Sunday. Did you get notification?" He waited. "If not, here is one, I would appreciate your being there," he said and pulled a black and gold card from his briefcase. "The gold is for her. She liked gold. The black is for the darkness of the occasion. Not very original."

Shelby took another sip.

"George told me. Two weeks ago. That's how I had to find out. You didn't call. I deserved more."

"I know. I just had so much going on."

"You had me fooled all along. You lied."

"I wouldn't do that, Shelby." The waiter delivered his favorite seafood assortment platter. He picked at it, looking forlorn.

"You know, thanks to you, I own my space. I'm grateful."

She smirked and piled the plate in front of her. He seemed to know that she was watching him and began to show signs of discomfort.

"I saw you on Catalina," she said, her eyes piercing through him.

She bit into the pickled octopus savoring it slowly while looking straight at him. She picked up the king prawn daintily with her forefinger and thumb, dipped it and unhurriedly let her tongue lick her lips while she swallowed each bite.

"Are you trying to excite me?" he said. "It's working. It always has."

"Your coded message came from your Los Angeles telephone number not from overseas. And why code it? Are we hiding?" Shelby was on a roll. She was not going to be his victim. "Why did you want to see me?"

"Originally, I was planning to charm you into resuming our relationship as it was. But some attorney sent me a couple of videos." He took a deep slow breath before continuing. "You're a better man than I am. Now, I have to thank you. I saw the video of your arrest. I also saw the video of your deposition. I know you love me and I love you, too."

Shelby chuckled. "So you want me?'

"I do, but crossing Alexandra could be extremely detrimental to my career. She can hurt me."

"You're in for one hell of a ride, Mr. Marshall."

"Shelby, dear. Don't be vindictive. It doesn't become you."

Shelby leaned back in her seat and measured him up. "Is she pregnant already? Did she get an early start? Is she going to have your babies and take all your money? That's what second wives in Hollywood do, isn't it? Moira told me. She knew."

"What's that supposed to mean?"

"It's a girl thing, Sidney. Young women make a career of getting their money by taking rich older men out of their marriages, getting pregnant and obligating the man to set them up for life. Say goodbye to your privacy and freedom. It's life. You're caught. No more fun fucking for you, Mister."

"Well, you're allowed this one more nasty remark," he said with a smile.

Shelby could not help but smile back. Not exactly a warm smile.

Unbeknownst to her, Alexandra arrived and walked toward their table. She went right over to Sidney and kissed him on the lips. She sat down next to him.

"Don't you know Sidney's eye-to-*eye theory*? Very important. Nobody sits next to him only across," said Shelby.

Alexandra looked to Sidney. She waited, but his moment to put his foot down and set rules had passed. He said nothing. She remained in her seat next to him.

"Oh, Shelby," said Alexandra. "I didn't recognize you from the back. I couldn't tell which one of his toys he's saying goodbye to."

"Let's not start calling each other names. I'm sure you have a few descriptive names trailing you like a long slimy tail."

Shelby got up. Gulped down the rest of her wine. "He will never stop thinking of me. He'll be in bed with you fantasizing about me. Maybe even call out my name. But I'm not going to rain on your parade, because there won't be a parade. You'll have to keep looking behind you all the time, because you'll never know who is moving in on you. Goodbye to both of you."

Shelby marched to the exit. In the front reception she ran into Jeff King, the owner she had met before.

"Shelby, great to see you. Can I get you anything?"

"You remember me, that is so nice. I can't believe it. My name and all," said Shelby, reaching for a handshake.

"Well, don't be a stranger. Just let me know when you will come and I'll take care of you," said Jeff.

"Not on a Thursday, Jeff. But I'll be back."

She walked outside, crossed the sunny street, and leisurely strolled toward her car.

"Hello, large me," she said out loud. "Large me," she repeated, stretching her arms toward the sun shining down on her.

# CHAPTER 38

Marc relaxed on the couch in her living room, his feet propped up, he could not stop staring at Shelby.

"You don't know how much I've missed you."

She smiled softly. "As much as I've missed you."

"You did?"

"To tell you the truth, you sort of got under my skin."

"You look so delicious standing there. I have always had a hard time not dragging you off to the bedroom."

She shyly touched her face to see whether she was blushing.

"There's something on my conscience." He was looking for the words and the tone of his voice alarmed her.

"I finally figured out the Voice, but it was too late."

Shelby had no idea what he was talking about.

"The night of the awards dinner, remember? I didn't mean to eavesdrop, but I happened to hear that strange message on your machine by this familiar voice. I couldn't place it for the life of me. Then in Milan, right after I met Sidney Marshall, it came to me.

He was very cordial. He told me how much he liked my work and how glad he was that I became available to adapt his novel to the screen. I told him how much I liked his work, then at our first dinner together, I'll never know what made me do it, but I said 'Brutus 22-17.' He got a shade paler, but his elegant composure never rumpled. He said 'That's not funny.' He didn't know that you didn't betray him and I couldn't tell him that that was all I knew. I felt like an idiot. So, the rest of the time he remained cordial, but I sensed he was always on guard around me."

Marc had tears in his eyes.

"You didn't know I remembered hearing that weird message. He didn't know that it was his voice that caught my attention. I didn't know how you knew him, yet it appears that we all knew everything. I still feel like an idiot and I always will."

Shelby's eyes were moist. She was silent: thinking, weighing, balancing.

"Sometimes some things have to die in order to give birth to something new."

She reached for his hand. He let her pull him close to her until he felt her lips on his. She unbuttoned his shirt. Pulled off her own Tee shirt and gently rubbed her bosom against his chest. He picked her up and carried her into the bedroom where they both fell on the bed. Marc gave into his desires, and like a flower, she opened up for him, feeling love in her every pore. They made the most gorgeous, all-consuming love either of them had ever experienced. They could not stop. They craved more and more. Walls tumbled. Man and woman became one. Time stood still.

"You're incredible," she told him, still in the afterglow of love.

"Just try harder. Unattractive men work harder."

"Unattractive? Says who?"

"It's true. It's all in the eyes of the beholder," he said with joyous emphasis.

A beautiful sunny California morning saw Shelby, Marc and Pamela driving the Malibu Canyon. Pamela was explaining everything she knew and liked about it. Marc listened intently. Shelby parked at the Surfrider Beach as usual.

"I'll show you what we do when we do nothing," said Shelby.

"We talk to people, meet dogs, laugh," said Pamela.

"So far I like it," said Marc.

Rolling their carry-all beach bag behind them they took the narrowing passage with flat rocks in the water leading through to the grounds of the Malibu Colony. Their destination was the area where they settled other times, not too close to any of the homes and enough distance away from the tourist spots. Pamela ran ahead.

Shelby walked up to the water's edge and took Boyd's medallion out of her bag. It read: "I'll love you as long as I'll live; I'll live as long as I love you. - B" She tossed it into the Pacific Ocean as far as her arm could throw. Marc was watching.

"Anything I should know?" he said.

"You should know that I have cleared the road for us. No obstacles. I'm the *large me* and the real me," she said.

Holding hands, they followed Pamela. Shelby knew that she was looking for Moira's house. They caught up to her.

"Mommy, this is where we played with the kids," she said.

She went closer to the house. The FOR SALE sign on the deck surprised her.

"Look, Mommy. Moira is not coming back."

Pamela walked closer to the house and under the deck she found the broken *travel time music box*. She carefully picked it up. Some of the mirrors were missing and it was filled with sand. She walked to the ocean with it. Marc started to follow but Shelby stopped him.

"She has to do this on her own," said Shelby.

"Moira?" said Marc.

"Sidney's wife," said Shelby and looked into Marc's eyes.

"May she rest in peace," said Marc.

Holding hands Shelby and Marc walked closer to Pamela but stopped far enough to give her space. Pamela was carefully washing the *mirror box* and when she was satisfied, she walked back to her mother. She held it up to show it to her.

"It looks like Moira forgot to take this with her."

"Yes. She must have."

"I want to keep it. May I?" said Pamela.

"Yes, honey."

They sat in the sand and looked at the ocean. Pamela reached out for her mother's hand and Shelby reached out for Marc's. It was a total rebirth on a beautiful sunny California day.